YOU CAN'T RUN

HOPE E. DAVIS

DEDICATION

For my grandmother,
Thanks for always being my biggest fan.

And for Taylor Largusa
Thanks for talking me down off a ledge.

DISCLAIMER

This is a work of fiction. Names, characters, businesses, places, events, locales, and incidents are either the products of the author's imagination or used in a fictitious manner. Any resemblance to actual persons, living or dead, or actual events is purely coincidental.

Denver, and La Junta, Colorado are real cities. However, all portrayals of either city are completely fictionalized.

ACKNOWLEDGMENTS

Cover by Victoria Cooper
Edited by K. Joyce

PROLOGUE
MARK

He pulled up in front of a dark multiple story condominium, glancing down at the phone in his hand to make sure he had the right address before putting his car into park.

It didn't look like anyone was awake at this hour, but as a precaution he straightened the collar around his neck and glanced in the mirror to make sure his hair was slicked back. Even though the darkness was on his side right now, the sun would be rising soon. He reached into the backseat and slid his black duffel bag over his shoulder. The clothing and computer in the bag were all he owned now. He had sold everything else to begin his new life.

Quietly, he walked up to the front door of the building, checking the rental app to find the check-in instructions. He had specifically chosen this rental because of the self check-in. He didn't want the hassle of dealing with people.

He typed in the number on the security pad to unlock the door, and stepped in while quietly closing it. The hallway was quiet, all the wooden doors were closed and the old light bulb buzzing above his head was the only sound. Directly in front of him was a rickety old silver elevator that didn't look like it could possibly work, to his left was a staircase. He chose to take the stairs.

Mark made his way to the third floor where he double checked the check in instructions once more. He turned to his right to find door 310 to be directly next to the staircase. He would have rather had a room at the end of the hall, but this would do.

He opened the lockbox next to the door with the code the landlord had provided. Two silver keys fell into his hand. He slid the first in the lock and swung the door open.

The apartment wasn't much, just a studio in the center of the city. It was modest, containing only a bedroom and cramped kitchen, but that was all he needed.

He set his duffel bag on the queen bed and crossed the room over to the window which overlooked the street. He didn't turn on any lights.

Mark looked at the empty street, lit only by an occasional street lamp. He grinned as a young copper haired woman emerged from around the corner and jogged nimbly past his window. He looked at his watch. She is up early, which probably meant she has a family she has to get up and ready to go at home. It's crazy how predictable people are.

Mark slides his window open, grinning as it opens without a squeak or shutter. This would indeed suit him well. He sticks his head out briefly into the dawn air and looks up and down the street.

The location of the apartment was perfect, now he could start his work.

Mark reluctantly turned away from the window and back to his duffel bag on the bed. He unzipped the side pocket and pulled out the new passport and driver's license he had purchased. He grinned as he regarded his face next to the new name he had chosen,, he pulled a box of hair dye from his bag and headed into the bathroom to begin his transformation.

No one here will know him. No one will recognize him. He will be a new man.

And he will be free to put his plan into action.
Mark will officially be gone.

1

NAYA

She took a deep breath as she slowly opened her car door and placed one foot on the cement outside. The fresh autumn air came rushing into the car, breaking the cocoon of warmth she had created for herself. She pinched her eyes shut quickly, taking in one more deep breath before she stood.

This was it, her first day at her new job.

Naya leaned her head back against the headrest of her drivers seat and looked up at the large brown office building in front of her, then turned to the backseat of her car to grab the cardboard box which contained all her things. It didn't hold much, just a photo for her desk, some favorite pens and a few manila file folders of cold cases she had been unable to solve but couldn't let go.

She had been the Sheriff of La Junta, a small town in the south east corner of Colorado. Assuming the title of Sheriff after her father, the previous Sheriff, retired. She had honestly planned to stay there forever, but her brother who lived in Denver had found out he had cancer, and Naya had immediately requested a transfer.

Being a detective in Denver was going to be much different than her job as sheriff in her humble home town. She had already gotten lost three times this morning on her way to the office, which had done quite a number on her already disheveled nerves. She was a small-town girl at heart and so far had been unable to see the "city charm" her brother had always gushed about when he returned home every Christmas.

Naya squared her shoulders and headed for the glass doors. She wasn't exceptionally tall standing at about five foot five, but she was both physically and mentally strong from years of being a cop and the backbone of her family. She caught a glimpse of her reflection in the glass, her long dark hair was tied into a tight bun at the base of her neck and her dark chocolate eyes looked more tired than normal. Her skin seemed to be slightly dull compared to its usual lightly tanned bronze tone. She made a mental note to make sure she took her vitamins when she got home, she couldn't risk getting sick this soon at a new job.

She reached the door and pushed it open, surprising herself when it swung inward swiftly, then she let go of the handle so that it could silently swing shut behind her. A thin blonde woman with her hair pulled back in a tight bun is sitting behind the desk directly inside the small foyer area. Naya surveyed the room taking in all the details, the woman's name tag said her name was Jean. Naya opened her mouth to greet the woman but Jean beat her to it.

"Hello, how can I help you today?"

"Yes," Naya cleared her throat when the word came out slightly garbled. "Can you please direct me to homicide? I'm detective Naya Largusa, I'm supposed to be starting today. "

Jean nodded. "Certainly, fourth floor, I'll buzz up and let them know you're coming. Welcome by the way."

"Thank you." Naya responded as she steered herself and her cardboard box towards the large shiny elevator. It amazed her how a building this imposing could be only one of many precincts in the department for downtown Denver. In La Junta they had only one precinct that consisted of three desks and a holding cell.

When the doors slid open she found herself in what appeared to be a busy office with an open floorplan. There were people chatting in groups at various points in the room, while others rushed from desk to desk delivering messages and possibly evidence. There had to be about fifteen desks, and the back wall was lined with doors which she assumed led to private offices, interview rooms and possibly even a holding cell. She was unsure how long she stood there drinking in the business of the room, but she suddenly became aware of all the eyes turned on her and blushed pink under their gaze.

"Hello, I'm detective Largusa, a transfer from La Junta?" Naya mentally slapped herself for sounding so dumb. Now no one would take her seriously here.

A kind looking gentleman stepped forward and held out his hand. He was tall, probably mid-forties, and in great shape. Naya could clearly see he took care of himself from the way he was trim and muscular while many men his age have let themselves go. "Stephen Atlas, I'm your partner, I'll take you to your desk."

Naya took his outstretched hand and gave it a quick firm shake then followed as he turned and led her towards the edge of the room. She took a quick catalog of Stephen Atlas' appearance, after hearing his voice she was now even more sure he had to be above forty as he spoke with a certain maturity. His hair was naturally a dark brown but was already peppered with a spattering of grey hairs. His complexion was light and his skin was healthy, indicating to Naya that he probably never smoked or did drugs—both characteristics of a typical cop.

"Here's your desk." He motioned to an empty desk with an opened laptop to his right. "And this one's mine," he gestured to the one next to it, there was no divider between them. "Everyone here just calls me Atlas, both on and off the radio."

Naya nodded. It was a bit awkward between them but she figured they would warm up to each other in time.

"I read your file." Atlas looked away as he admitted it. Cops generally didn't read one another's file out of respect, but she assumed he had been too curious to resist.

"And?" She asked, raising her eyebrow as she set her box on her desk.

He broke out in a grin. "It was pretty clean, even for a cop. I was actually a little disappointed."

Naya laughed. "You were hoping to get a transfer for political reasons or something?"

He shook his head. "Nah, those guys don't last long here, I just thought it was a weird career move from sheriff to detective."

"I didn't move for career reasons." She said somberly, Naya didn't elaborate and began to unpack her few belongings.

Atlas seemed to be waiting for her to continue but realized she never would. "Well, shall I give you the tour?"

Naya stopped unpacking and brushed off her hands, "Sure, just make sure you take me to your leader so I can get my new badge."

Atlas saluted her jokingly. "No problem your highness, and off we go!" He spun around and began to proclaim names as they passed desks in rapid-fire. Naya couldn't keep up and vowed she would go back to look at name plates later, but from what she could retain she was one of six detectives in the office, there were also various secretaries, assistant detectives, and a few tech guys who helped both on cases and around the office. There were more tech guys on another floor, but they used them so much these days a few had permanently moved to reside in homicide. There was a break room, the captain's office, a few rooms for interviews and family and friends', and then there was a sleep room, for when the shifts spilled past twenty-four-hours.

After his whirlwind of a tour he turned to Naya and pointed to the captain's office they had just passed. "Captain Brody is in there. Careful, he's a stickler for knocking."

Naya nodded in acknowledgment, thinkin that his last statement seemed like a joke but she wasn't actually sure if it was or not. Before she couls ask, Atlas sauntered back in the direction from which they had come. Naya stifled a yawn as she lifted her hand and knocked on the door.

"Come in." Came a baritone voice from the other side.

Naya swung the door open and took note of the Captain as he stood from behind his desk. He was significantly younger than she anticipated, with jet black hair and tanned skin. She presumed he was probably of Hispanic descent and in his mid-thirties. Like Atlas, he was in good shape, a far cry from the two plump, overweight officers Naya had been in charge of in La Junta.

She stuck out her hand as she approached him. "Detective Naya Largusa joining you from La Junta, Sir."

He shook her hand. "I've been expecting you." He reached into his drawer and placed her weapon, a badge, and the form for them on his desk for her. "I assume you've already met your partner and found your desk?"

"Yes sir." She replied as she deftly inspected her weapon, picked up her badge and signed the document. She slid the weapon into her side holster and the badge into her back pocket. She pulled out her weapons certification from her wallet and passed it to the captain for him to copy.

"No need to call me sir. We're pretty laid back around here, just call me Captain, Cap, or Brody." He smiled as he slid her ID through the scanner on his desk. Naya had never seen that technology before and she marveled at how easy it was as a copy of her ID and her personal information appeared on the screen. He handed her documents back to her. "Spend the rest of today getting acquainted with your desk and the office and be ready to answer calls tomorrow." He gave her a swift once over, taking in her jeans and buttoned up blouse. "I know you had no idea what to expect, but here in Denver I expect my Detectives to dress professionally. No jeans."

Naya nodded thinking about how this clearly contradicted how he had just said they were laid back in the office. But she wasn't going to argue on her first day. "Of course, Si-Brody."

The captain noticed and smiled. "You'll fit in here in no time. And don't let the others on the floor scare you, my door is always open. If you have questions, theories or concerns, bring 'em my way. Just make sure you knock first."

"I will." Naya smiled, her question from earlier having been answered, and turned to leave, hesitating outside the door just long enough to toss a quick "Thanks" over her shoulder.

"No problem." Brody replied and motioned for her to shut the door, which she did.

She made her way back to her desk and began to settle in. She pulled out her phone and opened the email she had received the day before with instructions on setting up her login. the directions were user friendly and straight forward and she was soon effortlessly trapezing through one of the most technologically advanced systems she had ever seen. She definitely wasn't in La Junta anymore.

Atlas came and went, having conversations with various other coworkers as they passed as well as making frequent trips to the coffee machine for refills. When he was at his desk they would converse a few minutes here and there as she explored the computer system. Before she knew it, it was five o'clock, Atlas rose and put on his jacket.

"You're free to leave." He said as he closed his laptop. "We are only required to work nine to five unless we've got an active case."

She nodded. "I know, but I think I'm going to spend a few more minutes exploring this system before I call it a night."

"Sure thing, see you tomorrow partner." He tipped his imaginary hat with a grin as he turned and headed for the precinct doors. As soon as he was out of sight, Naya reached for the folders she had slid into the bottom drawer.

Before she left La Junta she had taken copies of the three case files that she couldn't let go, the only ones she didn't solve. They were deaths that still haunted her to this day. She quickly flipped through each case file and began to enter their information into the computer system. It didn't take long, as they were cold cases for a reason and there was little to no evidence. At least now if a similar crime showed up it could flag one of them she reasoned. She logged out of her computer and slid her purse over her shoulder.

She was determined to solve those three cold cases. Even if it was the last thing she did.

2

NAYA

T he drive home was short, thankfully, as she didn't think she could handle too long in rush hour traffic yet. Coming from a small town it was still a shock to see so many cars on the road every day. Naya knew she had grown up sheltered, and even when she went to college she hadn't ventured further than Pueblo. Unlike her brother she hadn't been blessed with a sense of adventure, instead she felt powerful ties to her provincial home.

She parked in the driveway of the modestly sized, rundown, two-story house she now co-habited. Real estate in Denver was expensive, and she was glad her brother's place had been large enough for her to move in, so she didn't have to stress about finding something nearby. She slid her key into the worn-down lock and twisted open the door. She immediately heard voices coming from down the hall.

"Vance?" She called out.

"In here!" He replied from the den.

She set her purse down on the small table in the hall and walked over to the doorway to see her brother Vance, thin and frail, sitting on the couch in the den with an Xbox controller in his hands. Although she had barely recognized him when she first returned home, anyone could see they were clearly siblings. Their hair was a perfect match in color, and they both had the same dark eyes. They had once had the same skin tone, but Vance now had an unnaturally pale parlor which occasionally supported bruises from his various treatments. Another man was sitting cross legged on the floor with the other controller and they were both talking to the TV as they played what looked to be a tactical war game.

"Hey sis." Vance called over his shoulder after another minute of chatter. The man on the floor turned to look at Naya for a moment before turning back to the TV. She didn't get a good look but she thought she glimpsed blue eyes to match his curly, dirty blonde hair. "This is my buddy Kevin."

"Hello." Naya waived to the back of their heads before she turned and headed to the kitchen. The house was small, technically only a one bedroom, but the second floor contained a loft and half bathroom. Vance occupied the bedroom on the main floor and they shared the full bathroom off the hallway. Besides the cramped kitchen and den there wasn't much to the home. Naya had taken over the loft when she had moved in a day earlier, not that she had many possessions.

She opened the fridge to the lunch she had prepped for Vance sitting on the shelf uneaten. She sighed and gave the fridge a once over, it didn't appear he had eaten anything.

It was sad to see her older brother a shell of the man he once was. When he had left La Junta almost ten years ago, he had been broad shouldered, athletically built, energetic twenty-two-year-old with a quirky smile. Now he was thin, frail, and barely got out of bed most days.

At least he had made it to the couch today.

Naya pulled out a sauce pan and filled it with water from the tap. Quietly humming to herself, she quickly turned on the gas stove and salted the water so it would come to a boil faster. She pulled out all the ingredients to make her brother's favorite cheese pasta as she listened to the sounds of battle from the other room.

As she waited for the water to boil, she grabbed a glass of water and leaned against the door jamb to the living room.

"I'm making pasta for dinner, Kevin, would you like some?" She offered.

Kevin looked over his left shoulder and Naya observed the way his neck muscles moved as he opened his mouth to speak. "Sure, that would be great, thanks." He flashed her a stunningly straight smile then turned back to the game.

Naya couldn't tell how tall he was from the way he was sitting, but he was clearly fit and muscular. His complexion was fair to match his light hair, a sharp contrast to her and her brothers more bronze shade. She filed this information away as she turned and headed back to the kitchen to add the pasta to the pot.

She was stirring the hard noodles into the boiling water when the doorbell rang. Naya sighed and turned to head for the door only to see Kevin had beaten her to it. Now that he was standing in front of the door Naya could see he was almost a foot taller than her.

A second man stood in the doorway with a similar build and dressed in dusty jeans and a logoed shirt like Kevin but with straight and thick chestnut hair that fell into his eyes. Naya assumed they must work construction for the same company her brother used to and met him there. There was simply no other reason they would be wearing shirts from the construction company.

Kevin turned from the door and noticed her. "This is our buddy Trevor."

"Hello, I'm Naya, Vance's sister." She held out her hand and noticed how he maintained eye contact as they shook hands.

"Nice to meet you Naya." He said and Naya couldn't help but notice his warm and bright smile, chiseled jaw and broad shoulders similar to the way Vance's shoulders used to look. He was definitely an attractive man.

The men turned and headed for the living room as Naya returned to the kitchen and quickly added the rest of the box of pasta to the boiling water. Hopefully it would be enough for four. While she was pulling out a sauce pan to heat the sauce she heard someone clear their throat behind her. Startled, she spun around with a slight jump, she hadn't heard them come into the kitchen. Kevin was standing behind her with a sheepish smile.

"Sorry, Vance said it was okay for Trevor to join." He said as she placed the pot on the stove.

Naya rapidly regained her composure and forced a smile, "No worries, the more the merrier." She wasn't unhappy that Vance had invited friends over, just a little bummed he hadn't warned her.

"Okay, well Vance sent me in here to let you know that he also invited another person." Kevin seemed apologetic as he watched Naya's face for her reaction.

Interrogation class had prepared her for this, and she was careful not to show her annoyance. "Awesome, I'm glad Vance has such a great group of friends." She kept the fake smile in place as she quickly calculated if there was enough pasta in the pot for five or if she would need to make herself something else.

Kevin seemed to realize her dilemma. "Should I order a pizza or something?"

Naya paused, she was big on hospitality but there was no way she could feed four grown men on only what was in the pot. "That would probably be best yes."

In one smooth motion Kevin's phone was in his hand and he was typing quickly. "What toppings do you like?"

"Anything's fine, get whatever you all would like, I'm not picky." She smiled as she turned back to the pot. Now she was genuinely glad Vance had found such considerate and respectful friends. When he had called her parents to let them know he could no longer work his job in construction as a site manager Naya had been worried about his mental health, with him being home alone all day. But it seems her worries then had been unnecessary.

Kevin was still tapping away at his phone when the doorbell rang once more. Naya put down the spoon she was using to stir the pasta intending to answer, but Kevin held up a hand. "I got it." He said as he turned and left the kitchen.

Naya sighed as she pivoted back to the dinner which was about to be upstaged by the pizza Kevin was ordering.

When Vance had found out he was ill six months ago he had adequate savings and health insurance to cover his condition, but as he had quickly begun to deteriorate so had his savings and his ability to work, which cost him his healthcare. Naya made enough to support them now, and she had come to Denver with sufficient savings, but she knew with the medical bills her brother was destined to incur that she needed to save every penny she could. Luxuries like eating out didn't make the cut. She intended to ask about the possibility of overtime to compensate and allow some flexibility for splurges like pizza as soon as she felt it was appropriate without seeming desperate.

Kevin reentered the kitchen with another dark-haired man at his side. Just like Trevor, he was tall and muscled with a chiseled jaw but with lighter green eyes, he was wearing a shirt with the same logo as the others. It was obvious he was another of Vance's construction buddies.

"Naya this is Sebastian, Sebastian, this is Naya, Vance's sister."

"Nice to meet you." Sebastian flashed Naya a crooked smile as she held out her hand for yet another callused handshake.

Naya was quiet, almost expecting one of the men to hit on her as a number of Vance's friends had done when he was in college. To her surprise, they didn't say anything more and Sebastian turned and headed for the living room. Naya wasn't sure whether to be pleased that they were respectful or worried that she was losing her edge.

She was single by choice, as she had her share of boyfriends in La Junta, but she had wanted to come to the city unattached as she had known she would probably be here for the long term and that her brother would be her priority. She had been seeing a man for about six months prior to moving and it hadn't been serious enough for her to ask him to come with, nor had it been serious enough for her to feel a loss at letting him go. It felt proper to break it off.

After Sebastian left the room Kevin had pulled out his phone and resumed clicking buttons, after a moment he flipped the phone her way, interrupting her thoughts, "Ta-Da, pizza will be here in half an hour."

Naya returned her attention to the stove and made a split-second decision, put the second pot she was going to use for sauce away and instead spun to the fridge to grab some ranch dressing and bell peppers. "I think I'll make this into a pasta salad instead."

"Good idea." Kevin agreed, "Especially sinceI just ordered four pizzas."

"Four pizzas? You guys eat that much?" She sputtered.

Kevin laughed and shook his head "No but you weren't helping me decide so I wanted to get a range of options."

Naya laughed along with him. "Well I suppose everyone will have leftovers for lunch tomorrow."

"Perfect." Kevin chuckled as he turned and walked back to the living room. Naya heard whoops and cheers from the room, she smiled, they must have made some big achievement in whatever game they were playing.

She grabbed the pasta and turned to the sink to drain it, taking a deep breath as she watched the steaming water swirl down the drain. She sensed she would be happy here, even if things were stressful right now.

She felt certain of it.

3

MARK

He waited in his truck, tucked around a corner, his fingers trembling while he watched the dot on the phone screen move closer.

Yes. Come to me.

A grin spread across as his face as he felt the exhilaration from what he was about to do, what he had always wanted to do.

He reached over to the passenger seat and grabbed a cloth and the bottle of ether he had managed to procure. The dot on his phone was steadily approaching and he started to get ready.

Mark popped the lock on the door now so that the sound didn't startle her and cause her to change course. Not that he thought she would, she ran this route frequently it was clearly routine and felt familiar to her.

He checked again, the dot was almost next to him now, and he could see her approaching in the rearview mirror. He prepared to strike.

She jogged comfortably past the rearview mirror, and in one motion he was out of the truck, positioned himself behind her, and wrapped his arm around her shoulders to hold her still. She didn't have time to realize what was going on or make a sound before he placed the cloth over her mouth and prevented her from screaming as she breathed through the soaked cloth.

She tried to kick him feebly a few times, but he had the element of surprise on his side and she didn't have much use of her limbs in this position. With a smile he glanced around as she gradually gave up fighting and went limp. Checking behind him, he smoothly hoisted her over his shoulder in a fireman carry, keeping the cloth to her mouth and open the back door of the cab.

Placing her lightweight athletic frame in the compact back seat was easy and he hurriedly closed it in case any lookieloos were to happen upon them. Though it was doubtful at this hour, it was a school night afterall. Hadn't anyone taught the poor girl she shouldn't run once it was dark at night?

Mark climbed back into the driver's seat and started up the car, heading to a location he had picked out earlier that week.

He smiled into the rearview mirror.

Executing his plan was going to be easy. It was fool-proof.

4

NAYA

The pizza arrived, as had two more of Vance's friends. She had no idea her brother was this social. Then again, she shouldn't be surprised, he'd always been too large for life in their small town.

Naya had always kept to herself, content with it just being her and her best friend Hensely. They had been nearly inseparable in school and nothing had changed even though they had both recently celebrated their twenty ninth birthdays. Well almost nothing, except that Hensely was now married and expecting her first child.

She grabbed a slice of pizza and a scoop of pasta salad for her plate and quietly made her way up the stairs to her loft. She didn't really feel like being social this evening, the day had been overwhelming already.

Naya flipped on the lights and once again took in the space she would be calling home for the foreseeable future. The previous night had been her first in the small loft with the slanted roof. It wasn't anything special, but it had a queen bed, nightstand and dresser which filled most of the limited space, she could probably put a TV on the dresser if she wanted one. But honestly, she figured she would be too busy with Vance and work to need one. There was a small door next to the stairs she came up which opened to the small half bathroom with just a toilet and sink, and she had to go downstairs to shower.

She pulled out her laptop from the nightstand drawer as she sat down on the bed. She had made a list as she had packed in La Junta of all the things she would need to do once she got here, she now added 'go shopping for dress pants' to the list. She had brought her measly wardrobe with her, which apparently wouldn't suit Brody, as it was mostly nice jeans and blouses. She only owned one pair of slacks she now planned to wear the rest of the week, but she knew that wouldn't cut it long term.

Her eyes scanned up to the list and she sighed as she read the words she had written shortly after she had made the decision to come to Denver. She did a quick Google search then pulled out her cell phone. It rang a couple times before a woman answered.

"Home Health Care, how can I help you?"

"Yes, I need to see about getting some part-time assistance?" Naya shyly inquired, at the same time she pulled up the information she suspected the woman would need.

"Certainly, can you explain a bit about what kind of assistance you need and I'll look into matching you with one of our aides."

She could hear the woman typing on the keyboard in the background.

"Yes, my name is Naya Largusa and I need some help a few days a week with my brother, Vance Largusa, who has non-Hodgkin's lymphoma."

The woman was silent for a moment then her typing resumed. "Sure thing, I just need to ask, how old is he? And what is his level of mobility?"

"He's thirty-two. He can walk, but not far, and he can't stand for more than a few minutes at a time. The treatment has made him very weak."

"Ahh, yes."

The woman was quiet for a minute, seemingly trying to think of the best way to broach the next subject, she braced herself.

"Is the treatment…helping?"

She sighed, she knew this was something she needed to acknowledge, "It does not seem like it, no."

"Alright, I will put down a preference for a male assistant, that way they will more easily be able to lift Vance if necessary."

Naya pinched the bridge of her nose, blinking back the tears that came no matter how well she prepared herself for these difficult conversations. "Thank you."

"What is Vance's current height and weight, if you know?"

Naya references her notes from the chat she had with her brother the previous day. "He's about six foot, and approximately one hundred and sixty-five pounds I believe."

"And how often will you need assistance?"

"That's the thing, I'm a detective and so my hours will change quite a bit. I'd like to start at maybe three or four afternoons a week, and then if work gets busier, maybe every afternoon? And if…" she took a sharp breath, "If things get worse, I will need more help. Perhaps full days."

The woman typed for a moment. "Alright, I've got a couple of prospects, let me contact them and then I'll get back to you. If your brother needs more extensive care in the future, we will probably need to split the job between two nurses. Could you give me your address?"

Naya rattled off the address she had already memorized.

"Perfect. I will call you back sometime in the next two business days."

"Thank you." Naya wiped the moisture from her cheek.

"No problem, have a good evening." The woman replied, then the call was disconnected.

Naya jolted awake in the middle of the night to the sound of her phone ringing. She leaned over and squinted at the screen; recognizing the number, she rushed to answer before it could ring a third time. "Hello?"

"I know you just went home a couple of hours ago, but it looks like we already have our first case." Atlas' voice came over the line.

Naya glanced at her clock and noticed it was almost one in the morning.

"What's going on?" She asked as she began slipping out of her sleep shorts and into her slacks. She went to the closet and pulled a button-up blouse out to put on.

"Maybe something, maybe nothing. A girl from the local high school went out running around eight this evening and never came home. His parents started to get worried and called in at around midnight."

Naya balanced her phone between her ear and shoulder as she leaned to slide into her shoes. "Midnight? Seems a bit long for a run. How old is the girl?"

"That's the thing, she's eighteen, a high school senior on the cross country team, and supposed to graduate this year. She runs two or so hours a day for practice, so when she wasn't home by ten, her parents just figured she ran a little farther than normal, but then by midnight, they knew something was wrong."

"Did she have a cell phone with her?" She slid her weapon into her holster and headed into the bathroom to run her brush through her hair.

"Yes. But it was off when they tried to call."

"Ok." Cell phones in the recent years had made their jobs easier, but the criminals were learning to be smarter about them. "I'll be out the door in five. We meeting at the girl's house?"

"Yes, I'll text over the address. I'm going to have the tech check for any cell pings on my way."

Atlas was clearly going to be a great partner.

"Alright. See you in a few." Naya ended the call and grabbed her jacket, slowly walking down the stairs on the side she had discovered the previous morning creaked less.

Vance's bedroom door at the bottom of the stairs was open a

crack, and Naya peeked in. He was asleep in the middle of his bed, which seemed to grow bigger around him each day. He didn't stir as Naya inched the door closed. In the kitchen, she opened the fridge and grabbed a ziplock bag of the leftover pizza she had separated after everyone had left earlier, making sure the one for Vance's lunch was easy for him to find. Not that she expected he would eat it, but she left it for him anyway.

Naya hoped the Home Health Care company would get back to her quickly, if all it meant was that Vance would be forced to eat more often, it would be enough to make her feel better.

NAYA PULLED up in front of a large red brick house in the Cherry Creek neighborhood, noticing immediately that whoever these people were, they had money. As she cut the ignition, her vision zeroed in on Atlas, who was halfway up the walk. He heard her footsteps as she stepped out and turned around, waiting for her.

"Any developments in the past half hour?"

He shook his head. "The techs are still trying to get a final ping for her phone. The patrol officers have been sitting with the parents while they wait for us."

Naya stifled a yawn as they stood in front of the door, and Atlas made a quick call to the officers inside to come to the door.

The entry opened into the foyer, which was dominated by a grand staircase in the center and a mirrored chandelier, which reflected the light from the other room the family was gathered in. The officer led them to the kitchen, there was a tired-looking man with short greyed hair leaning against the counter, he was looking at his wife, a clearly frazzled and distraught blonde woman who was sitting at the table with an untouched cup of coffee in front of her, she was tapping on the table anxiously. A few seats down, a preteen boy was also at the table; he was staring blankly ahead while an officer, presumably the partner of the patrol officer who had answered the door for them, was asking him routine questions.

"These are Julia's parents. Roger and Lynn Charles, and her brother, Sean." Naya bowed her head in greeting as she made their acquaintance. She opened her mouth to introduce herself, but Atlas spoke first.

"I'm Detective Atlas, and this is Detective Largusa; we will be the lead detectives in charge of finding your daughter." Roger ventured forward and shook both of their hands. The officer who had answered the door filled two cups with coffee from a pot on the counter and handed them each one.

"We were just discussing if their daughter has any reason she would leave home without calling, to say, go to a friend's house," The officer at the table shared.

"And like I told them, that Julia isn't like that. She's a good kid, committed to her grades and cross country, so much so she doesn't even have a boyfriend. She would have no reason not to tell us where she was going!" Lynn sobbed.

Naya glanced at Atlas. They hadn't known each other for more than a day, but she could tell he was having the same thought as her. Just because a teenager said she didn't have a boyfriend didn't necessarily mean it was true.

"What about friends, does she have any she may spend the night with?" Naya prodded, as she jotted notes on her phone.

"Yes. She has her best friend Becca, but we know her parents, and we called her earlier. Becca was already in bed. I mean, it's a school night; neither of the girls would try to have a sleepover on a school night!"

"Not to be disrespectful, but did Becca's parents actually check the room to ensure Becca was sleeping? Just to make sure there wasn't a mix-up of some sort, and maybe she is there?" Atlas asked.

Lynn nodded frantically. "They even woke Becca up! They're worried too."

"Okay, can you go over your daughter's running route with me?" Naya slid into the chair next to Lynn and pulled up a map on her phone.

"That's the thing," Lynn lamented. "Roger and I are both runners ourselves, and it isn't safe to run the same path every night, so we've always instilled that knowledge in her. So, other than her starting and ending here, Julia was instructed to always switch up her routine. She could have been running any route, there's endless possibilities."

They were certainly right about that if that was the case, they would have to formulate a plan. "Does she have any favorite routes, maybe?" Naya asked.

Atlas was listening to the exchange from behind Naya and Lynn.

"Well, she would run on busier streets at night, they're more well-lit and safer. During the day she would often run by the creek, but because she left so late tonight since she had a lot of homework, I can't imagine she would run out that way where it would be empty, or on any unlit roads."

Naya turned her head, and she and Atlas locked eyes; Atlas swiftly stepped from the room to make some calls and see what they could do about getting an Amber alert out. Julia was technically eighteen, but because she was still in high school and lived with her parents, they might be able to push the envelope on the timelines.

"Does Julia have a car?" Naya inquired as she turned back to Lynn.

For the first time, Roger spoke up before his wife could "Yes, she has a black Jetta. It's in the driveway."

"Does she use the car to go out often?" Naya continued taking notes.

"What's that supposed to mean?" Challenged Lynn.

"I'm sorry, let me clarify, Would Julia often use the car to meet up with friends? Or do they usually pick her up?"

"Oh , well, most of kids in this neighborhood have cars by Julia's age, so I suppose both? But I've been trying to tell you, detective, my daughter doesn't go out much. She's really focused on trying to get a scholarship for college for cross country. When she does go out, it's on Saturdays, and it's usually with Becca. They usually go to the mall."

Naya conceded, she wished Atlas wasn't on the phone as he would know more about the area than she did to ask more about the possible routes the girl would have taken. "Can you show me your daughters' room?"

Lynn assented and, grabbing another tissue, she stood from her chair and led Naya to the stairs. "Do you think someone... grabbed her?"

Naya took a deep breath, trying to stay calm, and broached the subject delicately. "Well, first, Mrs. Charles, we must evaluate all possibilities, such as that your daughter simply forgot to communicate with you that she is with a friend or at some sort of event. Then there is also the possibility that she simply fell and twisted her ankle or something of that nature, and her phone is dead ---"

"That would never happen! Julia was addicted to her phone. She never let the battery get below twenty percent. And she certainly wouldn't go running with it below half! She wouldn't be able to listen to her music then..."

Naya smiled, keeping her tone understanding she continued. "Yes, I understand that, but we still have to make sure. And then yes, we will also look at the possibility that perhaps someone picked her up." Lynn looked at her with terrified eyes and Naya quickly tried to reassure her. "That doesn't have to be anything malicious. There's a possibility that someone she knew saw her running, and maybe they offered her a ride or something." She knew it was a stretch, but she was trying to not scare the poor woman, she was already a wreck.

Lynn opened the first door in the hallway to reveal a lavender-walled room. Clothes littered the floor, and the walls were covered with band posters and several pictures of two teenage girls, who Naya assumed were Julia and her friend Becca.

Naya slipped on a pair of vinyl gloves she had taken from her pocket and began to search for anything that might give her an idea of where Julia was.

Nothing seemed out of place. The room was a mess, but the normal type of messy that came with being a teenager. A laptop was plugged in and sitting on the nightstand, a phone charger sat empty next to it. A bookbag was tossed across the bed. It certainly looked like Julia had planned to come back.

"What are you looking for exactly?" Lynn protested, a note of suspicion in her tone.

Naya shrugged. "Just making sure everything is in order." She slid open the top drawer on the nightstand and combed through a hodge-podge of nail polish, hair ties, and notepads. There was nothing of interest. "What did your daughter normally take running with her?"

"Her phone and headphones, she for sure wouldn't leave without those. And she would slip her ID and credit card in her fanny pack. Yeah, she ran with a fanny pack to carry her water bottles and gels."

"Do you see any of those items here?" Naya motioned to the room.

Lynn glanced around, clearly looking in a few places where those items could usually be found. "No, I don't see them. And she was definitely wearing her running clothes when she left."

Naya agreed and turned to leave the room. "I don't think there anything more I need from here." Lynn's whole body relaxed as the words left Naya's mouth. It was clear that she was uncomfortable with Naya in her daughter's room.

As they were going down the stairs, Atlas was on his way up. Their eyes met and Naya shook her head.

"Alright Mrs. Charles, thank you for your cooperation, the two officers here are going to stay with you in case she comes back. Please do your best to stay off the phone lines that your daughter would be the most likely to call in case she tries to get through. Detective Largusa and I are going to start searching and we will check in later today, alright?"

Lynn nodded and yawned. She was visibly tired but probably wouldn't sleep, a fear of missing something and nerves to be sure. Naya just hoped this case would be a classic case where the teen girl shows up in the morning and was just goofing off, but something about it didn't feel right.

After agreeing to meet back at the station Naya and Atlas headed to their respective cars. She yawned as she slid behind the wheel, she was going to need to stop for a coffee on her way, because at this rate it was going to be a long night.

5

NAYA

Naya startled awake as her phone buzzed on the bunk beside her. She grabbed it as she sat up and tried her best to straighten her work clothes while letting her eyes gradually focus on the screen. "Hello?" she sighed.

"Hello, Ms. Largusa? This is Home Health Care and my name is Mary. I am just calling to let you know we have found a placement for you. Would it be possible for you to meet him sometime this evening?"

Naya glanced at her watch, it was only eleven, but she had been at the precinct since before three in the morning. She was sure she would be permitted to go home for at least an hour at some point. "Yes, would five work?"

There was silence where the representative clearly muted Naya to consult with someone. "Yes, it does. His name is Derek, he will be at the address you gave us at five then?"

"Perfect. Thank you, have a good day." Naya started to pull the phone away from her ear to hang up.

"Oh and Ms. Largusa?" interjected Mary.

"Yes?" She put the phone back to her ear.

"Keep in mind that we want him to be a good fit for you. If you don't think he will work out please let us know, and we can try someone else."

"Of course, thank you." Naya replied as they both said their good-byes and she finally got to hang up. Vance had always been an easy-going guy and Naya doubted he would put up much of a fight, just about anyone would be fine.

She smoothed her hair, pulled it back and glanced in the mirror by the door. She was a wreck, but when she had gone to take a nap an hour ago, the young Julia Charles had still been missing.

When she opened the sleep room door she was greeted by mass chaos in the precinct. People were darting every which way shouting and gesturing. Naya scanned the room for Atlas. She didn't have to look hard because he was making a beeline for her, she met him halfway and they headed towards their desks.

"Good, you're up. I was coming to get you."

"What happened?" She quickly turned and grabbed her jacket from her chair. She would kill for a coffee right now but doubted there would be time. And the look on Atlas' face told her he did not have good news.

"They found a body."

Naya felt her shoulders drop. "Crap."

Atlas nodded. "My thoughts exactly."

THEY PULLED up behind the coroner's van on the side of a dirt road. They were in the eastern part of the state, almost an hour's drive from Denver. The area was mostly farmland and consisted almost entirely of open fields, and you could go miles without seeing a person. Definitely an easy place to dump a body without being seen. She could see several police cruisers on the other side of the road. Clouds covered the glittering sun, giving the entire scene a somber feel as Naya stepped from the passenger seat and took in her surroundings.

There was a ditch running along one side of the road and an embankment on the other, the embankment was covered with grass and held a fence marking the property line of whoever's land it was. About twenty feet ahead of them, a man was standing next to a red pickup truck; Naya was willing to bet that this was his property. She and Atlas walked a little ways into the field to where the crime scene techs were huddled. She pulled up Julia's picture on her phone and held it up, for herself and Atlas. Unfortunately, there was a strong resemblance.

"It looks to be her." He said solemnly.

"I agree," Naya whispered.

The techs looked busy, she didn't want to disrupt them. She glanced back at the farmer a few paces ahead of them, on the road. "I'm going to go talk to him, we can get the details from these guys later." She nudged Atlas.

He nodded and followed her.

"Hello!" Naya called once they were back on the road, the man turned towards them and waved as they approached. They quickly made introductions and it turned out that the man was a farmer as she had suspected most in the area would be. He had a local plot on which he raised wheat and had been the one to find the body. Atlas began asking him questions about how and when he discovered Julia's body.

"I saw some hawks circling. And sometimes they do that you know? Especially when they see a large snake or rabbit. But there were several of them circling, at one point there were three. And hawks are solitary predators, so I knew something big had died, and I was a bit worried it was one of the cats I have on property to keep the mice at bay or someone's livestock, ya know? So I drove out here, and the minute I saw it was a person I called the police."

Atlas nodded. "Ok. And was she covered with anything when you found her?"

The farmer shook his head. "No, she was just as you see her now. She wasn't covered or buried or anything, so I dialed 911 immediately."

Naya was jotting down notes in her phone. "Did you check for a pulse or anything?"

"No. I didn't need to; I've been around a long time, and the moment I saw her, I knew she was dead. Didn't look to have a drop of blood left in her."

She made a note of that and figured she could check with forensics later. "Did you see anything else, any cars? People wandering around? Anything out of the ordinary?"

"No. But I'm a farmer, so although I've been up since the crack of dawn, I've been out in the fields working, not standing and watching the road."

Naya nodded, pulled her card out of her pocket, and handed it to the man. "Let me check with my associates, but I believe you're good to go back to your work. Just call me if you think of anything else or notice anything else unusual." The farmer nodded his agreement.

Naya turned to go back to the scene when he suddenly cleared his throat. "The girl...she's quite young?"

She knew immediately what the man was hinting at, she took a measured breath before turning around and putting on her most professional façade. "Yes sir. We still have to tell her family. But. If you would like more information you can certainly watch the news tonight."

He nodded again, a scolded look on his face.

Naya resumed walking towards the body and the crime scene techs, Atlas keeping up with her every stride. When they were out of ear shot but still a few paces away from the huddle around the body he opened his mouth. "You were very efficient about deflecting that."

She smiled, "You forget, I used to be sheriff. I had to give press conferences."

"You said you didn't move for career reasons?" He was prying but Naya wasn't ready to share that part of her life with him yet.

"Yes, that's correct." Luckily they joined the group at the body with perfect timing, giving her the opportunity to drop the subject without being suspicious..

Atlas began talking to one of the techs who he seemed to have built a rapport with on past cases. "Cause of death?"

She shrugged. "Hard to tell. One thing I can say for sure is there's hardly any blood."

"As in it was a clean crime scene?"

"No, as in most of it is missing. Not all of it, but enough that the girl is as white as a sheet and I don't see any dried blood at the scene. .She's been so drained of blood that had she been cut after, I don't think the wound would have bled."

Atlas sent Naya a stunned glance which she mirrored before he continued his inquiry with the young tech. "Any other observations you can tell us?"

The coroner chose this moment to speak. "Well, I can tell you the time of death was between ten and eleven last night."

"Damn," Naya murmured. It didn't matter how they worked the case. They were already too late by the time they had gotten to the Charles' household.

They exchanged a few more words with the coroner and tech before turning away from the scene and walking back towards the car.

"What do you think?" She asked Atlas, scanning the horizon and contemplating the information they had gathered.

"I don't like it. Not one bit. He only had her for a few hours. This was a cold, calculated murder. This wasn't an opportunistic kill. I think he is going to kill again."

Naya opened the door and slid into the passenger side, checking the time on her phone. She figured she could still make it in time for the Home Health Care meeting if she left directly from the station. "Yeah, I was thinking the same thing. Hey, listen, I know this case is just getting rolling, but I really need a shower. Mind if I head home for a couple of hours to freshen up and come back after?"

Atlas started the car. "Yeah, that's no problem. I mean, the girl is already dead, and I doubt our murderer will strike again so soon."

"I agree, I just feel bad asking for a personal favor already."

Atlas shook his head. "Don't even worry about it. You forget this isn't the three-man La Junta show anymore. There's a whole team of detectives and assistants I can have to help me build a board. Then you can take a look, and we can adjust it when you get back."

She felt a half smile brush her lips. He was right, she hadn't considered that. "I guess I'm just so used to being on the clock all the time."

"I noticed. But listen, I like to get to know my partner a bit if we are gonna work together and we got tossed on this before we could blink. So, mind if I ask you a few questions while we are stuck in the car anyway?"

"Sure." The half-smile instantly disappeared from her face. "But nothing too personal."

"Not too personal, okay, I can do that. One, how do you like your coffee?"

Naya chuckled, that was a something they would definitely need to know about each other, especially as more cases came across their desk. "Two sugars, the real kind. You?"

"Black." He winked over at her and then turned his eyes back to the road. "Favorite donut?"

She giggled at that; this was the quintessential cop quiz. "Glazed, you?"

"Don't laugh, but, pink with sprinkles." It was his turn to break out into a grin. "And I eat them because I somehow always get left with them in the break room, understand? If you ever insinuate otherwise to anyone in the precinct, you will find out just how sneaky I can be." He mocked a serious face at her before they both burst into laughter.

"Alright, alright, point taken. My turn, favorite takeout?"

"Chipotle, you?"

"Uh-oh, Qudoba."

"Uh oh, is right, seems like we will be rock paper scissoring a lot." it unintentionally sounded like an innuendo, and they both busted out laughing again. They were practically in tears when he choked out, "I did not mean it like that." They giggled a little longer before finally getting their breathing under control.

"Don't worry, I won't be reporting you for sexual harassment. It's not my style, and I can handle myself." Naya reassured, smiling as they pulled into the station parking lot.

"Well, besides the takeout battle, I think we will get along just fine." Atlas teased as he stepped out of the car.

"I agree."

She pulled up in front of her house just as a man dressed in scrubs was stepping out of his car. Naya stepped out of hers and waved. He waved back, and she could see the muscles flexing in his arm. He seemed strong enough to lift Vance, just as the representative had assured her. His dark hair was gelled back professionally so that strands wouldn't fall in his eyes.

"Hi! I'm Naya Largusa." She held out her hand as she walked up. He shook it, his grip was like iron, his handshake solid and professional.

"Hi, I'm Derek, from Home Health Care."

She smiled. "I assumed so, come right in. Hopefully, Vance is awake." She slid her key into the lock and pushed the door open, heading inside, Derek followed her.

"Vance?" She called out.

"In here." He replied from the den area, his voice scratchy.

They rounded the corner to find Vance sitting on the couch in the same place he had been the day before. Kevin was once again on the floor next to him and seemed a bit shocked to see a man walk in behind Naya. For a minute, Naya swore she saw an emotion cross his features but she couldn't identify it before it was gone.

"Vance, Kevin, this is Derek from Home Health Care."

The men greeted Derek.

"Well, since you're here to meet Vance I'll leave you two to talk and I'll be in the kitchen when you're finished." She tried to keep her voice even as she excused herself, even though the fact that she was hiring a caregiver for her thirty-two year old brother was splintering her insides to pieces.

"Kevin, join me in the kitchen?"

Kevin paused the game they were playing and followed her into the tiny kitchen. Naya opened the fridge to find Vance hadn't eaten lunch again. She took a deep breath and blinked back the tears that welled up behind her eyes before grabbing some leftover pizza for herself and turning around to face Kevin.

He clearly sensed something was up. "Who is that?" He asked, his tone slightly accusatory.

She grabbed a plate from the cupboard and began microwaving the pizza, swallowing the lump building in her throat and trying to keep her composure. She felt crazy; she could look at the dead body of an eighteen-year-old girl without blinking but couldn't face the brother's illness.

"He's from Home Health Care. I... I need help with Vance."

Kevin was silent. She was sure he knew Vance's condition, but she also wasn't sure how much her brother had disclosed and didn't want to violate his privacy.

But before she could stop herself, she felt the next words bubble from her lips, "He won't eat unless I'm here, it's getting harder for him to move, and I just—" She caught herself as a single tear slid down her cheek. She turned toward the sink to try to hide while she regained her composure. She felt embarrassed.

The microwave dinged, interrupting the moment.

Kevin took the interruption as his cue. "Is there anything I can do to help?" his voice was somber, closer than before. He had stepped toward her but hesitated, his posture visibly unsure what else to do now that he was there.

She took another few seconds to breathe and got her emotions under control, before turning to face him.

"Well, Derek will be here a couple of days a week now, but maybe when he isn't, you could make sure Vance at least tries to eat lunch. I always leave it in the fridge, I can start making extra for you as well—"

Kevin held up his hand. "No need. But yes, I will encourage him to try to eat more often. I promise."

Derek cleared his throat from the doorway. "Can I talk to you for a minute, Ms. Largusa?"

She nodded, and Kevin took his cue and headed back into the den.

"Vance and I seem to get along alright." Derek started.

"Yes?"

"Yeah, I mean, it's hard for any guy to admit they need help, but I explained to him that I want to be his friend, not just his assistant. So, I can help carry him to use the facilities, but then we can also play video games the rest of the time if that's what he wants."

It felt so weird to be discussing her older adult brother like this. "And he was okay with that?"

Derek nodded. "As okay with it as any man in his condition can be."

"Okay, well, do they have a set schedule for you, or..." She trailed off, she really hadn't any idea how this was supposed to work.

"No. You let me know your schedule, I am yours any three days of the week you choose. I'm just not available on Sundays or Tuesdays; I work with someone else on those days." Derek specified. "However, Home Health Care did explain to me that you want to start at part-time care, but at some point, you would likely need more full-time assistance. They already know my schedule, though, so it's likely that when that time comes, you will be assigned a second person who can fill in the gaps. But for now, when did you think would work best?"

Naya did some quick calculations. "Well, I guess let's do Monday, Wednesday, and Friday to start. Vance usually sleeps in late, but I would want you here when he wakes up to help him get ready if he needs. So how about ten in the morning? And your shifts are eight hours, correct?"

He nodded. "That works, and yes. I take a half-hour lunch, but I will stay from ten in the morning until six every night. My job is to help with medical care and household chores, errands, or whatever needs to be done that the person no longer can on their own, so I can assist with whatever Vance needs done on those days."

"Perfect. Well, no chores here. I do want you to make sure Vance eats lunch, I've been leaving it in the fridge and coming home to it untouched. And then on Fridays if you could take him to his chemo appointment at two in the afternoon? He was driving himself...but it's gotten too hard."

"I understand, and I can definitely do those."

"Other than that, whatever he wants you to do is up to him. He's an adult—" Her voice cracked. "—And this is his home."

"Yes ma'am. Well, I will report back to Home Health Care that things went well and that I'll start Friday since it's Wednesday?"

"Sounds great to me." She said as she suddenly remembered her forgotten pizza in the microwave and randomly popped open the door to her now cold slice, she would have to reheat it again.

"Perfect. Home Health Care will call you to verify, but if you want to give me the house key for tomorrow, I'll say bye to Vance and get out of your way in the evening."

"Certainly." Naya grabbed the spare house key off the wall and handed it to Derek. She would need to make another copy at some point. "Here you go."

"Thank you. I'll show myself out, have a good night."

Naya responded automatically and slipped her pizza back into the microwave, resting her elbows on the counter as it made its slow revolutions. She could still feel her emotions rippling right beneath her normally composed surface. She would need to figure herself out before she returned to work. She couldn't end up crying on her first case. She would never live it down.

She scarfed down her pizza as quickly as the temperature would allow, wishing like hell she could go for a run right now. It always helped to clear her mind, but duty was calling, and she had a murderer to find.

She had wanted to talk with Vance about Derek, but when she looked in the den, Kevin was still there, and they were clearly having a ball with the shooting game they were playing. So instead, she decided to settle for a quick goodbye. After all, Vance could text her if he wanted to.

"Later Vance." She called out as she walked to the door.

"See ya, catch those bad guys for me, will ya?"

"I will." She smiled at their inside joke. It started when she had first become sheriff.

She caught Kevin's eye just as she stepped out the door, and she couldn't be quite sure, but she thought she saw him wink at her. Maybe it was her imagination.

6

MARK

He was bored. Really bored. The young girl hadn't fought enough and it had been over too quickly for him. He missed the days when he could play mind games with women for years instead.

Now he was just sitting in his apartment, staring out the window, his disguise making his face unbearably itchy. Granted, he could probably take it off. He doubted anyone was really looking for him, especially here and on the third floor. But he was also a cautious man, and he knew the one time people let their guard down was often the time they got caught. He wasn't taking that chance, he had too much work to do.

He turned away from the window and looked at what he had spent all day setting up in his room. Granted, it was rough. But he could perfect it as the days went on.

If only he hadn't had to get a job! He would've been able to devote all his time to his work, but unfortunately he had to pay for his room somehow. And he needed to be a model tenant if he wanted to stay under the radar, so that meant he couldn't miss rent payments.

All in all the job wasn't too bad, he had some great coworkers. They had even invited him out for a beer after work the other night.

He had to decline though, he couldn't let anyone get to close, it would be too risky.

He surveyed his set up again. It definitely needed work. But even though he was bored he just didn't feel like devoting himself to it tonight. What he did feel like, was doing some scouting. He pulled out his phone and opened his favorite feature.

Of course, the phone hadn't come with this feature, but he had no problem programming it. Computer programming had always been his gift. He brushed his hand over the interface he had designed. He could have totally used his skills for good and spent time programming all kinds of fun apps for Google, Apple, and whatever other operating systems were out there.

He could have.

He had tried that however, and it was boring. Mind numbingly so.

Instead, he had decided to go out on his own. It was more fun that way.

Interesting.

And he didn't have to climb the corporate ladder.

And he could work on *his* project.

But the last girl. She was too easy. He needed someone older, more mature, with more fight this time.

Mark moved to his PC and popped open the Facebook tab and began making a number of requests. He requested several hundred friends in under a few minutes. Then he leaned back and rested his hands in his lap.

Now to wait.

It didn't take long, just a few minutes latera little red notification showed up.

He was in business.

7

NAYA

Naya dropped her head into her hands and grumbled in frustration. It had been nearly a week since Julia's Charles' body had been discovered, and they were absolutely no closer to finding her than they were that first night. There were no fingerprints, no footprints left on the scene, there was nothing that would give them a single hint as to what happened to the eighteen year old athlete.

Atlas leaned back in his chair and huffed. "I'm guessing you're just as stuck as me?"

She nodded without looking up from the coroners report she was reading for the umpteenth time. "It's like she was beamed up by aliens, got her blood sucked out, and was dumped in that field."

"I know." He replied, his dejection matching hers. "I haven't had a case like this in a long time. Usually people have at least one enemy, but everyone loved this girl. And I mean everyone."

Atlas wasn't exaggerating, after informing the parents they had found her body last week, they had gone to interview the best friend, as well as half of the girl's high school, and she didn't know if it was because the girl was dead, but no one had anything bad to say.

Maybe it was her prejudice from working in a small town, but in La Junta, whenever she had a case, especially a murder, there was always rumors and gossip to go with it. Everyone there had comments and opinions.

She flipped the pages of the report, looking for something, anything she hadn't see on her other passes. But no luck. "No leads on what happened to her phone?" she asked again.

Atlas shook his head as he rattled off the same thing they both knew. "Still hasn't surfaced. Has been off since about nine that evening, which is her estimated abduction time. Time of death was between ten and eleven that evening."

She'd heard it before, and she knew Atlas was humoring her by going over it again, but she couldn't help it. This case was getting under her skin.

Suddenly, she remembered the files she had tucked in the bottom of her desk drawer, she leaned down and dug around for them. Atlas must've thought she had found something because he raised an eyebrow in interest.

"Don't get too excited." She joked as she pulled out the three cold cases from La Junta.

"What are those?"

"Cases from my time as Sheriff in La Junta. They are the only three cases I never solved." She flipped open the top one, it was from five years earlier when she was still just officer Largusa, it detailed the sudden disappearance of a six year old girl.

"Do you think they have something to do with this case?" He asked incredulously.

Naya shook her head. "No, but sometimes it helps to focus on something else for a minute and then come back."

"You know most cops just use social media for that."

Naya smiled. "I'm not most cops. Besides, I don't want to flood my mind with new information, I want to look at this case I know everything about then look back at the case in question. You never know what might help jolt your mind to make connections."

He rolled his eyes but was smirking. "Well I'm going to look at something known as the breakroom. I need coffee, want a cup?"

"Please." She checked her watch, it was almost eight at night and she knew she needed to go home soon. Derek would have left a couple hours ago, and Vance needed dinner.

Life was much easier with Derek around and Vance seemed to be eating more. Naya had also noticed that on the days Derek came Vance was always dressed a bit nicer. Maybe they went out for walks or something, she wasn't sure, but it still made her happy.

As much of a blessing as Derek was, he had also been the bearer of bad news. After just two visits he had mentioned to Naya that she needed to purchase a wheelchair for Vance. She hadn't done it yet, mainly because when she opened the internet window to do so she had started crying inconsolably and had been unable to complete the order. She would have to try again when she got home tonight, but before she clocked out she wanted to take one more look at the report on Julia Charles.

She was scanning the part where it talked about the vast amount of blood which had been drained from her body, when it hit her. She hastily opened Google and began searching.

Atlas walked back over, noticing her enthusiasm as he placed a paper cup in front of her. "Did you seriously crack the case while I was getting coffee?" He joked.

"No, but I thought of something. Why would he drain her blood so completely?"

"Because he's a nutjob?" Atlas raised his eyebrow at her, a confused look on his face.

"Definitely, but I was thinking, it was done so completely, what if he also had a reason to? Like a use for the blood?" She closed the tab she was in and went back to the search results. "I mean it could be for something like a cult ritual, or science experiments or something. I don't know, that's what I'm searching now, possible reasons he might need that much blood."

"That's what you typed in?"

Naya chuckled. "No, but you get my point, right? I want to see if this goes anywhere."

"You're right." He conceded as he opened his own internet browsing window. "The removal was so clean. Manner of death was blood loss, do you think she was awake for it? And if she was, why didn't she struggle and how did he not get any on her? You may be on to something here Largusa."

They fell into a concentrated silence as they clicked through internet windows, the only sounds the clacking of keys between sips of coffee. What felt like moments later, she looked up at the clock and it was after nine. "Shit, I gotta head home, but I'll do some more before bed."

"Hot date?" Atlas joked.

Naya tried to paste on a smile. She hadn't told Atlas about her brother yet, but she knew she wouldn't be able to keep it from him much longer with these hours.

"Kinda, but I better not keep him waiting either way."

"So it is a him then? There was a rumor going around you batted for the other team." He teased.

Naya laughed and blushed. "You never can tell, can you?" And with a wink she turned and headed for the door.

SHE UNLOCKED the door and let herself in, she was surprised to find Kevin in the hallway in front of her. "Everything okay?" She asked, glancing at her phone wondering if something had happened and she had missed a call from Vance.

"Everything is fine, Vance, uh, wasn't feeling well, so he had Derek help him to bed hours ago. I was planning to stay only a few minutes but I must've fallen asleep on the couch. Your keys in the lock woke me up."

Naya had zoned out after hearing that Vance wasn't feeling well. "Did he say what was bothering him?"

"His stomach, I think." Kevin said as he followed her into the kitchen. Naya opened the fridge surveying the contents. The food she had made for Vance had been eaten, just like every other day Derek had been there this week.

"He ate at least."

"Yeah." Kevin confirmed.

They stood in silence for what seemed like forever but was probably only a few minutes. "Listen," he finally spoke, his voice cracking a bit. "Vance, well, he hasn't told me how bad it is, but I know it's bad, and well, since he's my best friend and all, do you think I could have your number? You know, for emergencies."

Naya surprised herself by giggling in response, to which she was immediately embarrassed by and slapped her hand over her mouth before apologizing. "I'm sorry, I didn't mean to laugh. I just got the mental image of you using that line to pick up a girl."

A smile broke out across Kevin's face. "I mean, it is a pretty good line, right? I've been rehearsing it all night."

With that they both broke out in laughter. They tried to stifle it as not to wake Vance, which of course made them both only laugh harder. Pretty soon they were sitting on the floor next to each other, in front of the refrigerator, trying to breathe deeply between giggles as they attempted to calm themselves down.

"Well, ridiculous line or not, you can have my number." Naya held out her phone in his direction with a new contact page pulled up.

"Yes! Success!" He hissed which only made them both laugh again. Once they had calmed down for the second time, he looked at her, "But really," he said somberly, as he handed her phone back and kept her hand in his. "Me and the guys, we know it's bad, and we want to be there for Vance any way we can. None of us have much extra money, but we're all in construction and fairly handy. So if you need help around the house or something, please let us know."

She nodded and stood up from the floor, reaching a hand out to help Kevin up, but he shooed her offer away and stood up on his own facing her with a small grin. "Well, since I have your number now. Do you think I could, you know, text you just for me sometimes?"

Naya raised an eyebrow but felt a smile spread across her face. "And just why would you want to text me for yourself?"

"Because I think you're kinda cute." He quipped, and then he turned and headed out the door, leaving her alone in the kitchen. Naya stood there for a moment after he left, a bit in shock at what he said. She hadn't lost her edge after all.

Making herself dinner now completely forgotten, she turned off the lights and headed up the stairs to prepare for bed. Tomorrow was likely to be another long day at the precinct.

HER PHONE JOLTED her awake in the middle of the night again. She sighed as she reached over to answer it. She definitely wasn't used to the pace of police work in the big city yet.

"Largusa?"

She was already sitting up and kicking her legs over the edge of the bed as she grunted in confirmation.

"You're not gonna believe this." It was Atlas.

"I think I can." She mumbled as she fumbled for the light. "Another girl?"

"Sort of. This one isn't quite a girl though. Shanice Woods. Thirty-two, mother of two. Her husband called when she didn't return from her run."

"So, he likes runners then." She considered this as she slid on her pants and placed her gun in its holster.

"It would seem so."

There was silence on the other end of the line for a minute, but Naya had an idea. "Listen Atlas, maybe I'm going out on a limb here. But I don't think we should waste time interviewing the husband and kids. I think we should let the patrol guys handle that this time."

"I agree."

"We should see if we can find out her regular route from them, head there and see if there could've been any witnesses around or anyone suspicious." Naya tiptoed down the stairs, looking in on

Vance as always. She was surprised to see him awake and sitting up in bed. She held up her finger and looked away from him. "I'll meet you at the station in twenty."

"Sure thing, hop in my car when you get here."

"Will do." Naya hung up the call and looked back towards Vance. He had a book open on his lap and she could see dark circles under his eyes, she wondered how long he had been having trouble sleeping.

"Everything okay?" She asked.

"I'm fine. Seems I can go to bed nice and early with as tired as I am these days.." A shy smile playing on his lips.

Naya went over and sat on the bed with him for a moment. "How are you liking Derek?" She asked reluctantly. It felt weird to have a conversation with her older brother about his caretaker.

He shrugged. "He's okay. I'm trying to stay positive about this whole thing," he motioned to his legs covered by the blanket, "But it's hard. Derek is cool though. Kevin and I got him into our Call of Duty rotation."

Naya nodded slowly, knowing what she had to say next. She looked away from her brother's face and towards the wall. "Derek wants me to get you a wheelchair..."

"That would be best, yes." He answered in a way that was so calm and collected; for a minute, Naya forgot what a serious topic this was. For a second he was just her brother again, having a mundane conversation about something like grocery shopping and not the impact of his cancer. It was hard to believe he was able to stay so objective about something so life-altering.

She turned back to look at his face, and all it took was seeing the dark circles under his eyes to remind her of where they were and their reality, and that she had to be going.

"Alright, I've got to go, but call me if there's an emergency okay? No Derek today, but there is still lunch in the fridge for you. Middle shelf." She said this as if he didn't know, though she knew he did.

"Thanks mom." Rolling his eyes, a half-smile back on his face.

"You're welcome, son." She joked right back, ruffling his hair like she used to do when they were kids. It wasn't until she locked the front door and looked down at her hand that she noticed it was covered in his hair.

Her breath caught and she fought back the tears that threatened to spill as she turned away from the door.

She had work to do, she would have to deal with her turmoil later.

8

NAYA

"Turn left on 88th." Naya directed, looking down at the hastily scribbled notes in her hand.

"Hmm..." Atlas surveyed the dark horizon. "This is so...rural."

Fields lined the road on either side, a single double yellow line reflected their headlights back at them, there were no streetlights, no sidewalks either.

"Are you sure this was the route Shanice's husband gave?" She glanced back at the notes, they weren't all that descriptive.

"Yeah. And I know this is a grown woman we're talking about, but I would be nervous to run this road at night." Atlas slowed the car as there was motion off to the left.

Naya leaned over to get a better look "Raccoon?"

"Yeah... This is weird, although, her husband did say she was a former long distance marathoner and fast. He said her average mile time could get as low as a six-minute mile."

She let out a low whistle. "And our guy managed to grab her? He'd have to be pretty fast himself?"

They were both quiet for a second. "I guess we shouldn't assume this is the same guy." Naya added. "After all, she's a full-grown woman, maybe she just went further than normal?"

"No." Atlas shook his head. "I know we're supposed to keep an open mind, but it's too similar. Two late night runners disappearing within a week of each other isn't a coincidence." He let out a huff. "And I don't care what anyone says. No mother of two children is still out at three in the morning when she told her husband she would be home at ten as always."

Naya shared his belief.

"Turn right."

Atlas did and Naya surveyed the area around them. They were almost back to the Woods' house. "I wish there was a chance that there was a witness, but I'm thinking not."

"Maybe we should've detained the raccoon." Atlas joked and Naya laughed.

"I don't think we have cuffs small enough." She yawned. "Well, we are almost back to her home, but I need coffee. We aren't going to be sleeping any time soon."

"You're right. I think there's a 24-hour drive-thru on the way back to the station."

"Thank god."

THEY LAID out everything they had on the conference room table, and then Atlas rearranged the pictures of Julia Charles he had taped to the whiteboard. Naya took a gulp of her coffee and tried not to yawn. She needed some sleep, badly. It would have to wait, though; she glanced at her watch and noticed it was now almost six in the morning.

She stifled another yawn and taped together the halves of the map she had printed, circling both sites of the victim's homes in yellow and the site where they had found Julia's body in red. She grabbed a few more pieces of tape and hung it up next to where Atlas was working on the board. He paused to look at her project.

"Damn. This is weird."

He didn't have to explain, she knew. Killers usually worked in a single convenient and familiar area, and they would be able to get an idea of where the killer lived or worked based on their abduction and dump sites. But the three circles Naya had made on the map were scattered and had no correlation to one another.

"Well, I guess we know he has transportation." She shrugged and turned to see what else they had accumulated on the table.

"Transportation. And he likes females who are in shape from running"

"Which is weird because the murder of Julia didn't seem to be sexually driven," Naya added while reading from the coroner's report on Julia Charles. "Well, I guess that could change with Shanice."

He shook his head in agreement. "I don't think he is a sexual predator at all. He doesn't seem to keep them alive long enough for that, I don't think..." He trailed off as they both thought of what was left unsaid.

"He crossed racial barriers." She interjected into the uncomfortable silence that had taken over; she said this while looking at the picture of the young Caucasian Julia Charles next to Shanice Woods, who was a black woman and mother and much older than Julia. She stood up and began to pace, they were so different. What could this man possibly be doing with these women? And with the blood? And how long did they have until Shanice showed up dead?

Atlas watched her pace as he sipped from his coffee. "Penny for your thoughts?"

"Honestly, I've got nothing." She admitted.

"Me neither." He looked a bit dejected. "I'm considering running this by Brody and getting his take on it."

"Couldn't hurt." She slid back into one of the chairs and took another gulp of her coffee.

She was feeling stuck, so she pulled out her phone and pulled up the website for wheelchairs, realizing she had no idea which one to pick. She scrolled through for a few moments before randomly selecting one. It would have to do. She quickly clicked to the checkout screen, then before she could put her card information in, she thought better of it and set her phone back down. When she looked up again, Atlas was staring intently at the board.

"Anything?" She asked.

He shook his head. "Nada. Honestly, as pessimistic as it is, I'm trying to guess where and when we will find the body this time. I expect him to be more careful. I really don't think he meant for us to find Julia so fast."

"I agree –." Her statement was cut off when she yawned again and this didn't escape Atlas' notice.

"You've been working long hours all week; why don't you head home and sleep for a few hours, and I'll call you if we have any leads?"

"Are you sure?" Naya still felt guilty leaving in the middle of a case.

"Again, you do realize we have lots of detectives here, right? You don't have to be here round-the-clock, you just have to be ready to go around the clock." He smirked as he turned back to the whiteboard and began reading something there.

She stood and slid her phone in her pocket. He was right, she needed sleep.

"How do you do it?"

"Do what?" He asked without turning around.

"You don't even look tired, meanwhile I'm dead on my feet."

He chuckled. "No wife, no kids, nothing to do but work and sleep."

"And you're assuming I have a wife and kids?" She gave him her most accusatory look.

"Nah." He chuckled. "I think you've got two. And that you're balancing both until it blows up in your face." With that, they both broke out in laughter as Naya left and shut the door to the conference room, headed for her car.

〜

SHE AWOKE hours later in her bed with only a vague idea of how she got there. She had a fuzzy memory of driving home, walking up the stairs, and crawling in bed. She did know she hadn't seen Vance when she had come in, he must've gone back to sleep after she had left. Atlas was right though, she was letting herself become way too worn out for her own good, she'd have to work a little harder on taking care of herself if she wanted to make this work long-term.

She sat up, suddenly realizing she hadn't bothered to change when she had gotten home and had instead just slept in her work clothes. As much as she was determined to go right back to the case, she knew she needed a shower. But first, she decided it was time to try one of her more unusual case-working methods.

Before she could talk herself out of it, she slipped into some running clothes and slid her work phone into her side pocket. She cued up her favorite playlist and slid a single earbud in her left ear.

As she walked down the stairs, she could hear Vance in the living room talking, but she didn't hear anyone answering so he was likely playing video games with his online friends. She smiled a little to herself as she realized how little he had changed.

She quietly made her way outside and shut the door, carefully locking it behind her and sliding the key into her pocket. Then she lightly jogged down the front walk and up the street. She was cautious not to overexert herself, she hadn't gone for a run since before the move, but her muscles and breathing easily found their old steady rhythm. She had always loved running, it helped to clear her mind.

As she was starting to work up a sweat and breathe a little heavier, she reached down and shut off her playlist, listening to the sound of her own breathing. As she did, she observed the world around her. Would she notice if a man jumped out in front of her right now? She glanced over her shoulder. What about cars? Would she hear one if she hadn't shut off her music? And what if both women were wearing both earbuds? How likely would they have been to hear someone approaching then?

These thoughts continued to swirl around in her head as she

turned and began to make her way back to the house. She hadn't come far, but that wasn't the point today. As she stretched out her muscles on the front lawn, she realized that she really missed running and decided that she should definitely start again. She pulled up her RunTracker app and looked at how long her last run had been, ten miles, but it had been over a month and a half ago. She closed the app and promised herself she would run that weekend, rain or shine.

As she walked up to the front door, she noticed a car pull up behind hers on the curb. It was a red pickup with dark-tinted windows. On instinct, her hand went to where her gun would normally be before she remembered that, of course, she didn't have it when wearing her running clothes.

Kevin chose that moment to step out from behind the driver's side and waved, Naya relaxed and waved back as Trevor stepped out of the passenger side. She unlocked the door and waited for the two men to make it up the steps.

"Hey, Vance invited us over," Kevin explained.

"I assumed," Naya replied, mock sternness on her face.

"What are you doing home during the day?" Trevor checked the clock on his phone, clearly confused to see her.

"Why? You guys doing something you wouldn't want a cop to know about?" She raised her eyebrow and tried to display the most authoritarian cop face she could imagine.

Both men smiled as they walked into the home.

"No, just not like you, is all." Trevor replied.

Naya watched as both men headed into the living room, Kevin turning around at the last second to give her a little wink. After they had disappeared, she dashed upstairs to grab her clothes and headed for the shower; she needed to get back to work. There was a serial killer to catch.

As she stepped in the shower, she realized it was almost one in the afternoon, and Atlas hadn't called her about finding a body, which meant that either their guy had gotten better, or maybe he had intended to keep them longer, and Julia had been a fluke.

She washed her hair and body as quickly as humanly possible, suddenly feeling like she had been away from the office too long. Although she knew Atlas was right, they didn't need her there all the time; even during a big case, she still couldn't shake the feeling of duty left over from her days in La Junta. She finished her shower, spurred by this obligation, and stepped into her second set of slacks. She missed the comfort of her jeans, but she needed to get more slacks. She had only bought two pairs, and it was clear she would be working more frequently than that would be sufficient for.

She slid her gun into her holster, immediately feeling whole again, and checked the mirror to run a brush through her hair. She briefly eyed her makeup bag next to the sink. She hadn't put on makeup in years, but for some reason, she suddenly had the urge. Before she could let herself waste time with indulgences, she swung open the bathroom door, tossed her dirty clothes and wet towel to the top of the stairs and slipped into her shoes. She could deal with exploring the reason for that impulse later, for now, she had a killer to catch.

"Bye Vance!" she called over her shoulder as she let herself out the door.

"Bye mom!" He called back, continuing their banter from that morning she could hear Kevin and Trevor chuckling at it. She smiled as she slid the door closed, she was grateful her brother had friends.

THE DRIVE WAS QUICK, and Naya was a bit surprised to find the precinct relatively calm when she arrived. It only occurred to her after she walked in the door that she should have called and asked if Atlas wanted coffee. She assumed he would have been there all morning, but realistically, she supposed he could have gone home for a nap as well.

She pulled her badge out and swiped it in front of the time clock, she smiled as she saw the amount of overtime hours she had already accumulated in the less than two weeks since starting.

It seemed that at least money wouldn't be a concern.

"Ah, you've decided to grace us with your presence again. May I ask how family number two is?"

"Hi, Atlas." Naya rolled her eyes as she dumped her keys on her desk and slid into her chair. "They kick you out of the conference room?"

"Nah, it was boring in there without you, so I came out here for a bit." He twirled his pen between his fingers. It made her want to laugh, although Naya knew he was older than her, sometimes his mannerisms made her feel he was younger. However, she supposed that men were often said to mature slower than women.

"Think of anything new?" She inquired.

"No. And to be honest, I was expecting a call any minute with some sort of information or a body, and that hasn't happened. So, now I'm wondering if she's already dead and no one has found her yet, or if last time really was a fluke and he didn't accomplish what he wanted with Julia."

"Well, what would you say to a drive?" She proposed.

"What are you thinking?"

"Well, last time that farmer said he only found her because of the hawks circling, right? What if that is his dumping ground, but the farmer isn't out in the fields today?"

Before she even finished, Atlas was already out of his chair with his jacket pulled halfway on. "You're right. Let's go." They both waved at Captain Brody as they turned and headed for the door.

"You really are a good detective." Atlas complimented her. "I see why they didn't have a problem transferring you here as one."

"What do you mean?" She asked as he held open the glass door and they both waved to the receptionist as they exited. Naya had never considered the fact that when she requested the transfer and position change it could be denied, she had just presumed it would be approved since the position was open.

"Well, typically, when someone wants to be a detective here, they have to start out as a regular officer and work their way up. Everyone was shocked when the position of detective, and my partner, which had been empty for three months and had several in-house officers vying for it, was suddenly given to a random person from La Junta."

"Oh." She hadn't considered that. "I guess, I assumed they gave it to me because I was a Sheriff." She opened the door to their department car while Atlas situated himself in the driver's seat.

"I'm sure that was part of it. That's why I asked you that first day though, because political transfers often take priority. So, if you had been in some shit as Sheriff, they would've hidden you up here as a detective, but when I looked at your file, I noticed it was clean, but you also had a near-perfect record for solving murder cases in La Junta. I think that's why you got the position over the others."

Yeah, perfect, except for three, she thought to herself.

"So, I guess I should ask. Does everyone who was vying for the job hate me now?"

He shrugged. "I don't think so. I mean, maybe. There are obviously a few hard feelings that you slipped in, but I also think they all understand you were clearly ahead in rank and more qualified. Also, there were three of them trying for it, so I think they were all prepared to be forced to relinquish the position to one another. The fact that the other was you doesn't make much difference, I would suppose."

She let that sink in for a minute. She hadn't realized her transfer would make so many waves. Things were so different than in La Junta. She had worked her way up there, but it had been, well, expected. Her father had been the sheriff before her and his father before that, the fact that Vance hadn't gone into the force and become sheriff had been more of a shock to people than her taking his place. Her leaving afterward had stunned and devastated everyone. Unfortunately, there wasn't the same kind of extensive medical care for Vance in La Junta. And now that she was here, she saw that even if there had been, removing him from the support of his friends would've been worse.

"I wouldn't worry about it if I was you," Atlas said, clearly thinking she was still worried as to whether people hated her or not.

"Oh, it's not that. Just thinking about how to keep my second family hidden from my first is all." She quipped, trying to lighten the mood.

"Might I recommend saying you have to work overtime?" He shot back, making her smile at the truth in his joke.

As they turned down the rural road flanked by fields where Julia Charles' body had been found, it suddenly occurred to Naya how little she actually knew about her partner, and she decided to work towards changing that.

"Wait, you don't even have one family?"

He shook his head "I've always been too married to this job to even consider romance."

"Really? Not even something noteworthy when you were fresh out of the academy?" She had a hard time believing someone as kind and thoughtful as Atlas had never had a romance, which impacted his life.

He shrugged. "They say men are like a fine wine, we get better as we age. And I think there is some truth to that. I wasn't a great person when I first graduated from the academy. I was cocky and full of myself, and I wasn't interested in having a woman for longer than one night. And women came easy then because I was a young cop, fit, with tons of energy, and fresh out of the academy."

"What changed?" She asked as Atlas slowed the car, and they both began looking for any signs of a body or disturbance in the area.

"This job. It changed me." He was solemn now. The conversation taking a serious turn with the admittance.

"It was great while I was a beat rookie, just pulling over speeders and giving tickets to kids who were drinking underage. But then, probably three or four years in, I was called to my first murder. A man had killed his wife..." Naya's eyebrows shot up. "But here's the thing. I had been called to that address multiple times, and every time, by the time we got there, the fighting had died down, and the wife would refuse to file a report. There was nothing we could do. The kids would report they had seen their father hit their mother, but—" He took a deep breath. "She would never corroborate or come with us. She didn't want to leave the kids and didn't think she had any other options. And when I was called there for the murder scene —" He paused for a second, "This job became real for me. I had failed that woman. I had failed those kids. It wasn't just tickets anymore, there were lives involved. So, from that point on, I swore I was going to take this job seriously. No more fucking around and using it to get laid."

Naya thought about saying something, but it seemed like it was better to just stay quiet. She understood all too well, and there was nothing to say.

"I've dated a few girls since, but they all couldn't stand the job coming first, so nothing ever made it past a few dates."

She didn't say anything, this wasn't the time for advice or agreement, it was the reality of their career. She continued to look outside as they passed field after empty field.

"I think we should get out of the car."

"There are miles of farmland out here. Are you crazy?" He was wide-eyed, but she had a hunch.

"Humor me. You don't have to join me."

He slowed to a stop, and Naya and Atlas stepped out; she looked to the west, where the sun was slowly beginning to sink below the mountains in a haze of yellows and pinks. She wasn't sure where they were exactly, but they were near the spot where they had found Julia's body just over a week ago.

She started walking in the grass along the side of the road. She shaded her eyes and looked into the distance, she could just see what might be a farmhouse or a barn rising into view. She was walking in the direction of it and assumed she would eventually encounter the road to turn onto the property it was on. She heard Atlas jump back in the car from where he had been watching her with curiosity, and he began to follow her slowly as she continued. She surveyed the horizon, looking for anything out of place, like hawks circling like the farmer had seen before. But nothing was standing out.

She finally encountered the dirt path turn that led to the building she had seen from afar. She motioned to Atlas, and he cut the engine and got out to join her. "And may I ask just what we are doing here?"

He was radiating skepticism and was openly unaccustomed to her methods.

"Investigating. Well, at least I am; I can't speak for you." He rolled his eyes and followed her up the path to the building. It was a run-down and dilapidated wooden structure in a state of disrepair, but now that she was up close, she was fairly certain it was once a home. There were no animals or vehicles around to suggest it was still occupied, not that she assumed it would be by its state. But, she lifted her hand to knock to be polite, just in case.

"Hello!" She called out. There was no answer. With her hand on her weapon, she tried the knob. It turned easily. She looked over her shoulder at Atlas, who already had his gun drawn and by his side for cover. He motioned for her to go for it.

"Anyone home?" She tried again as she stepped through the door.

The interior was musty and dark. It looked as if the building had previously been divided into two rooms, but what remained of the wooden interior wall was now on the floor in pieces. She scoped to her left and right as Atlas stepped in behind her and did his own visual check.

"Abandoned."

She nodded in agreement.

"Long time ago, too. Can't imagine this wall fell recently." There was a bed frame on one side of the wall and a gas stove on the other. At one point, they had clearly been a kitchen and a bedroom, but nothing else remained now. "No personal effects, probably left of their own free will." She noted.

"Agreed." Atlas used his boot to scrape at the floor, "Concrete foundation. That would've taken some time and money. Someone probably used to actually live here."

"I'll check the public records when we get back and see."

"Why the sudden interest in an abandoned farmhouse?" He questioned as they exited the small forgotten home back out into the open field, which was now strikingly beautiful in the deep orange evening glow.

"I don't know. Sometimes, I have hunches and feel like I should look into particular things. Most of the time, it's nothing, but every now and then, it's something, and that small percentage of the time that it is something is worth it."

He smiled. "Interesting. I'm not judging you, this is just definitely not how city cops work. We spend too much time on paperwork to go poking around on intuition like this."

"And you have too big of an area to know everything that is going on, so I get that. But I'm not ready to let go of the suspicion that our guy does everything with a purpose. I think he dumped her here for something more than convenience. Because, let's admit it, unless he lived in this building, this wasn't exactly a convenient location."

"You're right." He agreed as he looked towards the horizon. Suddenly, he froze. "Do you see what I see?"

Naya immediately turned to where he was looking. There was a hawk, and it was circling. In the direction they had just come from.

They both looked at each other before running to the car. Atlas already had the key in the ignition and the car in drive before she got her seatbelt on.

The hawk was a little ways back up the road, just past the place where she had asked to walk. Atlas put the car in park, and they both got out and ran toward the middle of the field where the hawk was. They didn't have to run far before they both stopped dead in their tracks.

"It's her," Naya whispered.

Atlas pulled out his phone and pushed a button on his speed dial, "Yeah, we need crime scene techs. We found her."

9

NAYA

She and Atlas watched as they loaded the body into a bag and onto the stretcher. They were almost certain it was Shanice Woods, but her husband would meet them at the morgue to make the final ID.

Processing the scene had taken a while, so there were white area lights set up so the techs could see as they checked the surrounding area. Naya and Atlas had already gotten almost all the answers they could from the scene, they would need the coroner and property reports to garner anything else. Now they were just waiting for the right time to slip out so they could head back to the station.

Naya looked towards the road where they had parked the car and wondered if Shanice had been here earlier and they had missed her because the hawk hadn't found her yet or, if he had dumped the body while they were inside the house. She was sure Atlas was going over the same thoughts in his head. According to the coroner, Shanice had been dead for hours before she was found, so either way it wouldn't have changed her fate.

Finally, after a few more minutes of watching the crime scene techs take pictures of the flattened grass splattered with blood for what felt like the hundredth time, Atlas made eye contact and did a slight head nod towards the car. She gave him her own slight nod back and they both turned and began to leave the scene.

When they got into the car they were both quiet, deep in their own thoughts, after a few somber moments Naya broke the silence.

"What are you thinking?" She asked as she watched the darkened scenery go by. It was now almost nine in the evening, it had been a long and draining day.

"I can't decide." Atlas rubbed his chin. "Either she was already there, and we were looking for a single blade of grass in a field, or he dumped her while we were looking into that abandoned house, both options are repulsive."

She nodded. "And we need to decide if this is the type of killer who wants to have his victims found, or if he's dumping them here as part of a ritual."

"We did learn something though..."

"The blood wasn't part of the ritual." Naya was glad this woman had not been drained of blood like the last, but it did ruin the only lead she had originally had and leave more questions than answers.

"Exactly. And we need to find out who owns this land—" Atlas yawned loudly. "I do think we need to get some rest though. Why don't we just start early tomorrow? Sleep on everything that we've learned and come back with a fresh perspective."

"Sure, as long as you let me put in for the land records for that property tonight. I want them on my desk first thing in the morning."

"Fair enough" Atlas yawned again and Naya was now almost certain he hadn't slept at all since one in the morning when they had been called in after Shanice had gone missing.

"Do you need me to drive?" She offered, they were still about 20 minutes from the station.

"Nah, I got it, just keep me talking."

She thought of the personal conversation they had gotten into earlier, but quickly decided she didn't think it was good timing to bring it back up and went with something basic as they continued to get to know each other a little.

"So, where do you live?"

"How familiar are you with the area?" He asked as he turned back onto the road that took them back to civilization.

"I mean I studied the area a bit before I moved up here since I knew I would be going into detective work and all. But I'm no local yet if that's what you're asking."

"Okay, well I'm actually in the neighborhood Denver locals call LoDo, for 'Lower Downtown."

"Oh wow!" She gasped. "I looked at some places down there and they were very expensive." She had originally looked at possibly getting a bigger place in a better neighborhood for Vance and herself as he lived in a rougher neighborhood, but the high costs had been a major factor that kept her from making the move. Besides, Vance was attached to his little home.

"Yes." He grinned. "Guess you could say that's a benefit of not having a wife or kids. There's not a lot of bills or extra expenses, and I can live happily in a one-bedroom apartment. And if you haven't noticed yet, there's an unending supply of overtime to be had here."

"Yeah." She was glad he had brought it up. "I meant to ask you if Brody cared about the amount of overtime we take."

He shook his head. "Not at all. In general, people tend to try to not be at the precinct whenever they can. I'm probably there more than anyone else and I think you and I are some of a select few who clocked overtime this week. Times have changed."

Now she was confused. "What do you mean about that?"

He looked at her, an incredulous look on his face. "I'm surprised you don't know, because it's taking place in your generation."

"You forget, I grew up in a small town, you might as well just think of me as an alien from another planet."

"Fair enough. Anyway," He continued, "The millennial generation, born between the early 1980's and 1995, generally don't want to work around the clock like me, generation X. They tend to place more value on experiencing life and making just enough money that they can be comfortable."

"Interesting." She supposed the same had been at play in La Junta, but there also weren't jobs to work around the clock there besides Sheriff and maybe a few others that had night shifts. Most of the town closed by eight in the evenings most days, besides the two bars. And considering it was a town with a population of only seven thousand, she was surprised it had two bars in the first place.

"Well either way, it's changed the way the precinct functions. Where they used to employ four detectives, now there's six of us. And where they used to have four or five crime scene techs, now I think there's ten."

"Hasn't the city grown as well?"

"Yes, of course, but I'm talking in our district specifically, there shouldn't be a need for two additional full-time detectives, except that most only work a maximum of fifty hours a week, even when they're on a case. That doesn't count the hours they put in thinking about a case at home, but when I first started detectives regularly put in many more hours. When I'm on a case I don't hesitate to pull eighty-hour weeks, but I'm the only one. "

"I noticed." She replied as he pulled up next to her car.

"Except you." He specified. "You seem to want overtime as badly as me."

She could tell this was a pointed question and she knew she would have to share about Vance sooner or later, but for now at least, time dictated their chat was over.

"Well, two families are expensive, you know." She joked as she stepped out of the car, but before closing the door she decided she better make sure he was okay to drive home.

"Do you need me to take you home? I could pick you up and bring you back to your car tomorrow?"

He shook his head and pulled a red bull from his center console. "That's what this baby is for. But thanks for checking."

She rolled her eyes. "Alright, well, if you want me to talk to you via Bluetooth to keep you awake, you have my number."

"Night, Largusa."

"Night Atlas." She shut his passenger door, and with that, he sped out of the parking lot as she stepped into her car and started the ignition. She was glad for the break she had taken earlier, otherwise she might be as tired as he was.

It didn't take her long to drive home, and when she pulled up in front of the house, Kevin's truck was still there, along with another car behind it.

When she walked through the doorway, she was immediately greeted by the smell of Indian takeout and the sound of grown men yelling at the TV. Ah, she had forgotten it was Thursday and that football was a thing to people with day jobs.

She was about to sneak up the stairs and call it a night when Vance just happened to look over his shoulder and spot her. "Hey sis, come join."

She couldn't say no to him, so she gestured for one minute and walked upstairs to lock her gun in its case and set it by her bed. She briefly considered changing her clothes, but she didn't plan to hang out longer than a few minutes, so she ultimately decided against it and headed back down in her slacks and blouse.

When she walked into the living room, Kevin, Trevor, and Sebastian were all eating plates filled with various curries and naan breads. Her stomach growled so loudly that the guys could hear it over the game.

"Go make yourself a plate already!" Vance laughed, though she could see his own plate had barely been touched. He pointed her to the kitchen, and when she walked in, she gasped. They had ordered the entire buffet to be delivered to their kitchen.

"Yeah, sorry, it was Sebastian's turn to buy, and he got carried away," Kevin said from the doorway where he stood with his plate in his hands.

Naya quickly went down the line and loaded her plate with a little of everything. She had to admit, it looked delicious.

"Well, let him know I said thank you."

Cheers erupted from the living room, clearly their team had scored. Naya cleared a spot for herself at the two-person table and sat down. To her surprise, Kevin followed suit, though he sat sideways and held his plate in his lap as a large vat of rice was occupying most of the small table.

"Not going to watch the game?" She asked.

He smiled. "I can watch the game whenever I want, but you're a hard lady to pin down."

"Oh, really now?" She was surprised at how flirtatious her own words sounded. She was so used to her work voice that it sounded foreign to her.

He smiled wider in return and took a large bite of curry.

"Was there a reason you wanted to pin me down?" After she said it she realized how it sounded and put a hand over her face. "I walked right into that one."

"That wasn't my intention, but yes, you did." Kevin smirked before taking another bite.

It was quiet for another minute as they both chewed on their dinners. "So, Kevin," Naya started, "You worked with Vance?"

He nodded. "I took his job, actually, when he quit or...was relieved of his duties," He corrected himself.

"It's okay. Vance has told me most of what happened."

"I figured. Did you move here just for him?" Kevin picked up his naan and began using it to clean up the leftover curry sauce on his plate.

Naya glanced towards the entry to the living room and smiled sadly. "Yeah, he's the only brother I've got, and my parents will visit, but they aren't cut out for big city life."

"It's not for everyone. How are you liking it?"

"Well considering I've done nothing but work the whole time I've been here, I guess you could say I'm fitting in fine. I actually like how busy I've been." She scooped what was left on her plate into one pile in the middle. "You seem to have a lot of time to spend with Vance."

"Yeah, I'm the supervisor. So, I can supervise sites a bit and then leave and check in on the site later. I manage three sites right now and Vance is centrally located between them, so it's convenient for me to swing by."

"I'm really thankful he has you. I worry what it would be like for him with a support system and sense of normalcy."

Naya finished clearing her plate and set it down in front of her, she had been much hungrier than she had thought. She was even thinking of filling a second plate.

"He's my best friend. We met in university, and he was the one who got me the job on the construction site. I owe him for a lot."

They were both quiet for a moment, and Naya eyed the rice in front of Kevin; it didn't escape his notice.

"Have more." He pushed the dish towards her. "God knows you need it. Always trying to get Vance to eat, and it looks like you're always forgetting to feed yourself."

Naya looked down at herself and knew there was truth in his words, she had already lost weight since she had come here. She hadn't expected to be thrown into work so quickly, and managing Vance had priority when she was home. She was still deep in her thoughts when she felt his hand lift her chin.

"You look beautiful though, don't worry. I was just commenting how you should take care of yourself too."

She didn't say anything as she found her eyes searching his face. He really was quite handsome. His eyes flickered down for a moment and before she could say anything or pull away, he used his hand on her chin to lean her forward and his lips connected with hers.

She was pleasantly surprised. The kiss was nice, not forceful, and he didn't try anything crazy like some men sometimes did. She actually enjoyed it. And when he did finally pull away, she found herself wanting more.

Kevin smiled sheepishly as he returned himself to his side of the table. Naya found herself at a loss for words.

"I've been wanting to do that for a while." "A while?! I've only been here a little over two weeks."

"And I've wanted to do it since that day you walked in wearing those cute jeans and a button-up." He glanced down at the slacks she was now wearing, and she answered his silent question.

"Apparently, jeans aren't allowed for detective work here, so I had to switch to slacks." She brushed off a piece of rice that was on her thigh and stood to throw away her plate, but Kevin beat her to it and took her plate from her hand.

"Well, I think you look great either way, but I was a fan of those jeans."

She caught his wink and began covering the buffet pans with the foil lids they had come with.

"Do you think Sebastian will take any of this with him?"

Kevin shook his head. "No way, he's also firmly on team make sure Vance eats."

She smiled as she began to slide the pans into the fridge; she was thankful. How did Vance come across such loyal friends?

As if he could read her mind, he answered.

"We take care of our own here."

"I can tell." She had always thought that small towns were unique, but apparently, finding a small-town group of people was possible in a large city. But she also wasn't surprised that Vance had managed to find them, his friendly personality was magnetic.

"Did you grow up here Kevin?" She asked as they continued to pack up the food.

"Yes ma'am, only a few blocks from here in fact, and now I live about twenty minutes away. Which is quite close by Denver standards. Lots of the guys commute over an hour for work because of the cost of housing in the center of the city. If you need more than a one-bedroom place, you're pretty much forced to live in the boondocks."

She finished loading the fridge, which was now filled to the brim, but she was appreciative since she doubted she would have time to go grocery shopping this week. She leaned herself against the counter, facing Kevin.

"Do you have any brothers or sisters?"

"I wish." He shrugged playfully and took a step closer to her.

"You wish?" She laughed.

"Yes, I was a lonely only child growing up." He clarified.

"Ah." She felt herself shift her weight in anticipation as he stepped even closer and leaned in to kiss her again. She enjoyed it just as much as before and didn't notice her hands had moved to his shoulders until she heard a whistle from the doorway, they broke apart instantly.

It was Sebastian. "I would ask if I'm interrupting anything, but clearly I am, so would be a moot point." he teased before going back to the living room to give them some privacy.

She and Kevin laughed, and Naya adjusted her shirt awkwardly, which she suddenly worried might be wrinkled, although she was sure it wasn't.

"I should go to bed anyway. Early day tomorrow." She walked towards the door and noticed the new key she had made to replace the copy she had given Derek. She picked it up and held it towards Kevin. "I think I should give you this. You know, in case Vance can't..." she found herself unable to say the words.

Kevin understood. "Of course. Thanks. Talk to you later." He smiled sheepishly as their hands brushed for a moment before she turned to head upstairs.

As she got undressed in her room, she couldn't believe how much she felt like a teenager who had just gotten caught by her father. It made her giggle a bit as she slid on some comfy clothes to sleep in and slid into bed. She had no idea how tired she was until she had laid down and she found herself immediately drifting off to sleep. She would have to think over the case tomorrow, she thought, before she drifted into dreamland.

10

MARK

This was annoying. It wasn't going according to the plan. He would probably have to start all over and try something different. It was infuriating.

He turned to his computer and pulled up the Facebook of one of the women who had accepted his friend request. He scrolled through the page for the signs he needed.

Nothing.

He'd even gone back three years. He looked at her profile picture again. He'd really thought she was a candidate, but he had been wrong before. He unfriended her and went to the next girl on his list. She wasn't what he was looking for either.

Delete.

He felt like his expectations were low, and it was upsetting that these women couldn't even meet them! He was about to start all over and that meant this would now take him much longer than he had anticipated.

He glanced at the clock, it was almost time for him to go to work. Stupid job. He grabbed his jacket from the back of the chair and slid it over his shoulders, and he slid his feet into his work shoes. When he stepped towards the door he noticed he was leaving bloody foot-prints on the pristine white carpet.

Well, now he was going to have to torch this Airbnb when he was done. He felt a little guilty but it couldn't be helped. Glancing over his shoulder, he eyed what he had collected for the project so far. maybe he would stop by the store on his way home, today was payday, and some new materials would do him good.

He wiped his shoes on the mat outside his door to make sure he wouldn't track blood down the hallway, looking around to make sure no nosy neighbors were getting too interested in what he was doing in his rental. Then he headed down the hall and down the stairs, he had to be on his best behavior.

As he exited the building to the street, he passed a beautiful blonde who was stretching by the door. She had earbuds in and was wearing running gear. Mark was intrigued. She didn't even glance his direction as she pulled out her phone and pressed a few buttons, he was a few feet away, but he could clearly see what she was doing.

Perfect.

As she straightened he began to walk in the other direction, hoping she hadn't noticed him pause to watch her. As soon as she was partially in the building, he quickly turned around, feigning like he forgot something he followed her into the lobby.

He listened to her sneakers squeak as she jogged up the cement stairs. it sounded like she lived on the third floor.

Yes. She was perfect.

Before anyone could notice him standing around and wonder what he was doing, he turned and left the building while checking his watch.

He liked her. And he would get her later. For now, he had to put in his eight hours of work like everyone else on this godforsaken planet.

If only others could see his vision.

11

NAYA

Her alarm woke her at five. She knew she wasn't expected in the office until around seven or eight, but she wanted to solve this case before another woman went missing. She quickly pulled on her clothes deciding to order another pair of slacks on her lunch break. She really should've expected that she would need more than two pairs; with the hours she was pulling, they wouldn't cut it.

She slipped down the stairs as quietly as they allowed, peering in on Vance when she reached the bottom, he was fast asleep. She was a bit worried to look into the living room, but when she did, she was pleasantly surprised to see Vance's friends had cleaned up their mess. She shook her head at herself. It's not like they were teenage boys! They were adults, of course, they had cleaned up after themselves.

As quickly as she could, she scooped Indian leftovers into a container and slid the fridge shut. She was glad Derek was coming today; he could help them eat some of these leftovers before they went bad; how many they had was out of control.

She was out the door and in the office within 30 minutes, she was surprised by how short her commute was without traffic.

She wasn't the first one in the office, but she had beat Atlas for once, a small victory. She hoped he had made it home safely the night before and that he would feel rested this morning. Naya didn't even stop at her desk, she headed straight for the conference room and began analyzing the map she had put on the board. She used her phone to get the exact location where they found Shanice's body, and then she stepped back and stared at it.

"Anything?" Atlas' voice interrupted. If she hadn't been a cop for so long, she might have jumped from surprise.

"Nothing. And the techs haven't emailed me the property transfer paperwork for that land yet."

"I'm impressed you beat me here, but at least I didn't miss much," Atlas replied as he slid into a seat and set his coffee in front of him. She could see the steam still rising from it.

"I have an idea." She bit her lip as she looked back at the board closely.

"I'm all ears." Atlas took a sip of coffee and pinched his eyes shut.

"Remember how I was looking for uses for blood?"

"Mhm."

"What if he still removed it for a reason? It might not be for a ritual, but maybe he drugged her or something, and he knew the drug would show on a toxicology report. And he was worried it could be traced back to him?" Atlas let out a sigh she knew without looking he was about to poke a hole in her theory.

"I mean, it's a thought. But he didn't remove all traces of blood and something like that could still show up in the traces." Atlas shuffled the papers in front of him, looking for the toxicology report.

Naya wasn't willing to let go of her theory so easily, but she didn't want to argue with her partner so she bit her lip and studied the board instead. She looked again at the two circles where the women had been found and took the liberty of writing the words 'burial ground' with a question mark. She really needed to see those farm records.

"What if what he injected her with was already in the bloodstream?"

"Hm?" Atlas was sipping his coffee and quickly set it down. "What do you mean by that?"

She spun around and grabbed the toxicology report from him, flipping to the page about the blood. "What if he injected her with something which is found in the human body naturally, but can kill someone in large doses?" She heard Atlas saying something, but she was too busy skimming the report now to listen. "So, he removed the blood so we wouldn't notice?"

There was nothing on the page that jumped out at her, but she had Atlas' full attention now. He had his phone in his hand and was already dialing.

"Yes, this is Detective Atlas...

"Put me through to the morgue please, and see if one of the coroners who did the report on Julia Charles is available...

"Thanks..." He flipped the phone to speaker and set it on the table.

This is Dr. Ouray. I heard you had questions about the Julia Charles case?

Atlas looked at Naya pointedly.

"Uh, yes sir, I was thinking, Julia Charles was drained of most of her blood correct?"

Yes.

"And what remained seemed like normal blood?"

Also yes.

He answered cleanly and professionally. He was probably ready to get back to his work and just wanted her to get to the point.

"Is it possible that something which is normally found in the blood could have been injected in toxic levels, and then subsequently hidden by removing that blood?"

The other end of the line was quiet for a minute. Naya made eye contact with Atlas and shrugged. Maybe she was barking up the wrong tree after all.

Actually,

They could hear Dr. Ouray take a deep breath.

There are a number of naturally occurring minerals in the human body that could be toxic in large quantities. Potassium, iron, copper, magnesium, and zinc to name just a few.

"Would there be any ways to tell if she had been given large amounts of any of those minerals before death?"

Well, if they were administered via injection the majority would be somewhat untraceable, besides magnesium, which would lead to cardiac arrest. Zinc usually irritates the stomach lining, but I didn't see anything unusual there, which only tells me she didn't consume it orally...

He trailed off a bit and it took Naya a minute to realize he was done talking and not just lost in thought.

"Did you see any needle marks on the body? Possible injection sites, I mean?" Atlas finally spoke up.

Well, I'm sure you have the report in front of you. We found the single cut on the back of the leg that we believe the blood was drained through, which we did think was a weird spot to choose. The neck would have seemed like a better place to remove blood. But now that you mention this, I'm wondering if he injected her there and cut the same spot to hide what he had done.

Naya flipped through the report. "And you still stand by blood loss as the cause of death? As in, she was alive when the blood was removed?"

Yes ma'am, it wouldn't have made sense for him to kill her first, because it would be difficult to drain the blood without the propulsion of the heart. But that doesn't necessarily mean she was conscious.

Atlas piped up then. "But the time of death was so close to the abduction?"

Dr. Ouray cleared his throat.

That is true. I'm afraid I don't have any more information for you, and we've already released the body to the family. I can see about getting it back if you...need it that badly?"

Atlas and Naya had a silent argument, Atlas was shaking his head yes while Naya was mouthing 'no way.' She felt that the poor Charles family had been through enough already. Finally, he relented.

"No sir, that's alright, I would assume she has already been embalmed by this point, it has been a week. Thank you for your help." He hung up the phone before the doctor replied.

"Well, we've got quite the puzzle here." Naya refreshed her email. "And it's unlikely we will get the report on Shanice anytime soon."

"I put a rush on it, but you're right, probably not until tomorrow at least."

A woman Naya didn't recognize knocked on the open door. "Atlas, this was just faxed through for you."

He stood up and grabbed the papers from the woman, almost knocking over his coffee in the process, he would have if Naya hadn't been faster and moved it out of the way first. He sat back down and placed the stack of documents he had been handed in front of Naya.

"Our land transfer records."

All the papers were scans of old documents and were handwritten, in cursive. "There aren't typed versions?" She asked, knowing there probably weren't if they had been given these. She had dealt with handwritten property transfer records in La Junta, but that was a much smaller area and a much less technologically savvy operation. She expected Denver to be more advanced with everything she had seen so far. And, well, this stack seemed huge.

"Not for the area we're looking into. That area hasn't really been of interest to the government ever. And they had a scribe working to type everything still handwritten up, but unfortunately, they were cut years ago due to budget. Didn't seem necessary to the officials."

"Until now." She grumbled as she grabbed a stack. Land transfer records were often written in a difficult-to-understand shorthand. "What quadrant am I looking for?"

Atlas checked something on his phone and scribbled down three different 16-digit identifiers.

"It's one of these three. The grid has been reassigned a few times."

"Of course." Naya stood and headed towards the door. "Want another coffee before we start?"

"Please."

THEY LOOKED through the old property documents for the rest of the day, flagging entries as they pertained and putting them aside. After hours of cross-referencing and elimination, they finally narrowed it down to three potential owners. Atlas grabbed his laptop from his desk and brought it into the room, and they used it to pull up the DMV database. The first result was the farmer who had found the body, Benjamin Rodgers. The other two were also farmers in the area, but no one either of the detectives were familiar with.

Atlas checked his watch. "It's only five, lets head out there and see if we can get some interviews in?"

"Sounds good." Naya grabbed her jacket, thankful that today was a day Derek was around, so she didn't have to worry about her brother too much. It was also Friday, and she figured one or more of Vance's friends would come over to hang out after they got off work, so he wouldn't be alone even if she stayed late.

They hopped into the car, Naya in the passenger side, like usual.

"I'm surprised," Atlas said without elaborating.

Naya waited a minute, but eventually, she asked, "At?"

"The sheriff never asks to drive."

She smiled at his tone. "Less liability. I haven't ever used the fancy driving skills they teach at the academy. La Junta was so small and the area around it so barren, you could run, but you literally couldn't hide." She joked. "But really, most of the cases I had were mind games. They weren't about finding a needle in a haystack, they were about who wasn't who they pretended to be."

"That makes sense, I suppose." They turned from the main highway onto the same empty stretch of road as before.

This time when she surveyed the landscape she felt a small pang of homesickness. She should call and update her parents, she hadn't been here that long, but it was weird to not see them every weekend. She had seen them every Sunday for dinner for the past twenty-nine years, excluding when she had been in the academy, so to go two weeks was a long time.

He phone buzzed and she glanced down to see a text from Kevin. Without her permission, her face broke out into a huge grin.

"That one of the husbands?" Atlas asked, clearly noticing the change.

"Maybe." She joked as they turned off the single-lane cement road and onto a dirt one, which abruptly ended as they came up to a farmhouse. At least this one looked like it was regularly kept up, unlike the abandoned one from the night before.

By the time they stepped out of the truck, Benjamin Rodgers had come out and was standing on the porch with a beer in his hand, eyeing them.

"Hey Ben!" Atlas called out in a friendly tone. Naya could see he was trying to start things off lighthearted instead of confrontationally, and she couldn't agree more.

"Ah, detectives." Ben lifted his beer to them. "Can I get you two a cold one?"

Naya shook her head. "Afraid we're on the clock Ben."

He smiled sadly. "I was afraid of that. Everything okay?"

Atlas pulled a map out of his pocket that Naya hadn't even seen him slip in there, it was map of the area almost identical to the one they had on the whiteboard. The only difference was that on this one, only the places where the bodies were found had been circled.

"I'm afraid not. I'm not sure if you've seen the news, but we found another body."

"Jesus," He muttered, taking a long pull from his beer. "You think it was the same person?"

"There are some similarities in the case." Atlas said noncommittally as he laid the map on the porch railing, and Ben came to stand next to him. "You see here is where you found that young girl. And we found another woman here," He pointed to the circle, "Last night. But here's our problem. Whose land is this here?" Atlas gestured to the area encompassing both circles.

Ben held out his hand. "May I?"

Atlas lifted his hand off the map so Ben could bring it closer to his face. "This one's a toughie. You see, I'm the only active farmer around here anymore. Most of the other guys have died or given up and moved away to the city for an easier life. There just isn't much demand for homegrown wheat anymore." He moved the map a bit before holding it up to the lone, bare porch light. "You see here," he drew an imaginary line down the map. "This is where my land ends. Where you found that second woman, well, that was old Dave's plot. But, he's been dead for ten years."

Naya glanced down at her notes where she had written the names. David Smith was next on their list. "Do you know who owns the land now?" she asked.

Ben shrugged. "Some of the guys out here have family, but most of us don't. So, I don't know what happens to the land when no one shows up to claim it. But whatever that process is, that's probably what happened to old Dave's land. I ain't never seen a soul out here checking on it, though."

Naya raised an eyebrow, she questioned how reliable that was, since for as well as he claimed to keep an eye on the land, he clearly hadn't seen Atlas and her out here the other night. Or had he?

She couldn't tell if Atlas was thinking the same thing or not, but she decided to wait to confer with him when they were back in the car.

"Anyone else still out here?" Atlas asked, looking over his shoulder for no apparent reason.

Ben shrugged. "I know there's another guy. I haven't talked to him, though. I see him sometimes, though, when I go to town to buy supplies. He's the only other person I've seen work the land out here in decades."

"And whereabouts is his farm located?" Naya was now standing on Ben's other side, looking at the map as well.

"Beats me. But If I had to say where I saw him farming, I would say about ten miles down the road. Well past old Dave's plot and a few other abandoned farms, too, I'm sure."

She felt defeated. It was unlikely that would be the third person on their list, since whoever the third person was had to be located nearby. She was starting to think the third person they had found was probably whoever Dave had his land transferred to upon his death.

"Well, thanks, Ben, that's all we needed. We'll get out of your hair, enjoy your Friday night." Atlas folded up the map and slid it back in his pocket.

"No problem. Listen, if you two ever take a Friday night off, feel free to come back out here and have a beer, it does get lonely."

"Thanks Ben." Naya gave him a wave as she stepped into the car. The minute they were back on the road, she turned to Atlas. "He's... nice."

"You say that like it's a bad thing." He kept his eyes on the road and didn't look at her. They were almost back to the abandoned building they had investigated the evening before.

"Well, I did think one thing he said was weird."

"What's that?" Atlas pulled to the dirt turn off, illuminating the small structure with their headlights.

"Well, he says he's so observant. Yet, he said he'd never seen anyone at Old Dave's place...so, then did he not see us here last night?"

Atlas considered her statement for a moment and cut the engine. "You're right. That is a bit odd."

"I mean it could be that he just doesn't realize what he's missing or is less attentive than he thinks. But I think we need to ask him for an alibi for both disappearances."

"Which he won't have, because he's a solo farmer."

"Exactly." Naya looked at the building in front of them. It looked much more imposing in the dark.

"I guess we officially have our first suspect then."

"That we do." Naya stood to step out of the car when her phone buzzed again. She pulled it out of her pocket to notice it was Kevin again. What she read on the screen made her heart drop.

"God, no." She whispered and pressed dial before she even realized what she was doing.

She forgot where she was, oblivious to the fact that Atlas was watching her intently as the phone rang and rang.

"Answer, goddamit!" She muttered to the other end.

Finally, after what felt like years, Kevin picked up.

"Is he okay?! Where are you? What happened? What —" The questions shot at him in succession, and so fast he couldn't possibly answer, but she couldn't stop herself.

"Whoa, calm down. We're at the hospital down the street. He's okay." He cut in when he realized she wasn't going to stop.

Naya let out the breath she didn't even realize she was holding.

"Thank God." She breathed. "You can't just text me that."

"I'm sorry. I sent it without thinking as we were on our way here. We had been just playing video games like always when Vance got up to use the bathroom, and a few minutes later, Trevor and I heard a crash and rushed in."

"Oh no," Naya whispered.

"He was unconscious when we found him, but he regained consciousness on our way here. I think he stood up too fast and got light-headed or disoriented and fell against the toilet. He doesn't remember what happened, but they're checking him out now. They wouldn't let me go back with him, but I'm in the waiting room with Trevor."

Naya glanced at her watch, the case still completely forgotten. "I think I can be there in thirty. Send me the address, please?"

Atlas heard enough of the conversation and was climbing in the driver's seat. As Naya climbed into the passenger side she hung up the phone, waiting for the text to come through with the hospital address. By the time it came through Atlas was already turning back on to the main road with the lights and siren blaring.

"I'm sorry." Naya was at a loss of what else to say or where to start.

"No problem. Seems serious, we can come back here later. But you're gonna need to tell me what's going on so when Brody asks me why we're at the hospital I'll have an answer."

Naya grimaced. She had known this moment would come, she would have to tell her partner about her brother. She had just hoped it could wait a bit longer.

"Well..." She took a deep breath, begging her emotions to stay in check. "You asked why I transferred here. And I transferred, because, well, my brother—" She had to take another breath. "Is in the final —" She choked on her words. "Final stages of cancer." It came out as a whisper, but it was no longer a secret.

"He can't really care for himself anymore, he can't work. So, I'm here to help support him."

Just as she didn't question his story, Atlas understood this was the time to stay silent and just drove while she continued.

"And I guess, he fell today, and his friends were there luckily, that's who called. I still just..." She looked at her lap dejectedly. She knew once she said the next part, she would have to face the reality of the situation.

"When Vance would call home, he didn't seem so bad, you know? He seemed like he was doing okay. Then he told us he lost his job and —" She felt a single tear run down her cheek and quickly brushed it away before Atlas could notice. "And I knew it was bad, but I had no idea it was...this bad."

Atlas paused, giving her time to collect herself and making sure she was done talking before saying anything.

"So...no juicy two-family story?"

"No." She felt a small smile ghost her lips. "Sorry if I ruined your fun."

"Good thing I only bet the guys $50."

She couldn't help but smile at his teasing despite her nerves, she had dreaded this conversation, but it made it much more bearable. As Atlas turned on the highway, civilization rose in front of them. Naya was glad they were almost there because she didn't know if her heart could take this racing much longer. And thanks to Atlas' crazy, but precise driving, and the help of the siren, they were in front of the hospital in record time. Naya scrambled out and headed into the lobby, Atlas hot at her heels.

When she turned the corner into the waiting area, she immediately spotted Trevor. "Where's Kevin?" She asked.

Trevor feigned looking hurt. "Hello to you too. He went to grab us some coffee, he'll be right back."

Atlas glanced at his watch, "I think I'll do the same. Seems like it'll be a late night."

"You really don't have to stay. Trevor and Kevin can take Vance and I home."

"But your car is at the precinct?"

She hadn't thought of that, that threw a wrench in things. "Well, what time did you want to start tomorrow?"

"It's Saturday, so I was thinking I might sleep in until six." He joked glancing at his watch again. Naya did the same and noticed it was already almost eight.

"Well, give me a call, and maybe you could swing by and grab me on your way to the station? Or I can call an Uber."

"No need to Uber, I'll give you a call when I'm on my way. Maybe we can just pick up where we left off. Might be easier."

"Good point."

She was surprised when Atlas suddenly enveloped her in a hug.

"Call me if you need anything, and let me know if you need a half day tomorrow. Seriously. I understand."

"Thanks. I appreciate it." Naya said as he pulled away. She caught a glimpse of Kevin out of the corner of her eye, and if she wasn't mistaken, he almost looked jealous.

"No problem." He gave a small wave as he strode back out to his car.

Kevin came over, clearly trying to fight the urge to ask who the man hugging her had been. He had a tray with three coffees in his hand and slid one into her hands.

"I figured you would need this."

"Thanks." She smiled at him. "And thanks so much for being there for Vance. I don't know what he would've done without you two tonight."

She looked between Kevin and Trevor for the first time, taking in the cramped waiting room and stained blue chairs with the same décor that seemed to be in every hospital in the country. "I'm going to go see if they will let me see him or at least give me an update. If they plan on keeping him all night, you guys can probably go, get some sleep, and come back in the morning.

They two nodded, and before she could walk away, Kevin grabbed her arm gently.

"I just wanted to give you a heads up, I gave the key you gave me to Sebastian for the night. When Vance fell, he fell onto the toilet and broke it. There was quite a mess, and the toilet was unusable. Sebastian was going to stop by Home Depot before they closed to buy a new one and have it installed for you, hopefully before you get home tonight."

She was shocked, she wouldn't have expected that Vance's frail body could do that much damage.

"Thank you so much. I don't know how we will ever repay you guys."

"No worries. That's what friends are for." Kevin winked at her as he let go of her arm.

"I'll make a new key for you." She turned to focus her eyes on Trevor, "And one for you as well, that way you won't have to worry about passing keys around to hang out with Vance."

"Sounds like a plan to me." The smile still hadn't left Kevin's face, and Naya managed to return a half smile as she turned her back towards the two men and walked forward.

She approached the receptionist, and after checking Vance's medical records to confirm that Naya was listed as his next of kin and power of attorney, she called and had a nurse come to take her to the back.

While they walked down the sterile white hall lined with rooms filled with patients and charts tacked to doors, Naya asked the nurse how Vance was doing.

"He isn't my patient, so I unfortunately don't have too much information for you, but I believe it's just a concussion. He does have a private room; however, considering the risk to his immune system, the doctor will fill you in when he comes in, though."

When they entered the room, Vance was laying on the bed with his eyes closed, hooked to a bunch of machines filling the space with a constant cacophony of beeps and buzzing that reminded her both that he was alive and that they were in a hospital. The nurse left, closing the door behind her.

"Are you sleeping?" Naya asked, knowing full well that he wasn't.

"No." He opened one eye to look at her. "How can you always tell?"

"Twenty-nine years of you fake sleeping so you wouldn't be roped into playing with me." She grinned at the memories.

Vance smiled, too, and opened his other eye. "I forget about that. It pretty much stopped working the day you turned seven. You've always had an investigative mindset and wouldn't take me sleeping at face value."

Both chuckled as Naya moved to sit in the chair by his bed. "So, are you going to tell me what happened? Or do I have to wait for the doctor?"

He rolled his eyes. "Well, Mom, I had my chemo today, and you know how sick that makes me, so I think I just got dehydrated from all the vomiting," He lifted his arm to motion to the room."Here we are."

"Not much could've been prevented there; we will just have to be more aware next time, I suppose." She admitted.

They sat in silence for a minute before Naya spoke again. "I think," Her voice broke for what felt like the millionth time that night and she started again. "I think we need to get around-the-clock care for you. Because I can't imagine what would've happened if your friends weren't there tonight."

Vance didn't attempt to disagree. "I think that would be best." As her older brother, he could sense how hard this was on her, so he pushed the button to bring himself into a sitting position and patted the spot next to him. Naya moved from the chair to sit next to him on the bed and leaned her head on his shoulder like she always had when she was upset when they were younger.

"I'll call in the morning." She said quietly. Vance didn't respond, and the two of them sat in silence for so long that if she didn't know better, she would've thought he'd fallen asleep.

"I think you should call mom and dad too." He eventually whispered.

She was too choked up to respond and simply nodded into his shoulder.

12

MARK

It was Saturday. A good day for Blondie to go for a run. That's what he was referring to her as now. Blondie.

He had moved his chair over in front of the window and was sitting with his laptop on his lap and his phone in his hand. Not having her as a Facebook friend first made this a little bit more difficult.

But he liked a challenge.

He had hacked the WiFi of the Airbnb owner weeks ago. And the WiFi next door. Okay, he had hacked everyone on the floor, but he still wasn't sure which one was hers. So far, every modem he had hacked he was inclined to believe belonged to a guy, because of the devices hooked up to them. He could go into the individual devices to find out more which might change that opinion, but he hadn't had the chance yet. The hacking work was time consuming. And it was also possible that she could be living with a man.

There she was!

He watched as she began stretching by the door as she had been doing last time he had spotted her. He pulled out his interceptor, he was hoping she was wearing Bluetooth headphones like before.

She was.

"Hello Alia." He smirked.

No last name, her phone was only labeled "Alia's iPhone" in the menu, but it was enough. The interceptor he had programed went to work, coming up with her IP address and cell provider in a matter of moments. He typed her first name into Facebook using the city of Denver as a filter. A long list of names showed up. He was familiar with the algorithm though, and he knew because of her close proximity that she should be the first after the "mutual friends" suggestions. She was.

So convenient.

He clicked on her page, but he didn't even have to friend request her, what he was looking for was right there. He wrote down the information he needed from the picture and plugged it into the jailbroken RunTracker app he had modified on his phone. Alia's running path and pace illuminated his screen.

"Ah, you aren't as fast as the other two." He gloated as he watched her turn a corner. He licked his lips, this was going to be fun.

He went to her run history, looked like she ran about twice a week and her next run was likely to be Monday or Tuesday based on her pattern. She always ran in the mornings, which could complicate things. Alia was proving a challenge, but he liked it.

"Enjoy your second to last run." He threatened before drawing the curtain.

13

NAYA

Her phone alarm woke her at seven the next morning, Naya was surprised. She had fully expected to receive a call from Atlas waking her before now. Maybe he hadn't been kidding when he'd said he was going to sleep in.

They had been discharged from the hospital at about eleven the night before. Turned out Vance's fluids and blood sugar were low, which confirmed his own suspicions for the cause of the fall. So, after an IV, he was discharged and sent home with orders to rest, as he did have a mild concussion.

She sent a quick text to Atlas letting him know she would be ready at nine or later, then she slid on her running clothes and headed down the stairs.

Running had helped Naya clear her mind ever since she was a little girl. She had never been crazy fast, but she was fast enough to become a police officer and that was all that mattered to her.

After lacing up her shoes she started the tracker app on her phone and slid it into her pocket. She was aiming for six miles this morning and she had just under an hour to complete them.

There was a light drizzle, typical for Denver this time of year, or so she'd been told. The moisture felt cool and invigorating on her face as she picked up speed. She had discovered there was a park about two miles from her house and she planned to run there to check it out.

As she jogged past the houses in her neighborhood, she couldn't help but think they looked sad. She couldn't tell if this was because of her dismal mood, or because a number of them were missing things, paint, porch railings, and some even siding and they felt neglected. She had often questioned why Vance had chosen the house he did but jogging through streets lined with houses like him she thought about it and decided he had probably intended to fix it up. That, and the newer properties in the area, were much more expensive than he could afford, especially because he had always preferred stand-alone homes to apartment buildings.

After a few minutes, she turned a corner and saw the park stretched ahead of her. It was nothing fancy, she could see a grassy field, a play area for kids, and what looked to be a charming trail that crossed the creek and headed into the neighborhood on the other side. She jogged in place while she waited for the light to change, when it finally did, she sped up a bit, frivolously jumping over the puddle on her path and heading towards the trail. She didn't know what it was about running in the rain, but she could feel all the negative emotions leaving her body. She was feeling revitalized and full of life.

When the voice in her ear notified her that she had run three miles she made a quick circle and headed back the way she had come. As she came back through the park, it was empty except for a woman with a black umbrella and her small dog, who was having a blast splashing in a puddle. Naya smiled. She had always wanted a dog, but her lifestyle had never allowed it. Maybe someday when she retired.

She passed the same houses on the way back as she had before, and despite her improved mood, they still looked sad. She was fairly certain now that it was the houses themselves and not her.

A smile broke out across her face as her house came into view, and as she came up on the walkway, the voice in her ear chimed that she had completed six miles in fifty-four minutes and change. She stretched out as quickly as she could on the front porch before unlocking the door and heading inside.

The house was still dark, and Naya was sure Vance would sleep until noon after the eventful night he had.

After a quick shower, Naya sat on her bed and pulled out her phone. There was a message from Atlas saying he would see her at nine. Perfect. That gave her just about an hour to make her phone calls and get ready for work.

She dialed the first number and the same woman from Home Health Care who had helped her before answered.

"Hi, it's Naya Largusa."

"Ah yes! I was just about to call you to check in, how is everything going with Derek? Well, I hope?" She sounded concerned and Naya was willing to bet people usually only called with complaints.

"Everything is great with Derek, he's not why I'm calling." She took a deep breath. "I'm calling because Vance needs full-time care now. I wanted to see if we could up Derek to ten, or maybe even twelve-hour days, and then I would like to request that we have someone else assigned to us for the other four days as well."

She didn't say anything for a second, and Naya could hear her typing.

"Okay, well, I can up Derek to three ten-hour days, but that will max him out since he has another contract. Let me see who else we have, one moment."

Naya waited patiently.

"Okay, I've got Elliot. He could take on the other four, ten-hour days? Or would you rather him do three twelve-hour shifts and I find you another aide for the last day?"

She rubbed her temples. This was all so stressful. She really didn't want to have to make Vance get used to three people, two around all day every day already seemed like a lot. And either Kevin, Trevor, or Sebastian were all usually around in the evenings.

"Let's just do Elliot and Derek. From eight in the morning until six at night every day please." She would have to watch her time a bit better at work and try to leave a bit earlier, but with everyone, she reasoned, they would manage the ten-hour days.

"Okay, no problem. I will contact them both. Is it okay if I send Elliot along with Derek on Monday to get acquainted and they can start the new schedule then?"

"Yeah, that sounds great. Thanks so much." Naya was a bit worried about what she was going to do tomorrow, but it was Sunday so it seemed likely the guys would be over to watch football.

"No problem. And if, in the future, you decide you need overnight care, just give us a call back. Okay?"

She cringed. "I will thank you."

She hung up the phone, it pained her to think of overnight care, but she was sure it would be their reality at some point. But hopefully not anytime soon.

Time for the next call; she wasn't looking forward to this any more than the last, but for different reasons. She glanced at her watch and realized it was a bit early for her parents, but she didn't have another option. The phone rang five times before her mother picked up.

"Naya." It sounded like she had just woken up and Naya was sure she had, unfortunately she didn't have time to feel guilty.

"Hey, mom."

Her mom would definitely be able to tell something was up, even though she was overdue for a call, Naya knew her tone would give her away.

"What's wrong?" She sounded more alert already.

Naya took a deep breath. "I think you and dad should come visit. Soon." She couldn't bring herself to say it any harsher than that.

"What's going on?"

"It's Vance, he's...well, he's much worse than he led us to believe. He asked me to call you last night." She could hear rustling in the background, and she figured her mom was shaking her father to wake him up.

"How long do you think?" Her mother's voice was the one to crack this time.

"He's still lucid. But I've hired round-the-clock care. And after I hang up I'm going to order him a wheelchair. I think he wants you to see him before...before it gets worse." Naya knew that even though he was as accepting of his condition as someone could be, Vance did not want his parents to see him helpless. He had always prided himself on his strength and independence and he wanted to maintain that image in their memories.

"Your father is awake now, let me see what he has planned for the week, but we will be up in the next few days."

"And mom? The house is very small."

Vance had always come home to visit their parents; they had never been up to visit him in Denver, and she knew they had grander expectations of his house since homes in La Junta were much cheaper.

"I think you and dad should get a hotel, there's an inexpensive one not too far. It's nothing fancy, but for a few nights I think it'll do."

"Send me a link and we'll book it." She could hear her mom's voice shaking. "Is there anything you want us to bring you? What about Vance, does he want anything."

She pinched the bridge of her nose and squeezed her eyes shut. Why was this so damn hard?

"Can you bring some pictures of Vance as a kid? And maybe anything else you think would be important to him from our childhood?"

"No problem." She could hear her mom sniffle, she was definitely crying now. "I'll—I'll have your dad look through some of the boxes in the attic."

Naya glanced at her watch, she had to hurry if she wanted to order the wheelchair and get dressed before Atlas showed up.

"Listen mom, I gotta go to work, but text me the days you will be here when you know, okay? And Vance had a late night but maybe give him a call and let him know when you're coming as well?"

"We will. Hang in there, honey. We will be there as soon as we can."

"Thanks mom. Love you, give dad my love too, please." After

quick goodbyes, she hung up and hurried to step into her pants and slide her shirt on. She could always order the wheelchair during the drive to work, but she wanted to at least be dressed and ready to go when Atlas showed up.

She ran a brush through her hair, deciding she didn't have time to blow dry it and it would have to air dry; she could pull it back if it got to be too much. They had a decent drive ahead of them, plenty of time for it to dry naturally.

Her phone buzzed. Atlas was here. Good thing she had gotten dressed.

She sent a text to Kevin, asking him to check in on Vance in a few hours if he could. She felt bad relying on him so much, but he didn't seem to mind, and she hadn't expected her job to be this demanding from day one.

She rushed to grab her credentials and weapon and jogged down the stairs and out the door.

"Morning." She greeted as she slid into the passenger seat.

"You look chipper." He commented. "I'm guessing that means you didn't spend the night at the hospital?"

"Nope, got off easy, he just has a minor concussion. They gave him an IV and sent him home with instructions to rest and be more careful. It was still a late night, but nothing I can't handle." Her phone blinked with a response from Kevin and she opened it. What she saw made her blush.

KEVIN: Of course. Anything for you beautiful. How would you feel about dinner tomorrow night while Trevor and Sebastian are with Vance for the game?

SHE SMILED as she texted back.

NAYA: Yes. It's about time you asked me on a proper date.

. . .

His response was immediate..

Kevin: Better late than never. Be ready at 4.

The smile didn't leave her face even as she opened her internet browser to finally finish ordering the wheelchair for Vance.

"Must be good news with that smile."

"Well kind of I guess." She tried to play it off so she wouldn't have to explain, but Atlas wouldn't let her off that easy.

"Come on, after last night you should be able to talk to me a little."

Naya started laughing. "Now you're talking like we're in a relationship or something. But if you must know, I have a date tomorrow afternoon."

Atlas chuckled. "Well, I guess we better solve this case tonight then, huh?"

She rolled her eyes. "Come on, we can do a half day on Sunday."

"Correction, you can. I do whatever I want, I'm not the one with a date."

"Oh right, I forgot." Naya laughed and was still smiling as they pulled off the highway onto the same long stretch of road that was starting to feel familiar with how often they'd been down it lately. She finished selecting a wheelchair, not that she knew much about them, and just went based on reviews, and used her Apple Pay to pay for expedited shipping. The chair would be delivered on Tuesday.

"Did you look into the process of what happens to land when there is no next of kin?" She felt a little bad she hadn't had time to look it up herself, but she felt the night before had been an extenuating circumstance.

Atlas shook his head. "I shouldn't say that I didn't because I did. More so, I couldn't find a procedure. It looks like everyone who has land has some sort of next of kin, or a designated beneficiary of some kind in a will. Even if they have to notify a second cousin twice removed or it's donated to charity or something. So, someone out there owns that land, it's just a matter of figuring out who."

"Time to dive into David Smith's life?"

"Exactly. And we will do that as soon as we get another look at this dilapidated house. See if we can find any clues." He exaggerated the last part, as if they were characters on a children's TV show, it made Naya's mind wander...

"Did you always plan on being a detective when you got older?" she asked hesitantly.

"I guess. Like you, I've always had a knack and drive for it I guess."

She accepted his answer and watched as Benjamin's house went by. She sensed something off about that guy; she wished she could put her finger on what it was.

"What the?!"

Naya's head snapped up at the exclamation just as Atlas sped closer and then slammed the car into park on the dirt path. Her eyes immediately met the reason for his shouting as she took in the structure.

It was on fire.

They both ran out of the car and towards the building, coughing as smoke blew in their face. By the time they were a football field away they could both tell it was too late, even if there was someone inside there was nothing they could do.

Always quick on his feet, Atlas was already on his phone describing where they were to the fire department. It would take them fifteen minutes to get there. Hopefully, the fire would stay contained to just the building until then.

Just then, a loud crack sliced through the air, and Naya watched in slow motion as the ceiling of the building fell in. She covered her nose and mouth with her shirt and backed away from the fire, careful not to turn her back to it, Atlas following suit and standing next to her.

"Are you thinking what I'm thinking?" He asked after a moment.

"Yep." She was indeed.

"He was the only person besides police personnel who knew we were looking into this."

"Exactly." Naya watched as the outside walls of the house began to crumble, unable to stand any longer. Their evidence, whatever that could've been, was literally burning to the ground in front of their eyes.

They were still standing there when the fire trucks came blaring in with their sirens a few minutes later. They soon had the fire under control, and it was swiftly put out. Atlas and Naya described the situation to the fire chief who promised to keep them clued-in during his investigation. With nothing left for them to do there, they returned to the car.

"Well," She looked towards Atlas, "Why don't we go pay a visit to our favorite farmer?"

"We really do think on the same wavelength. Let's go." He put the car into reverse to avoid the firetrucks parked along the dirt road in front of them, they pulled away as the firemen continued sifting through the rubble that remained of the homestead.

He turned onto the road and they were both quiet as they made the short drive to Benjamin's place.

He parked a little ways back from the house, effectively blocking the dirt access road with the vehicle.

"I'm not taking any chances. You go to the front and knock. I'm going around back."

"Copy that."

They both climbed out of the vehicle and Naya walked towards the front door.

"Mr. Rodgers?" She called out as she knocked. There was a red truck sitting unoccupied in the driveway. "Are you home? It's detective Largusa." Atlas who was waiting by the corner of the house motioned for her to knock again, so she did.

"Mr. Rodgers? Can we talk to you please?" She tried the knob, it was locked.

When there was still no answer, Atlas motioned that he was going around back and that she should give him time to get to the other side and then kick down the door. She gave him one last chance.

"Mr. Rodgers? I'm coming in!" The door buckled like it was made of kindling, giving way much less resistance than she expected.

The room was dingy and dark, the only light from the two windows that were covered with dirty old curtains that might've been white once. The back door knob spun and opened, revealing Atlas, walked in and they made eye contact. The front door had been locked, but not the back.

As if he could read her mind Atlas shrugged and continued to poke around.

They explored the room; there was a kitchen with a stove and a fridge and not much else. There was a small table that only had one chair, and across the way, there was an ugly and torn plaid loveseat facing the most archaic TV set Naya had ever seen. It had to be from the 50's. Other than that, the only other thing was a door behind the couch.

Atlas was way ahead of her and was already across the room, turning the knob, he pushed open the door and stood back to reveal a bed that was made, and it looked like it hadn't been touched since. The only other door was across the room and she presumed it was a bathroom. Atlas stepped across the room and opened it, it was empty.

"He's not here."

"I wonder where he could've gone." Naya let the hand that was holding her weapon relax by her side. They both cautiously made their way back to the front of the house and looked around.

"I don't see a barn or anything."

"Me neither. I did see a small shed outback with some farming equipment in it, but I cleared it and there wasn't anyone hiding."

"I don't like this."

"Me neither." Atlas agreed. "And his car is here." They stared at the car as if it would move any second. Naya and Atlas glanced in the cab and the bed, both were completely devoid of anything of use.

"So, where would our farmer friend go without a car when the closest sign of civilization is over ten miles away?" Naya surveyed the fields of wheat which approached the homestead from every side.

"Beats me." Atlas took one last glance around the driveway area and then turned towards the car.

Without another word, they got back in and headed towards the precinct.

14

NAYA

The next afternoon Naya stood in front of her mirror for what felt like forever. She felt a bit like she was back in high school. Honestly, that was probably the last time she cared this much about a date.

When she moved here she hadn't brought any cute clothes that would work for a date with her. She had planned to work most of the time, and then hang out at home with Vance in her loungewear, like any average woman. So, when she came home from work the reality of the situation set in. She had realized she had no idea if she had anything to wear on a date.

She had tried asking Kevin where they were going, but he wouldn't relent. He had said it was a surprise, and he was intent on keeping it that way. After about an hour of staring at her measly wardrobe in disdain, Naya decided on her favorite pair of jeans pairing it with the most elegant long-sleeved blouse she had, it was a deep emerald. She still looked a little more professional than cute, but this was as good as it was going to get. Kevin had said that her jeans looked great on her at least.

As she was grabbing her jacket and purse she heard a commotion from downstairs, she assumed that meant the guys had arrived. She stopped in front of her mirror for a split-second and debated putting on some makeup for the second time since she had moved to Denver, but she knew that if the others were there then Kevin was probably already waiting. Besides, he'd already seen her on numerous occasions without makeup.

Kevin was waiting at the bottom of the stairs when she went down. She couldn't tell if he had done it on purpose or not, but he seemed slightly more dressed up than normal. He was wearing dark jeans, a navy collared shirt, and a gray pullover sweater. Naya felt herself blush, he looked good, hot even, her mind supplemented.

"Are you ready?" He held out his hand and bowed ever so slightly, as if this was a scene from some old movie, it made her want to giggle.

"I am, I should just say goodbye to Vance."

"You can, but we won't be gone that long. And Sebastian and Trevor are with him."

Naya's mouth quirked to the side. Kevin was right, Vance wasn't a child, he would survive for a few hours while she went out on a date.

"You're right, shall we go?"

He smiled and continued to be the perfect gentleman, opening the door for her, even though it was her house.

"Do I get to know where we are going now?" She asked as they got into the car.

"Nope. And don't even try to guess. You're lucky I didn't go as far as to try blindfolding you."

"Yeah, I'm a cop, we don't like that type of stuff." Naya teased, she eyeballed Kevin as he navigated the side streets, his large hands moving smoothly over the leather wheel.

"I know, I'm not an idiot."

It was quiet in the car, so Naya decided to start a conversation the only way she could think to do so.

"So, is this the part where I ask what your favorite movie is or something?

"Sounds about right. But I suppose I haven't been on a proper date in a while."

She raised her eyebrows. "A fine specimen like yourself doesn't have a date every weekend?"

"That the type of guy you pinned me as?" He asked in surprise.

She shrugged. "I'm not going to lie, a bit, yeah. You came across so confident when you were talking to me that it seemed you had a bit of experience talking to women, like, flirting with them."

His eyes flickered in her direction. "Well, I guess your detective skills are a bit off. I don't think I've been out with a girl in six months. And before that, I was single for almost two years."

Naya decided to be cheeky. "And you're how old?"

"Thirty-two, same as Vance."

"Hmm..." She mocked, rubbing her chin melodramatically. "The math doesn't quite add up there Einstein." She pivoted, and made it clear she expected a more thorough answer.

"You're right." He simultaneously smiled and sighed. "Well about two and a half years ago, before I was single, I dated the same woman for six years."

"Six years and no marriage?" Even for someone who was as hesitant to commit as Naya, that was a bit long to only date.

"That's what she said." He checked his blind spot and merged over to the right lane, clearly planning to get off the highway. Naya looked around and spotted a suspiciously tall plastic volcano.

"You didn't want to marry her?" Trying to get answers out of Kevin felt a little too much like an interrogation to her, it was starting to get on her nerves.

He seemed to sense her shift in mood and rushed to fill in the rest of the story as they parked.

"We met when we were in our early twenties and fresh out of college. Honestly, the first few years we were together, we were both working so hard towards our careers that we rarely saw each other. I mean, we were together, but I personally feel like our relationship didn't get serious until three years later, but she didn't see it that way. So, three years later she got mad at me for not marrying her, and I just didn't feel ready. She couldn't understand that; she thought because she was ready that, I automatically should be too for some reason. And I wasn't." He shut off the car and looked at her directly in the eyes, "And I'm the type of guy where when you try to force me to do something I will pull as hard as possible in the opposite direction. Or at least I was then."

"I understand," Naya answered seriously as they stepped out of the car. She quickly spotted the sign for adventure golf. She should've guessed.

"I did date a bit afterward. But six years, well," He reached down and grabbed her hand and began leading her towards the entrance. "I couldn't get over it. I still loved her, and I had really wanted it to work out. And I couldn't let it go and it encroached on any other relationship I tried to start."

They got in line behind a couple of families and Kevin lowered his voice to just above a whisper. "And so finally, I just accepted. I wasn't ready yet."

"And now?" Naya stared him directly in the eyes.

"I'm ready now." He smiled as they moved forward a spot in line; they were two from the front row.

"What changed?"

"That day you walked in the living room and I first laid eyes on you." He leaned in so close their faces were almost touching.

"Are you messing with me?" This sounded like something straight out of a romance movie. They moved forward a spot and were now next in line.

"No, I'm not."

"You didn't seem that enamored by me then." She pointed out.

"I hide my emotions well."

The cashier called them forward and Kevin quickly paid for two rounds of golf.

"And now you pick your favorite color ball." The cashier motioned to the paper taped to the desktop and Naya leaned over to have a look.

"I'll take orange I think." The young cashier reached under the counter and handed her a neon orange golf ball.

"I'll do the lime green, please." Kevin collected his golf ball and then handed her a miniature golf club. "Shall we?" He motioned to the path, which was outlined with lights, leading to the park with a big sign labeled 'Hole 1' directly in front of them.

He waited for her to go first. Naya leaned down and lined up her ball on one of the divots in the mat. The first hole seemed pretty easy, well, it was putt-putt, so it was relative, but it seemed much easier than whatever level the volcano she had spotted on their way in.

As she aligned herself with the ball and got ready to swing, Kevin interrupted her. "I believe it's your turn."

Naya hit the ball, watching as it landed near the hole but not quite making it in. She would score a two for this hole for sure. "I just went."

He shook his head. "No, I mean your turn to tell me why someone as beautiful, smart, and accomplished as you is single."

She shrugged as he got ready to take his shot. "I was so focused on my career for so long, I mean, I had boyfriends here and there, but in a town like La Junta they all wanted to settle down right away and have kids, and that just wasn't in the cards for me." His ball landed near where hers had and they made their way over. She lined up her ball and lightly putted it directly into the hole.

"I met a man about eight months ago, and things were going well, but then I found out about Vance and there was just no way our relationship was at the point where he would want to move to Denver for me, so we split."

Kevin putt his ball in, then leaned down and collected both from the cup. "You know La Junta and Denver aren't that far apart, right? Why not do the long-distance thing?"

She shook her head as they approached the next hole. "Not my thing. I enjoy having free time from my phone when I'm off work. It's become especially important to me as the years go on and my job relies more and more on electronics."

"Ah, that makes sense."

They finished the second hole and moved on to the third. Turns out mini-golf went much quicker as an adult.

"I haven't mentioned this," she gestured between them, "To Vance yet, but I assume you did since I figure he would ask why you're not there today."

He smiled. "You assume correct. That's basic guy code, sisters are off limits without permission."

"And?"

Kevin got a hole in one. "He's more than okay with it. He knows I'm a good guy."

"Oh really?" She finished taking her turn, getting another hole in two shots.

"Yes, really, those were his exact words, actually."

They were almost done with the fourth hole. "So, then, Kevin, good guy, what are your plans for the future?"

He was quiet for a moment while he took his shot. "Well, I guess keep working my way up in the construction world. I'd like to eventually buy a few rental properties, and that way, those could be a bit of income insurance when I retire." Naya watched him without saying anything. "Is this your way of asking me if I want kids?"

She shook her head. "Not necessarily. I mean, I suppose if that's what you wanted, you would mention it? I'm asking what you want out of life, and clearly, kids didn't make the cut."

He grabbed both of their balls again and headed for the next hole. He handed Naya hers and she began to line up her swing. "I guess I should ask you the same question."

She watched where her ball went, thinking for a moment about her answer.

"If you had asked me a year ago, I would've had an answer for you. But now I'm not sure."

"What do you mean?" His eyes searched her face as if he could find the answer himself.

"A year ago, I was happy as sheriff of a small town and ready to start looking for a man, maybe buy a nice house, or build my own to my exact specifications...and now, well my whole life has been turned upside down and is hanging in limbo." Kevin knew what she was referring to, she didn't have to explain.

They finished the eighth hole and headed for the ninth. Naya couldn't believe how fast time was going by, she felt like she could spend forever just talking to Kevin.

"So, you already know a lot about my family life thanks to Vance, but tell me a little bit about yours?" She looked at Kevin, loving the way the setting sun was reflecting off his blond hair turning his curls golden.

"Well, that's easy. I'm a lonely only child as you already know. Vance is the closest thing I've ever had to a brother. That's why I'm always around. I know we didn't have an entire childhood together like the two of you, but I feel like I'm part of Vance's family, and he's part of mine."

He watched from the sidelines, and she lined up her ball on the next hole. This one had a tricky windmill that you had to time; if you shot early or late, the blade would send the ball right back to the start.

"And where are your parents?" She took the shot, pumping the air when she got it through the windmill obstacle on the first try.

Kevin chuckled at her little victory dance and began to line up his own shot. "My mom was a single mom, she did everything for me herself. And she's in Castle Rock. She's actually been wanting to visit Vance at some point soon, so maybe you'll be able to meet her.

"Is Vance close to your mom?"

Kevin shrugged. "When Vance first moved here, he would spend the smaller holidays and occasional weekend he couldn't make it home for with us, like the 4th of July, so I guess you could say so? Honestly, you'd have to ask Vance."

Naya was beginning to realize just how off her perception of her brother had been. She leaned down to line up her ball on what was now the fourteenth hole. When she had moved up here, she had done so thinking Vance had no support because his family was so far away.

"Penny for your thoughts?" Kevin watched her cautiously, seemingly worried he had said something wrong.

"Oh, I was just thinking. When I moved up here, I did so because I thought Vance didn't have anyone. I mean I assumed he had friends, but I guess I just pictured a bunch of college guys who still go out for beers once a month. But you and Vance, you're so close, it's just a bit surprising for me to see someone who is as close as family who isn't of relation, you know?"

"That doesn't happen in La Junta?" He shaded his eyes and looked towards the setting sun crowned in pink before glancing at the time on his phone.

"I mean, yes and no. There are some friends who are inseparable, but that's more in school. Once you grow up, it's expected you get married and have kids and that's your new support system, you know? Are we late for something?"

"We have reservations for dinner at six. If you aren't too attached to this game, maybe we should call it a draw? Or we can take our chances on missing our reservation and go as walk-ins."

She shook her head. "As much as it pains me to leave this golf game, I think food is going to take precedence here. Should I even ask what's for dinner?"

He took her ball and club from her hands and began heading to the return hut. "Nope, so don't even try."

He returned their supplies and grabbed her hand to lead her back to the parking lot. As they reached the car, he spun her around to face him, and faster than she could ask what he was doing, he leaned in and kissed her.

Just like the first time, it felt entirely natural, and she kissed him back, running her hands through his soft hair and along the stubble that went down the back of his neck.

He ended the kiss all too soon.

"As much as I would love for this to continue, we really do need to go." She nodded mutely and went around the car to get in the passenger side.

The drive to the restaurant was surprisingly quick and Naya smiled when they pulled up in front of a packed Mexican restaurant.

"How did you know?" Mexican food was her favorite.

"Vance told me." He smiled and leaned over for a quick peck on the lips.

THROUGHOUT THE COURSE OF DINNER, the conversation continued to flow naturally. Naya found that she and Kevin actually had a lot in common, beyond just the clear sexual chemistry. When the bill came, she went to reach for it, but he blocked her hand.

"Don't even try." He chastised; he picked up the little black book, and slid his card inside without even looking.

"But you paid for golf." She didn't feel he was obligated to pay.

"And I asked you on the date, so it is my treat." The server walked by and Kevin handed her the book.

"But—" he put his finger to her lips, stopping her retort.

"I would also love if you would consider going on another date with me?" He reached down and grabbed her hand, waiting patiently for her answer.

She smiled tenderly. "Next weekend? They tend to work better with my schedule unless something crazy happens at the precinct." She hoped that they would find their culprit before next weekend, but she was starting to doubt that was realistic.

"Works for me." He was smiling as the server came over and handed him back the check, thanking them for coming in. As Kevin signed the receipt Naya stood to put on her jacket. She took a moment to glance around the room; there were lots of families dining here, as well as a fair number of couples, and there wasn't a single empty seat. This place was popular.

"Shall we?" Naya turned to find Kevin holding out his hand and she didn't hesitate to slide her hand into his.

"Yes, let's find out what Sebastian and Trevor have done with my kitchen." She hoped they hadn't ordered anything too messy.

"They had specific instructions to order a more reasonable quantity than last time. I think they were planning on Chinese." They climbed in the car and Kevin backed out of the parking space to head back.

"Perfect."

Naya was surprised by how thoughtful Kevin was, maybe it was just because she hadn't dated in a while and the guy she had been dating in La Junta hadn't been all that great. Either way, Kevin seemed like a catch. As the thought passed through her head, Naya began to doubt. If he was such a catch, why was he single at their age? There had to be something wrong with him; it seemed there always was; anyone without major flaws seemed to be scooped up much younger than them.

"Penny for your thoughts?" Kevin interrupted her musings.

"Oh, just thinking about work."

"Jesus, I'm sorry the date was that bad." Kevin said with mock offense, the smile on his face giving him away.

"Yep, it was just the worst, I think I'm gonna have to wash my mouth out with soap when I get home."

Kevin laughed so hard he shook the car. "But really, have you ever had a date so bad, that you felt that way?" His words sank in a minute later. "Sorry, you don't have to answer that." He ran a hand awkwardly through his hair, refusing to look at her.

"I'm an open book. So, yes, if you must know." She replied, not bothered by his blunt question. "It was while I was in the academy, I went on a date with an older cop. Everything was going well, and we were really hitting it off; conversation was flowing smoothly, and for a moment, I really thought there was something there..." She sighed loudly. "But then, he walked me to my door and leaned in to kiss me...and awful! He basically started making out with my face. And I mean all over! I felt slobbered on and had to wash my face afterward. It was gross."

When she finished, Kevin was laughing so hard that he was out of breath; Naya smiled at the memory. It was remarkable how, as you got older, moments that had felt embarrassing at the time became amusing anecdotes instead.

By the time they pulled up in front of the house, Kevin was finally starting to catch his breath.

"Well, I'd like to ask you for a goodnight kiss, which I hope will be granted as long as I promise not to slobber all over your face."

"Request granted." This time she leaned in first, until her lips met his. It felt like they had barely started when they were interrupted by a tap at the passenger window. It was Sebastian. Again. Naya grabbed her purse and opened her door.

"Jesus, I thought the two of you were never going to stop." Sebastian groaned as Naya stifled a giggle. Maybe it had been longer than she thought. She turned to see that Kevin had gotten out.

"Whatever, did you guys clean up like I asked you too?"

Sebastian rolled his eyes. "Yes, dad, now can we go home? I'm tired and have to work tomorrow."

This time Kevin was the one to roll his eyes. "Where's Trevor?"

"He was helping Vance to bed, I thought he would be out by now, with how long you two were sucking face, but I guess I was wrong."

"I should go in and help." Naya wished Sebastian wasn't there so she could say a proper goodbye to Kevin, but he was, so she sheepishly waved and said,' See you later.' Like a teen girl, she turned and went inside. Some things never changed.

Just as she was walking through the doorway, she saw that Trevor was closing the door to Vance's room.

"Perfect timing." He greeted as he grabbed his keys.

"Was everything okay?" Naya hushed her voice, knowing her brother was still awake.

"Yep, just a little shaky on the walk into the room, but he had a few beers and relaxed with us."

Naya felt apprehensive about Vance drinking. She watched Trevor head for the door, she gave him a little wave as he walked out and grimaced as she was reminded of her awkward goodbye to Kevin.

She was torn between checking on the kitchen or Vance first, but ultimately chose Vance and softly knocked on his door.

"Come in."

She slowly pushed the door open to see her brother sitting up in his bed, and he looked like he had been about to read; a book was sitting open across his lap. He didn't look drunk. "Hey, just wanted to make sure they didn't get you too drunk."

Vance chuckled. "Is that what they told you? I only had two beers; I was just a little shaky when I stood up, just tired, I think, so Trevor insisted on helping me to bed." Vance rolled his eyes in feigned annoyance, she knew he appreciated his friends. "So, how was the big date?"

Naya turned red. "Going right for the jugular I see."

He shrugged. "Kevin's a nice guy, Naya; I really think you two could be good together."

She smiled sheepishly. "Sounds a bit weird coming from my big brother who used to threaten to beat up any guys who would dare to even look at me."

Vance grinned wide at his antics. "Well, that's because I know Kevin, and I know he would never do anything to hurt you. He really is a great man."

"I'm glad you approve."

"I do." He picked up the book on his lap. "Now if you don't mind, I'm going to read a bit before bed."

Naya was taken aback when she suddenly noticed what he was reading. "Wait, is that the Bible?" No one in her family had ever been religious.

"Yep, figured it was high time I see what all this mumbo-jumbo is about."

"And?"

He chuckled. "It's mumbo-jumbo alright. I think I might try the Quran next. Or maybe the Torah."

Naya rolled her eyes. "Isn't the Torah the same as the first few books of the Bible?"

"Maybe, but it'll be quite the challenge to read it in Hebrew."

"At least learning Hebrew is more constructive than playing video games."

"Goodnight," Vance replied in bluffing rudeness, the smile still on his face. "Have to get back to the good word."

Naya said goodnight back and closed the door with a laugh, heading up the stairs to her room. She decided she could worry about the kitchen tomorrow. As she got undressed, she couldn't help but smile as the events of the evening came back to her. Vance was right, Kevin was a nice guy.

As she slid into bed, she pulled out her phone to set an alarm for the morning she saw her mother's text. It said she and their father would be coming to town on Tuesday. That would be perfect.

With a sigh, she remembered that Derek would be bringing the second aide, Elliot, with him tomorrow, and she had forgotten to mention it to Vance. Oh well, she would just leave him a note in the morning and she slipped into a dreamless sleep.

15

NAYA

Naya stifled a yawn as she shuffled the stack of papers on her desk. Paperwork was the worst and most boring part of being a cop, and she dreaded it. All they did was checkout a simple house on Saturday, and now they were required to write an entire essay of what they found, which hadn't even been anything of value, just a sparsely furnished house of a man they weren't even sure was connected to anything.

Atlas who had been away from his desk was suddenly standing right next to her.

"Guess what I have?"

"Hm?" She asked without looking up she assumed it was something mundane.

A paper-clipped stack of papers suddenly landed on her desk where she had been working. It was the autopsy report on Shanice.

"Wow! That was quick." She picked it up and began to rifle through it.

"Captain called the lab to ask for a favor, even after I asked for a rush on it since this guy barely had a cooling off period, and you know his carries more weight."

Naya huffed, flipping to the page she wanted. "Damn"

Atlas already knew. "Yeah, now the blood thing really does make no sense."

"Nothing unusual, so what reason would he have to drain one but not the other? Did he just not have to drug Shanice?" Naya rested her head on her hands as she scanned the document.

Atlas rubbed his chin. "My guess? I think one of them was a mistake, and the other was exactly what he wanted."

"So, we need to figure out which abduction went as planned and which one didn't" Naya surmised and scribbled a few notes on a sticky note and attached it to the autopsy report. "And I hate to say it, but we might have a tiebreaker soon if he keeps his pace."

He grimaced. "I hope not, but you're probably right. Did you see the cause of death?"

Naya flipped back a page. "That's odd. A heart attack?"

"Yep. I'm not sure if it happened during the abduction or while this guy was doing whatever he does, but I have a feeling Shanice might've died before he could do what he wanted."

"You're probably on to something." Naya looked at the coroner's notes. "It does say she was in tip-top shape and that a natural heart attack would be unlikely?"

"But whatever could've caused it is no longer in her blood, she came back completely clean."

"Maybe it was something her body metabolized?" Naya ran through a mental list of chemicals she was familiar with in her head that might be able to do that, it was short. She now wished that she had paid more attention in chemistry.

"Maybe." Atlas flipped through his own copy of the autopsy.

"Any sign of Ben Rodgers?" She continued to jot down notes, attaching them to the autopsy.

"Nah, I had a squad car go out there last night, they did so very begrudgingly since it's so far out of the way, and there wasn't any sign of the man, nor has the truck been moved since we were there."

Naya groaned.

"You're telling me." Atlas sunk into his desk chair. "I don't think

I've had a case this frustratingly bizarre in a long time. The murders I have are usually pretty cut and dry."

"Don't tell me, you always find the perpetrator in 48 hours?" That show was the bane of her existence, convincing the public that solving murders was easy.

"How did you know?" He smirked. "I've been trying to find out information on who would have inherited old Dave's plot and I've formulated a potential theory."

"What's that?" Naya turned to face Atlas, closing her report, giving his idea her attention, and allowing herself to digest what she'd read so she could go back with fresh eyes after.

"Well, our computer says that David Smith owns that land, right?"

"Yes."

"And granted, the Denver Police Department isn't always up to date, but what do we always upload in the system fairly promptly?"

A piece of the puzzle slid into place in Naya's mind, and she gasped. "Death certificates."

"Exactly." Atlas smiled. "But guess what is conveniently missing about David Smith?"

"And who would benefit from his death by not informing anyone?" She couldn't believe they had missed it for this long.

"You got it, his good old neighbor and our infamous lone farmer, Benjamin Rodgers."

Naya spun towards her computer, feeling like she should Google something, but not quite sure what. "I don't think Benjamin Rodgers is our killer though."

"I don't think so either. According to the computer, David Smith would be about ninety-six now, so it doesn't surprise me much that he would be dead. But I do think that Rodgers has been secretly farming his land for years, and probably buried his body, convincing himself that David had no family. And maybe he didn't, I didn't know the guy." He tapped his lip with his pen. "But what I do think happened is Ben realized he had told us too much, and that we would find out that David Smith was never reported dead, and he got spooked."

"I agree." Naya really hadn't thought Rodgers was the killer in the first place, just that he had been hiding something. "Benjamin Rodgers doesn't seem like the kind of guy to abduct physically fit women, and if we agree he isn't involved just his land, do you think we should stop focusing on him?"

"Yes." Atlas also turned towards his computer and then looked at her over his right shoulder. "I'm not ruling out that something has happened to our friend Ben, but I think if anything he's hiding out, and if something did happen to him, all I can think it would be is our actual killer, because he saw us talking to him and didn't like it."

"So, do you think the burning house is still our killer?"

Atlas scrunched up his forehead. "I'm not sure about that one. I'm sort of waiting for the arson report to come back for me to make my decision. I can't decide if that was Ben trying to hide the evidence, or if that was the killer warning us off."

Naya bit her lip. "This guy doesn't seem like the type to be scared by the cops."

He raised his eyebrows.

She had a feeling she couldn't explain. "I just think this killer is in his own little world. I think he has a mission. Because if he was scared of us, why dump in the same field, possibly while we were there? If he did see us, then he's clearly not scared at all, but either way, he knew we had found that location and would be monitoring it."

"I see."

They sat in silence for a few moments staring into space.

"I guess there's nothing to do but wait for the arson report."

"Which means it's lunchtime!" Atlas jumped up and grabbed his coat.

"Are you ever not thinking of food or coffee?" Naya grabbed her jacket as well, she was sort of hungry as well, now that she thought about it

"Maybe when I...um well, when.... No, I guess not. C'mon, let's go." They were laughing as they walked out to their squad car.

NAYA SIGHED as she unlocked her front door. Despite their brainstorming and looking over the autopsy for the entire afternoon, nothing more had jumped out at either of them. They were at another dead end. There were no fingerprints, no hairs, and the killer had left no traceable evidence behind.

As she stepped in the hall and slid off her shoes, she could hear talking in the living room. She wasn't sure if it was Vance with Kevin or maybe Elliot and Derek, but she really wasn't in the mood to see anyone; her mind was filled with the case and burnout. Instead of saying hello, she slipped upstairs as stealthily as she could; once there, she quickly pulled on her running clothes and grabbed her headphones.

Before she headed back down the stairs, she grabbed her work pants and pulled out the spare keys she had stopped to make on her way home. One for Elliot, and two additional keys for Trevor and Sebastian, or whoever didn't have one already. She set them on the table in the hall on her way out.

She stepped silently back out of the door and locked it before anyone could notice she had even been there. Outside, she started up RunTracker and then headed to the left, her only desire was to be away from her home.

For the next hour everything stressing her out, Vance, the case, her parents coming, it all melted away as she pounded the pavement harder and harder. She had her running playlist playing, the pace of her steps syncing with the beat. She was breathing heavily and her heart thumping furiously in her chest, but she didn't care; it felt great to let all the stress fall off her shoulders temporarily. Nothing mattered in this moment but her feet hitting the ground.

When she got back to her house, she began to stretch out on the front porch, only taking the time for what was necessary to prevent injury; she was eager to go straight to her room. She wasn't sure why, but she really didn't feel like talking to Kevin or Vance tonight. It was unusual for her.

She quickly and quietly unlocked the door again and stepped back in the house. There were still voices in the living room, and for a second, Naya tried to remember which cars she had seen out front to determine if one of the voices was Kevin or not, but ultimately, she decided she didn't care either way, and snuck back upstairs. Afterwards she texted Vance and told him to holler if he needed and that the extra keys for him to hand out were on the table by the door.

When he didn't respond she worried for a moment, then reassured herself he wasn't alone and that someone would call her if there was an issue. She slipped into her most comfortable pajamas and lay on her side, facing the wall.

As if she didn't have enough on her plate lately, one of her old cases haunting her thoughts today and wouldn't leave. The three unsolved cases she kept in her drawer at work were connected, and they were all children. Her heart hurt every time she thought about it. It had been over a year, did the pain ever go away? Naya knew that guys like the killer she was currently trying to find, those kind of guys didn't stop until they were caught or died, whichever came first. Tomorrow was Tuesday, which meant it was about time for their current killer to act again. And there was absolutely nothing she could do to stop it and it was reminding her too much of how powerless she felt when it came to her old cases.

"Knock-knock" She heard Kevin's voice from the top of the stairs. She considered pretending to be asleep, but knew he would never buy it.

"Is Vance okay?" She asked, really not wanting to have a stupid 'how are you' small talk conversation.

"Are you okay?" She heard him step on the final step, which creaked, come through the doorway, and cross the room to sit on the bed behind her. "I was surprised you didn't come to check on Vance when you got home or at least look to see if he'd eaten."

"I heard voices and assumed he was okay. I'm not really in the mood to talk to anyone, it was a long day."

She heard some rustling and almost turned around to see what he was doing when she felt the bed shift. Next thing she knew, his arms were encircling her.

"That's fine, we don't have to talk." He whispered next to her ear.

Naya felt herself relax in his embrace, and they settled into a comfortable silence. He was right, they didn't need to talk.

He lay with her for a while; she wasn't sure how long because she didn't want to break the peaceful embrace to check the time on her phone, but eventually, she began to drift off. Not a deep sleep, a light doze where she was still aware of her surroundings.

Kevin must've thought she had fallen asleep though, because she felt him shift away from her and start to put on his shoes. She found herself thinking that he truly was a gentleman.

As quietly as he could she heard him leave, even skipping the step that had creaked as he came up. She could hear hushed voices in the hallway and wondered if he was talking to Vance. That was the last conscious thought she had before she finally fell into a deep slumber.

16

MARK

Tuesday morning.

It was time.

He had hoped that Alia would go for a run yesterday, but when it hadn't happened he knew today would be the day. It had to be.

This was going to be difficult. Much more difficult than the others.

But he had a plan.

He propped his door ajar, waiting to hear her leave her apartment. Since it was morning, he had a couple of false alarms as other people left for work. Finally, he heard a door and, when he peeked out, was rewarded with Alia looking beautiful in her designer running wear.

Perfect.

She jogged lightly down the stairs and he moved over to his computer, quickly accessing her phone through the Bluetooth connection again. Modern technology made this almost too easy.

He watched as she stretched just outside the door and then headed west. He watched as the line on his screen turned around corners and sped up across street crossings. Yes, he liked technology, a lot.

After what seemed like forever to his building anticipation, her line began to head back towards him. He pulled out the rag he had ready and dipped it in the ether solution, once she came back into view and began stretching in the same place she had stretched before her run, he knew it was time and quietly slid out of his apartment. He left the door propped open with another rag; that way, he wouldn't have to worry about trying to open it with his hands full.

He stood in the hallway and looked around, this was the only part of his plan he hadn't perfected yet. He hoped what he had thought of would work. He briefly glanced down the stairwell, which was in the center of the building, to see if there were any busybodies loitering. There didn't appear to be any. He smiled. This was much more exhilarating than normal.

He heard footsteps coming up the stairs, this was going perfectly.

He stayed by the opposite wall until he heard her feet reach the third level. Then he began to amble towards the staircase.

He stepped to the side to let her pass, and she smiled at him.

As she looked back in the direction of his door he made his move. Grabbing her from behind and putting the rag over her mouth before she could scream, she started kicking violently and he held her securely while she squirmed, careful not to be too close to any of the walls or doors. He didn't want her foot to make contact and alert anyone to what was happening under their noses.

It seemed to take forever for her to fall unconscious, his adrenaline racing at the possibility of being caught. As soon as she was completely still dead weight in his arms, he dragged her to his door and brought her inside. He set her on the table he had set up, went back to close the door, and slid the lock into place. He closed the curtains and then turned to Alia's unconscious form. He would have to be quick.

He pulled out the solutions he would be testing this time and expertly filled up a few syringes. He injected them into her calf muscles one after another.

Then, his active participation done, he sat back in his chair to observe, waiting to see if anything happened. He was worried that she might wake up, so he had taken extra precautions to tie her down, but chances were, even if she woke up, she wouldn't be able to do anything anyway.

With a smirk, he pulled up the notes app on his phone and began typing the patient's condition and his observations.

He was such a brilliant scientist.

17

NAYA

She was driving to work the next morning when the call came in. She answered over her car's Bluetooth.

"Detective Largusa."

"He got another one."

Naya groaned and felt herself press the gas pedal a little harder. "Send me the details, I'll meet you there."

"Alia Larson, she lives on the third floor of a building on Blake Street. Her boyfriend called it in. I guess she is really religious about her running routine and he says that she was due back at eight, and it's now nine."

Naya thought it was a bit premature, but she also knew that this fit their guy's M.O. A text with an address came through and she clicked it, it opened in her GPS and she pushed the button to redirect.

"I know it's too soon to be sure she was taken; she's only an hour late, but he was adamant that she was never late. And he said he keeps trying to call her phone and it's been shut off. He says she never shuts it off while she runs because she listens to music and tracks her run with it."

"And there's no possibility her phone could have died?" Naya took the next corner a little too fast, but she recovered and pressed the gas even harder, her department-issued light flickering on her dash.

"He says she was religious about charging it and that it and I quote, 'straight up wouldn't happen.' I'm telling you; this kid gave 9-1-1 a rough time."

"How old?" Naya turned onto Blake Street, heading towards the tall building up ahead, which she felt instinctively was the one Atlas was talking about.

"Twenty-five, she and the boyfriend have been living together for two years, says they were about to get married."

"Damn. This guy is all over the map. The only thing we know is that he likes female runners."

"There has to be a reason…" Atlas thought aloud. "I see your car. Park on the curb next to me." She saw him waving, she pulled towards him and parked where she was told.

"Wow, this is a fancy building." She said as they walked into the lobby.

He nodded. "I think it's one of the few affordable high rises in the downtown area. Mostly because it's so old and the neighborhood, normally these kinds of apartments cost thousands a month."

The door had been unlocked for them but there had been a security pad, and Naya surveyed the lobby she noticed there were also security cameras in plain sight, though the lobby itself seemed unmanned. She assumed the security cameras were probably monitored off-site by a contract company or that the building was owned by another company that monitored all their properties from a central location. Naya pointed them out to Atlas.

He nodded. "I'll request the tapes."

Behind the lobby was a hall with a single freight elevator, and behind it was an open doorway to a staircase that went up to the residences. Atlas pressed the button for the elevator while Naya walked over to the bottom of the stairs and looked up; she noticed that the stairs circled and stopped at every floor; she could see all the way up to the top.

"Damn. This elevator is taking forever." Atlas complained.

Naya looked around and noticed the lack of an additional elevator. "One elevator for an entire building?"

"Yeah, but these old buildings usually only have one elevator shaft since elevators were expensive to build at the time."

"What floor?" She placed her foot on the bottom step.

Atlas looked down at his phone. "Third."

"No problem." She started up the stairs and heard Atlas follow her lead shortly thereafter. They reached the third floor in no time.

"I bet she takes the stairs a lot." Atlas commented as he noticed her door was only a few down and to the left from where they came out. He knocked on her door.

The officer who had answered the boyfriend's call opened the door, and after they flashed their badges, he motioned them inside.

Just as before, Atlas talked to the officer while Naya walked into the kitchen where the boyfriend was standing, his eyes wide in thought and red-rimmed.

"Hello, I'm Detective Largusa." She held out her. The young man looked at her, lost for a moment; when he recovered, he hastened to shake her hand, almost stumbling as he did so. He was an absolute mess.

"Justin." He said and leaned on the counter behind him. "I know you all think I'm nuts, but this is not like Alia. She's a smart girl, she knows how dangerous running alone is. That's why she always tells me exactly when she will be back."

Naya nodded in sympathy. "I understand. Does she always run the same route?"

"No, almost never. I mean she has favorite routes, but she always changes the exact streets in case anyone's watching. She even changes up the days. She runs two to three times a week, either Monday or Tuesday, then Thursday or Friday, and sometimes a run on the weekend. And she does it at random depending on her work schedule. She tries to be as unpredictable as possible."

Wow, Naya had to admit, this girl had done everything right when it came to running safety. The guy they were looking for must have some other way of finding these women. Naya was beginning to think that maybe he was a runner himself who was meeting them and running with them.

"Did she ever run with anyone?" She pried.

"No, never." Justin didn't hesitate. "I wanted her to. But running was her safe space. She liked the alone time."

Naya wondered if perhaps their killer was an attractive young man and that maybe these women didn't want to tell their significant others they were running with him. Then her mind snapped back to Julia Charles and she realized that the theory didn't fit that narrative. Julia would have probably mentioned it to her parents she was running with an older man. Unless he perhaps looked like a high school or college kid, but that seemed improbable, and she still might've said something.

The more Naya thought about it, the more she was sure that there had to be a personal connection she was missing. How could this guy abduct so many women so easily, and without leaving a trace?

"Was she a fast runner?"

Justin nodded. "Average, but fast enough, that's why I was generally okay with her running alone as long as she took precautions, she can speed up pretty randomly as needed and that's why I didn't think anyone would ever really be able to catch her if she ran into problems."

Atlas came up behind Naya, placing an arm on her shoulder. "Justin, my colleague Officer Bartel will be staying here with you if you need anything." He grabbed a card out of his pocket. "Give us a call if you think of anything else, or if she comes back after Bartel has left."

"Where are you going?" He challenged.

"To go look for her," Atlas answered in a calm and collected tone, which Naya knew was to diffuse him.

"Oh okay. Cool. Find her, please. She's my whole life." He turned and leaned his elbows on the counter and covered his face. It was clear he was trying to hide his emotions from them.

Atlas nodded and took Naya's wrist to lead her out of the apartment and give the young man some privacy. Once they were out, he glanced around the hallway. It looked like there were six apartments on each floor.

"Generally, I would say we should canvas, beginning with the neighbors, but that is just going to take too long here."

"Agreed. Let's head out to the street." Naya concurred and they jogged down the stairs and out the front door.

"So, like the others, she's a smart runner. No typical path runs at random times..." Atlas said, and Naya mirrored his frustration.

"I don't care what Brody wants, I think it's time he held a press conference and warned female runners in the area."

Atlas nodded. "I think he might already be on it. After all, he called me while I was on my way to work this morning, and he sounded just as frustrated as we are."

"Good," Naya grumbled as she looked up and down the street. "Now how is he getting these girls? None of them make the typical mistake predators capitalize on where they run the same path at the same time."

Atlas shrugged, but when he spotted a corner store imbedded in the building to the right began to beeline for it. Naya followed.

Before going in he stopped and looked up at the eave, looking for cameras, Naya did the same and noticed that there was one pointed at the door. Maybe that could help.

Atlas went inside to ask for the tapes while Naya watched the people meandering on the street. It seemed fairly active and it was daylight. How did no one notice a woman getting abducted?

She sighed, she knew exactly how. There were countless stories of women being drugged and then people on the street thinking the woman was just drunk and with her boyfriend. It was possible he was drugging these girls. It was also possible that he was threatening them and they appeared to be going willingly. People were not as observant as one would think.

Atlas came out and stood right next to her, placing a cup of gas station-quality coffee in her hand.

"Really? Coffee?" She laughed as she took a sip.

"I felt bad for the guy, doesn't seem like he has much business around here. Cameras are fake by the way. Well, they are real, but he didn't have the money to hook them to anything. He says it still helps deter crime though."

Naya grumbled as she took another sip. "I guess we better find out who monitors those apartment building cameras, and fast." Naya looked at her watch and grimaced. Her parents would've arrived in Denver by now, and they were probably on their way to spend time with Vance. She felt bad that she couldn't be there, but there was no way she could leave the case now. With a sigh she sent a quick apology text to both her mother and Vance, promising to catch up with them later in the week.

"I haven't had a case this bad in a long time," Atlas muttered as they started walking down Blake Street.

"Me neither," Naya replied, mentally shuddering at the memory of the children whose cases she had been thinking about the night before.

"I don't like it."

Naya could tell he meant something more than what he was saying. They turned a corner and began looking around the area for more cameras as they went.

"There's too many loose ends in this case. We're missing something. Or...I don't know, but something isn't right."

Atlas was right but she didn't know what either. Naya pulled out her phone and began noting the cameras on the block, she noticed Atlas was doing the same, they could compare notes later. They would find out where this girl had run. Her own run from the night before came back to her and then it hit her like a brick wall. She stopped dead in her tracks.

"Wait."

Atlas turned and stared, waiting.

"The boyfriend." She choked out, her mind spinning at a million miles a minute while she tried to keep up. She began walking back towards the building, and Atlas followed, although he was clearly confused.

"He mentioned Alia used an app to track her runs. Instead of going off on a wild goose chase, let's just find out which one and contact the company to see if we can get the records."

Atlas shook his head with a smile on his face, visibly pissed he didn't think of that but also pleased she had. As she ran up the stairs to talk to the boyfriend about which app his girlfriend used, Atlas stayed in the lobby and was already on the phone asking for a warrant to be drafted. She met Atlas back down at the bottom of the stairs.

"She uses RunTracker."

He cocked his head.

"I use it too. It's actually quite convenient, you just turn it on, and it tracks your run as you go, giving you updates right in your ear..." More thoughts hit her, a theory coming together.

"Maybe Julia and Shanice used similar apps?"

Atlas hit redial. "I'll have a warrant created for each girl. Contact the Woods and Charles families and find out what apps those girls used."

"On it." Naya was already dialing her own phone.

Now they were getting somewhere.

18

MARK

This new girl was also a dud. He could already tell. Nothing had happened.

He was pretty sure she had just died.

He groaned loudly as he stood to look out the window. He looked out and saw the pretty little detective standing on the sidewalk next to who he assumed was her partner.

Originally, he hadn't wanted to take her because it seemed a bit risky, most of the girls he grabbed were easily forgotten.

The detective would be missed.

But the more he looked at her, the more perfect he thought she was. And he knew she was a runner.

With a grin on his face, he sat in his chair and spun towards his computer. He began mapping out just how and when he would grab the detective. It would take a while, that was unfortunate. But it would be much easier than all of his other abductions.

The grin wouldn't leave Mark's face. He couldn't believe he hadn't thought of this sooner. It was perfect.

With a chuckle, he slid open the top drawer of the desk and pulled out his secret weapon.

A key to the cute little detectives' front door. And he didn't even have to steal it.

With a glance at the clock, he realized he would be late for work unless he left right now. He hated his stupid job. He slid on his work clothes and checked the girl once more for a pulse. Nothing.

Dead.

Well. She could hang here for the day then, he would deal with her when he got back. He slid the detective's key into his pocket and peeked at the mirror that hung by the door. He was tiring of this disguise, but it was the one the detective knew him as.

That would be a positive of getting rid of the detective. He could change his look. Yes. This plan was looking more and more attractive with each passing minute

"You'd better watch out Detective Largusa. I'm coming for yah." He winked at the end, which made him chuckle. He really was hilarious.

19

NAYA

The second breakthrough came after lunch. They were at their desks digging through side leads while they waited for the camera footage to come back when it happened.

"Ah-ha!" Atlas jumped up from his chair, excitement all over his face.

"What?!"

"I found out more information about our little farmer friend."

"Mr. Rodgers? What is he up to this time?" Naya crossed her legs one over the other and leaned back. She couldn't believe how tired she was, but it had already been quite the day.

"So, Mr. Rodgers tried to buy Old Dave's farm when he was alive but ill. The man must've said no, because then he called the records department to find out if Old Dave had any family. My guess is he wanted the man reported as senile."

"And they noted the call?" Naya was surprised, the records department usually didn't care that much.

"That's the thing. He called so many times, trying to pose as so many different people to get the information. But that's the thing, there was no information to get. It didn't matter if he was Dave's brother or neighbor or wife." He chuckled at the last one. "But you're right, the records department just shrugged it off and didn't make a note or think to call us, because why would they? But then today when I called and asked for records on Benjamin Rodgers' property the lady was surprised and mentioned it, because the records were still on her desk. He had called so many times that she had made a mental note of him for the girl who works on her day off."

"And..."

"Well, here's the deal, turns out that besides Dave's farm, Benjamin Rodgers owns all those properties out there. There is no third farmer. It's just him. And I bet that's where he's hiding out right now."

Naya sighed, the answer had been staring them in the face all along. She glanced at her watch and noticed it should, on a normal day, be almost time to clock out. Her family would be upset if she missed dinner.

Nothing escaped Atlas' notice. "You need to go?"

"Yes, but let's go. We can drive separately, I'll leave for home from there." She slid on her jacket and grabbed her keys.

Atlas put a hand on her shoulder. "You know this job doesn't have to be your whole life, right? I can ask another detective to go with me."

She shook her head, the case from her past surfacing again. "No. This is something I need to be there for. My family will understand."

"You know you only have one family, right?" He asked somberly.

Naya nodded. She was well aware. The pain of Vance's unfortunate future making her heart stop for a second. She shrugged off the feeling. These girls had families too. And there was no later for them any longer.

As soon as she got to the car, she attached her phone to Bluetooth and dialed her mom, following Atlas out of the parking lot as the phone rang. After a few rings, her mom answered.

"Hey, Mom."

Her mom audibly sighed. "Let me guess, you aren't going to make our six-o-clock dinner reservations?"

Naya frowned. Now, she felt even more guilty. "I have one more thing I need to do mom, think you can hold the boys off until eight? I'll meet you at the restaurant."

"Of course, Naya, but if I'm changing the reservation, you better be there."

Naya grimaced again. Her mom knew her all too well.

"I will mom. I'm just driving to interview a man real quick, and then I will head straight there." She heard laughing in the background of the phone call that didn't sound like her Dad or Vance. "Who's there?"

"Oh!" Her mom seemed surprised she noticed. "Well, Vance's friend Kevin came over; he really is quite the sweetheart, and Elliot or Derek? I can't remember which is which, is still here."

Naya she still hadn't met Elliot. "Were both of them there today?"

"This morning, yes, I guess there were a few more things to go over. Just one is here now though, and like I said, I forget which one exactly."

She rolled her eyes, it was typical of her mom to forget names. "Can you find out for me mom? That way, I don't look like an idiot later?" She tried to remember the schedule Home Health Care had given her, but her brain was too tired to function.

"Yeah, no problem, dear. I'll ask and then call the restaurant, okay? I'll text you if I'm able to move the reservation."

"Thanks mom."

"Okay, see you soon." Her mom replied, and the line went dead. The timing was perfect, they had just turned down the long two-lane road that headed towards Ben's farm and she wasn't sure how reception would have been.

It was a Tuesday evening, and she doubted her mom would have any issue changing the reservation. This was Denver, not New York City, but her parents certainly acted like they were in the big city. The thought made her smile. They were such small-town people.

THIS TIME NAYA and Atlas drove past his farm, then the one that had burned down, afterwards slowing to a crawl as they looked from their respective cars for some sort of structure he might be using to hide. The land transfer rights outlined which acres belonged to Rodgers but didn't go into detail about where things had been built.

Atlas suddenly veered left off the road, and she quickly followed. She drove for about fifty more feet before the building came into view. She wondered how Atlas had seen the small house from the street, it was well off the road and didn't stand out as much as the other two farms.

Naya and Atlas stopped their vehicles in tandem, blocking the road out, and climbed out while making eye contact. Naya shrugged to indicate she didn't think they would need force, Atlas mouthed "your funeral" with his pistol unholstered in his right hand hanging down by his side as they walked towards the door.

Granted, as she reached her left hand up to knock, her right was resting on her weapon, she didn't think she needed it but was prepared to change her opinion in an instant.

She heard a lock disengage, and the door swung open to reveal none other than their friend, Benjamin Rodgers.

"Ah. It's you." He said, certainly not looking like he was planning to run.

Naya nodded, her hand still on her pistol. "It is. Want to come out here and chat with us?"

Benjamin audibly gulped. "Sure thing." He stepped out on the porch and closed the door behind him. He motioned to the two rocking chairs, which occupied most of the small space. "Did you want to sit down?" He asked, a gracious host despite the circumstances.

"No thanks. We'll just cut to the chase. What happened to David Smith?" She didn't have time for pleasantries. As if on cue, her phone vibrated in her pocket, letting her know she had a text. Probably her mom, as promised.

He sighed. "Ah, so you found out about that."

Atlas cut in. "You knew we would, that's why you're hiding out here. On your property, after you lied to us and told us there was a third farmer out."

Benjamin looked genuinely shocked. "I'm not hiding. I switch where I live frequently. I've just been at this place this week."

"Without your truck?" Atlas accused.

"I drove my tractor out here. It's parked behind the house if you want to check."

Naya wasn't too sure, but he hadn't run when they had knocked on the door, so it didn't seem like he had much to hide. "Then why lie about who owns this property? And about David Smith?"

He ran a hand through his hair and let out a breath. "I didn't really mean to lie about David. Okay, you're right, I knew he was dead, and I've been working his land. But to be fair, I tried to call numerous times to find his next of kin, and they wouldn't give me any information."

Naya and Atlas' eyes met. His story matched up, though it sounded different from his perspective. "Why didn't you report that he was dead?" Atlas pushed.

"I didn't know I had to?" He lifted his hands and shrugged.

Naya almost believed him. "So, he died, and you just buried him and called it good?"

"No, it wasn't like that." He shook his head vehemently. "Dave started getting sick long before, and I couldn't care for him and the farm. So, I called the records place to find out if there was anyone who could come and care for him, but I never got any info. Nor did he have health insurance or any kind of will that I could find; Dave was old-fashioned like that. A while before he died he told me how and where he wanted to be buried. So, when he passed, I buried him on the north side of his land. There's a few trees over there, it's real peaceful. And well, I gave up on the records department and I've been farming both pieces of land ever since."

"Why didn't you tell us that the first time we were out here?" Atlas still had a stern look on his face, but he had holstered his weapon. He didn't seem to think Benjamin was a threat to their safety anymore at least.

"Because I'm not actually stupid, and I know I was supposed to report his death. I just had a lot on my plate, okay? And I knew the city would probably keep his body forever looking for whatever relatives that were out there that didn't exist."

He sighed. "Fair enough. I'm not going to arrest you, but we do need to have you report his death." Although his gun wasn't in his hand, he was still using a voice that meant he was all business.

"I will." Benjamin promised, nodding frantically.

"Now, why did you lie about the third farmer?"

Benjamin pursed his lips. "I didn't lie, okay? There was a third farmer out here. But he disappeared years ago. So kinda like with Dave, I just started working his land."

Naya knew that in farming, the amount of land you had to work was basically the same as cash. "How long ago did he disappear?"

He shrugged again, "Ten years, maybe. It's been a while. I don't usually take over a farm unless I'm absolutely sure it's been abandoned, and I think I started working this land about seven years ago."

"And you farm all of these acres all by yourself?" Atlas was clearly reading Naya's mind.

"No, I hire transient farm hands for the harvest, same with the planting. In between, I will hire people as needed, but wheat doesn't need as much care as it used to thanks to genetic modifications which make it pest and weather-resistant."

Atlas and Naya met gazes again. She couldn't tell if he wanted to ask more questions or not, so she said nothing. She didn't see any holes in the man's story. Apparently, he had been waiting for the same thing, so when she said nothing either, he spoke up.

"Alright, Benjamin, thank you for talking with us. Now please, come to the police station and report that death sometime this week. And no more disappearing on us."

He nodded. "I am sorry. I had no idea you were looking for me."

They quickly said their farewells and headed back to their respective cars, but Naya's eyes were drawn to the sky, where a couple of large dark birds were circling.

"Atlas."

It came out as a whisper, but he looked to where her eyes were and swore before they took off at a sprint.

The body was about a hundred and fifty yards from the house where they had just spoken to Benjamin. It was a beautiful young blonde woman who looked to be in her mid-twenties. Naya was sure it was Alia Larson. Her eyes swept the area as she caught her breath. He was so far ahead of them, and she was so angry she wanted to scream.

Atlas called the crime scene techs while Naya checked for a pulse, even though she knew it was futile. The girl was ghostly pale and definitely dead. She lifted her head and scanned the horizon for Ben's house, trying to do some quick distance calculations in her head.

Atlas came up next to her. "What are you thinking?"

"I think he knows we're out here. I think he leaves them for us. There is no other explanation."

"I think you're right. This is starting to feel a bit personal."

Naya looked down at the woman who was so white she was almost transparent.

"I think we answered one question, though."

He looked at her with a question in his eyes, and she gestured to the body.

"She looks almost bloodless. That is part of his ritual."

"I hate that it took another young woman to die before we found out, but you're right."

"I hate it too." Naya looked at her watch and shook her head. If she didn't leave soon, she would not be making those dinner reservations.

Atlas shielded his eyes and looked out at the horizon. "As soon as the crime scene techs arrive, you can go. I'll stay here while they process the scene, and we can reconvene in the morning."

"Are you sure?"

"Positive. It's not like we do much except stand awkwardly out of the way anyway."

"Good point."

A few minutes later, the forensics and coroner's vans turned off the main road and headed towards them.

Shortly after, Naya gave a brief statement as to how they found the body, she was in her car and speeding towards the restaurant. She would just barely make it.

Her stomach grumbled, and she had to admit she was a bit excited about the restaurant her parents had chosen; the restaurant was known for its large portions and delicious cannolis.

She pulled up in the parking lot just as her parents were helping Vance into his wheelchair. She noticed there was a fourth figure with them, and even from behind, she could tell it was Kevin. She wondered how he had found himself with an invite to dinner.

She stepped out of her car, and Kevin gave her a small wave. She waved back as she walked over and her parents both smiled when they saw her, she gave them each a long overdue hug.

"Naya." Her dad whispered in her ear. "It's good to see you." She smiled and said the same thing back to him.

She knew he was curious about her case, but she really didn't want to discuss the case with him at dinner when she had just spent the last ten hours on it. Especially since she knew that she would go home and think about it more, only to wake up tomorrow to go to work again.

Kevin wheeled Vance into the restaurant, and Naya was a bit surprised he hadn't tried to walk, but then again, this was probably better for him.

They were greeted by the host and led to a table in the corner for five. One chair was quickly removed so that Vance could be pushed directly up to the table.

"Wow, this is quite convenient." He laughed, spreading his napkin over his lap as everyone else took their seats. Their mother tried to force a chuckle at his joke, but she could tell that her parents didn't think Vance's condition was a laughing matter.

Vance rolled his eyes. "Oh, come on, that was a great joke."

"It was." Naya agreed.

Naya conveniently ended up with Vance on her left and Kevin on her right.

As she began to skim the menu, her eyes caught on the eggplant parmesan. The server came over to ask about drinks, and her parents ordered two bottles of red wine for the table in short order.

"Just water for me." She whispered to the server as they went to set a wine glass in front of her.

"No wine?" Her mother questioned, she knew it had once been Naya's favorite.

She shook her head. "It's been a rough day. I've got to keep my head clear, and I'll probably have to be up early tomorrow." She took a quick peek at her phone to see if there was an update from Atlas. Nothing yet. Not that she expected much from the scene, it was probably just as clean as the last two.

She picked the menu back up, and Kevin lifted his eyebrow as she caught his eye. She shook her head slightly. She didn't feel like discussing it with him right now. She had noticed he had texted her a couple of times throughout the day, but she had just been too busy to look at the texts. Now, she felt a little guilty about not answering with him sitting beside her.

"Anyone want eggplant parmesan with me?" Naya asked. The portions here were family style, so she needed at least one person to go in with her for her to be able to justify ordering it.

"I'm in." Vance smiled and put down his menu. "Everything looks so good that I'll just dive right in with Naya."

Naya smiled, but it felt fake, she knew Vance would eat next to nothing.

The server approached the table with the wine and quickly poured everyone except her a glass. Her parents ordered the classic spaghetti, and Naya ordered the eggplant parmesan for her and Vance; Kevin decided to go big and try to conquer the clam spaghetti all by himself. The server offered to see if the kitchen could do a half-portion, but he told her not to bother and that he would enjoy the leftovers.

After the waitress left the table, Kevin and her parents began to chat about the weather and the differences between La Junta and Denver. Naya took the opportunity to talk with Vance.

"So, how do you like Elliot?" She took a sip of her water.

"He's nice. He and Derek are both great."

"You're not just trying to make me feel less guilty, right?" Naya searched his face, looking for any sort of deception.

"Now, would I ever do that?" He teased, reaching for a slice of bread from the basket the server had set in the center of the table. Naya did the same and passed the basket to Kevin.

"Hmm...would my brother deceive me? Nah! I don't think that's a possibility." She bantered back, glad when she found herself smiling for real this time.

"But really. I don't like what this case is doing to you. You're starting to look as bad as me." He motioned to his pale face and sunken eyes.

"Geez, thanks. I'll work on that." She rolled her eyes, she wanted to tell her family that another girl had just died and that was why she was late, but she couldn't disclose that sort of information until the girl's family had been notified.

The rest of dinner went smoothly, but Naya had been right, and Vance barely touched his half of the eggplant parmesan. She was positive she only saw him have two bites, if that. Kevin, on the other hand, had somehow eaten almost all of his clam spaghetti by himself. It was quite the feat.

Naya thought her parents would ask for the check, but when the server came back, they ordered another bottle of wine instead. When Naya raised her eyebrow, her mother simply replied, "When in Rome," and patiently waited for the server to refill her glass.

It was already almost ten, though, and Naya had to leave. "Well, if you will excuse me, I'm going to head out. I've got a long day ahead." She announced to the table as she stood, surprised to see Kevin stand too.

"I'll hitch a ride back with you, if that's okay?" When Naya nodded in agreement, he turned to her father. "Can you manage the wheelchair on your own?"

"Yeah, we got it. You worker bees go ahead and get home."

Naya gave her parents each a hug and headed for the door, Kevin wasn't far behind. Once they were outside, she turned to speak.

"I'm sorry." When Kevin didn't answer, she elaborated. "For not answering your texts. Yesterday was rough and then today was worse. But thanks for being there last night, I mean." She felt silly babbling and tripping over her words as if she were still a teenage girl.

"No problem." He replied as they got into her car and left. "I get it. Life isn't really going your way right now."

"Still. I should respond to your texts. It's disrespectful when I don't."

"It would be disrespectful if you were doing nothing, but you're busy with work. And your work is important to the city. I understand." He reached over and ran his hand gently along her arm. "I'm the last person you have to explain yourself too."

"I appreciate that." And she did, it was such a nice difference from her parents.

When they pulled up in front of the house, Naya turned off the ignition and took a deep breath, hoping some of the tension from her shoulders would release.

"Come on. Let's go upstairs, and I'll give you a backrub."

"How did you know?" How did this man always seem to read her mind?

"You were rubbing your shoulders all through dinner. Last I checked, I don't think people do that sort of stuff unless they're sore." They stepped out of the car and made their way towards the house, Kevin using his key to unlock the door for her.

She smiled as he held the door for her, then followed her in and locked it behind them. They walked up the stairs, and Naya collapsed on her bed in exhaustion.

Kevin sat down next to her, patiently waiting as she rolled over on her side. Before she knew it his strong callused hands were making quick work of the knots in her shoulders and upper back.

"You're so good at this." She almost moaned as he worked out a particularly bad knot near her right shoulder blade.

"Thanks." She could hear the smile in his voice.

Naya closed her eyes and could feel herself drifting towards sleep. She almost wondered if Kevin had offered the back rub in order to make his move, but if that were the case it would backfire, she would be asleep before that happened.

Just before she entered the world of dreamland, she heard a car door. Her parents and Vance must be home. Kevin stopped the massage and laid the throw blanket from the end of the bed on top of her since she was lying on top of the comforter. She wanted to thank him, but she was too close to sleep.

The last thing she heard was the creak of the top step as he headed down the stairs.

~

It wasn't until Friday that the autopsy report landed on her desk. And it was a bit of a welcome relief to confirm what Atlas and she had already assumed.

Naya yawned as she read through the documents, it had been a long week with her parents in town. She had assumed they would spend most of their time with Vance, but they also seemed to want to spend an inordinate amount of time with her as well. And a case like this, as well as family demands, was messing with her sleep schedule big time.

She continued to skim the document, stopping as she noticed something she hadn't noticed in the field.

"Puncture wounds?" She whispered mostly to herself.

"I thought the same thing." Atlas pipped up next to her, either eavesdropping or her whisper had been louder than Naya thought. "Two of them too. What do you make of that?"

"I think it solves our question of what he's doing with the blood."

Naya jotted some notes down on a sticky note. "He's not doing anything; he's just disposing of it to hide evidence."

"Which means whatever he is doing could be seen in the blood."

Naya pulled out her notes from the last two autopsy reports. "Can you call down and have them find out if there are any traces of 'potassium, iron, copper, magnesium, or zinc' in the body that would indicate her having higher than normal levels?" She read from her Julia Charles note.

Atlas picked up the phone and dialed. "You know, if you're going to stick around, you should probably learn all the extensions and program all the numbers into your phone, so I don't have to be your secretary."

She chuckled. "I've been meaning to do exactly that. But this case got dumped on me so fast."

He opened his mouth as if he was about to argue with her, but whoever was on the other end of the line must've picked up, so Atlas began asking for the additional tests to be run before the body was released to the family.

Naya was glad she hadn't had to be the one to notify Alia's boyfriend, how she meant everything to him rang deafeningly loud in her head. This had to have crushed him.

Atlas hung up the phone and turned, only for his phone to ring in his hands. He rolled his eyes, "Detective Atlas?... Mhm... Perfect, thanks."

"What was that?" Naya asked, her fingers crossed that it was what she hoped it was.

"Our tapes." He smiled and rose from his chair. "They're emailing the ones with our victim in them, should be here in about a minute. I'm gonna grab some coffee, want a viewing drink?"

She shook her head, "No, thank you." He seemed surprised but turned and headed for the break room regardless. She turned back to her computer and checked the time. It was just after two, Vance should have just finished chemotherapy. Naya hoped it went better than it had the week before. At least he wouldn't be alone since their parents weren't planning to leave for a few more days. She thought about texting Kevin, who she was sure would be over this evening, but quickly talked herself out of it. Coincidentally, her phone chose that moment to vibrate; she looked down, surprised to see it was a text from the man himself.

KEVIN: Can I take you to dinner tonight? Please?

NAYA COULDN'T HELP but smile, it was amusing that he had apparently thought of her at the same time she had thought of him.

NAYA: I need to see if my parents will let me get away first.

SHE PRESSED SEND and wondered what she would say, but she was a grown woman, and it wasn't as if her parents controlled her. She did a mental facepalm as she realized how nervous she felt. What was it about Kevin that made her turn back into an awkward and shy teenager? The reply came while she was berating herself.

KEVIN: They said it's fine as long as I have you home at a decent hour ;)

NAYA KNEW that the last part had to be a joke, but she couldn't help but chuckle as she replied.

NAYA: Alright, I'll plan on leaving the station at 6.

· · ·

She put her phone back in her pocket so she wasn't tempted to look at it again and resumed her reading and notations. Atlas returned a moment later with a coffee in one hand and a bag of microwave popcorn in the other.

"You didn't tell me you were making popcorn!" She said incredulously as she grabbed her notepad and pen and followed him into the conference room that had their whiteboard. Naya had updated the map the day before and added Alia Larson's picture and information.

"You didn't ask." He replied smartly, although he handed her the open bag as he got the computer set up and logged into his email.

"Alright, here she is leaving the building at about seven, just as her boyfriend said."

Naya watched as Alia came from the direction of the stairs and passed through the lobby, earbuds in; she appeared to be texting on her phone.

"And here she is stretching outside."

The next video was footage from the camera right outside the door, and sure enough, there was Alia doing a runner's lunge.

"And then she runs out of view for about an hour..." Atlas pulled up the next clip. "Then look, here she is at about eight, doing some after-run stretches outside."

"So, she made it back?" Naya was confused and bit her lip as Atlas pulled up the last video.

"Not only did she make it back, but she made it through the lobby..."

Both watched as her figure walked past the elevator again and towards the stairs. "Which means our killer either lives in the building or knew her patterns and came in before her and was lying in wait." Atlas theorized.

"You really think this guy would kill a girl in the building he lived in?"

"It seems daring." Atlas agreed. "It's unlikely but possible, I guess. I'm going request they look over the footage again and send stills of anyone who walked in the building that morning."

"Good idea. And we should see if we can get a full list of tenants in the building."

Atlas was already at his computer typing the first email but nodded a quick yes. After he finished typing and hit send, he pulled out his phone and made a call, probably to the same judge who had acquired the warrant for the tapes for them.

Naya looked at the girl's form, frozen on the screen on the edge of the frame, about to walk out of view. She was looking at her phone, no idea what lay in wait for her. She stood and walked towards the screen, wishing that she could've stopped this guy before he got to her.

She checked her phone to see if any of the emails they were waiting for had come in. There was nothing. They didn't have the records from RunTracker yet, of course, they were futile for Alia Larson since they now knew she completed her run. But Julia Charles and Shanice Woods had also used RunTracker, according to their families. They had submitted the requirements for the warrant a few days before, the company had sent a warning that it would be difficult to trace users, as accounts were only attached to an email, with a first name and last initial, but they did say they would work on it. It was already past four, which meant they probably wouldn't hear until Monday at this point.

Atlas hung up his phone. "They'll get us the rental list, but it probably won't get to us until Monday."

"That's what I was just thinking about the RunTracker info."

"Yeah, I almost forgot about that." Atlas grabbed the popcorn bag back from Naya and began munching on what was left.

"Do you think those other girls finished their runs too? And they were grabbed before they reached their door?" He speculated.

"It's possible, I mean, all the families said the women practiced runners safety techniques and didn't take predictable routes. It would make sense that he saw them leave their house's then waited for them to get back. But what I can't figure out is, just how is he finding these women?" She moved to the whiteboard which held their pictures.

"I mean, they're all so different, they're from different stages of life, different neighborhoods, and ran different routes. We have the almost adult child of affluent parents in Cherry Creek, the middle-class mom who is a track champion from Thornton, and now a young woman who lives in a neglected area of Downtown. What could these women possibly have in common?"

Atlas was getting to the bottom of the popcorn bag, and instead of grabbing the last few pieces, he lifted the bag to his mouth and dumped them in. He thought for a moment while he chewed and swallowed, then opened his mouth. "Your guess is as good as mine. I can't see anything besides the fact that all three women were runners and used the RunTracker App."

"Wait!" Naya pulled out her phone and pulled up her Run Tracker app. "You can have friends on here, look." She showed him the friends tab. Hers was empty because she preferred to keep her runs private.

"Let me see that." He held out his hand for her phone, and she handed it to him. "So, if I wanted to add friends, I would click here, right?" He pointed to the little plus in the upper right-hand corner.

"I think so, I never have. Give it a try." She watched as he pressed it, and a white screen came up with a grey bar asking her to type in her friend's name.

Atlas quickly typed in Alia and watched as the screen filled with names and pictures of over a hundred Alia's.

"How does he search through this? Especially with a name like Julia, which I'm sure there are millions of?" He quickly typed in 'Shanice', and over two hundred people named Shanice popped up. Above the search bar where he had been typing names was an invite tab. He clicked on it and saw you could invite people via SMS or Email.

"I mean with their last initial, that could help." Naya suggested. Atlas quickly typed in Julia C. and angled Naya the screen even though she had already been watching.

"No way, there are three hundred, or more, Julia C's here. This guy must be finding them another way."

Naya considered that as she watched as Atlas clicked around her app a bit more, looking for a way you could get more information. He opened her running history and let out a low whistle.

"Damn, you're fast."

"Thanks."

"But look here, each of your runs comes with a little map, see? If you had any friends, they would be able to see where you ran. And the routes all clearly start and end in your neighborhood." He pointed out.

"You're right. Which is why I don't. Even if you don't post your runs until after you're done, someone can get an idea of where I live, the times I run, and the general directions I like to run in, even if I switch it up..." She agreed. "So, what, is this guy was just randomly friending a bunch of people via SMS or email? And the girls that took the bait and accepted became his victims?"

"Maybe." Atlas scratched his neck. "Maybe what these women have in common is that they agreed to be friends with the killer on RunTracker."

"Since it's only a person's first name and last initial, if they had a friend with that same first name, they may say yes even if they weren't sure it was them. I mean, most people don't have pictures on here." Naya showed him the same screen he had typed the women's names in, and sure enough, only about every tenth account had a photo.

"That means our killer uses a fairly common name." He mused, turning to write 'Common name' on the board under the suspect profile.

"That would explain why he abducts from everywhere rather than sticking to a comfort zone, like most killers do. He actually is opportunistic." Naya glanced down at her phone and saw it was almost five.

"Exactly."

They were both silent for a moment, thinking about the reality of what they just discovered. Naya broke the silence. "Let's release this information to the press. Tell women not to add anyone they don't know to their RunTracker."

"I'll go talk to Captain Brody now." Atlas put down the dry-erase marker and walked towards the door. Naya stood and followed.

"I'm going to head out Atlas, but I'll be in tomorrow. Even if we don't have the information we requested, I have some ideas I want to check out."

"Fair enough." He agreed, taking the time to glance at his own watch. "I actually think I'll call it an early night myself. I've spent entirely too much time in this building this week. And that's saying a lot for me."

"It is." Naya smiled as she turned and headed to clock out. "See you tomorrow!" She called over her shoulder as she exited the door and walked towards her car. She felt relieved, she finally felt like they were getting somewhere with this case besides chasing their tails.

THE DRIVE HOME was quicker than she expected for five on a Friday, and when she pulled up in front of her house, she noticed there were quite a few cars out front. It made her wonder if her family was having a party.

When she walked in the door, she heard voices in the living room and decided to poke her head in really quickly before going to change for her date. She noticed that her parents were actually not there for once, but Vance was on the couch watching as Trevor, Kevin, and Sebastian played some sort of shooting game. It was early, so Derek was still there as well, a controller in his hands. There was also another man she had never seen before, but he was dressed in scrubs, so she assumed it was Elliot. It was a bit weird that both aides were there at the same time.

"Is there some sort of party I missed the invite for?"

Vance looked over his shoulder to see her, his face eerily pale like it usually was after a day of chemotherapy. "Oh, you're here, now we can start." He joked feebly. Naya could tell he felt weak.

The man she didn't recognize quickly crossed the room and held out his hand.

"Hi, I'm Elliot from Home Health Care. I don't believe we've met, but I assume you're Naya, Vance's sister?"

"You are correct." She replied as she shook his hand. Elliot looked to be quite a bit younger than the rest of them, but like Derek, clearly had the muscles required to lift a full-grown man if needed. "Nice to meet you."

He quickly volunteered the information she had wondered about. "Derek had me come in today to learn the chemotherapy routine, so that way if we ever needed to switch days, or if Vance had his appointments switched, we would both be trained."

"That's smart." She smiled, glancing over her shoulder to see Kevin looking at her. "Well, if you men don't need me for anything, I'm going to go change."

The entire group smiled, giving 'no thank you's over their shoulders while focused on their game, and Elliot went and sat back down.

Naya went up the stairs and changed into an oversized sweater with leggings. She wished she had something a little dressier, but she simply didn't. Besides, he knew it had been a long week, cute and comfortable would have to do.

She was about to walk down the stairs when she noticed a new urgent email had come through on her phone. She opened it up to find the report on the house fire in Dave Smith's home. She skimmed through it, being thoroughly disappointed by how short it was. And she was more disappointed still when she reached the end to read that the fire chief was pretty sure it had just been a shorted wire. Crazy timing for a wire to short out, but there were no signs of an accelerant to lead them to consider it as arson.

Naya checked to see that Atlas received the same email, laughing when a text came in from him just as she did so. Apparently, he had been reading the email, too.

ATLAS: Back to square one I guess

· · ·

THE TEXT also had a shrugging emoji, which made Naya giggle. For some reason she hadn't figured Atlas as the emoji type of person. She quickly sent an emoji she thought looked annoyed back to him and slid her phone into her pocket.

With a small sigh and a last check in her mirror, she walked back down the stairs to find Kevin standing by the door, dangling her keys.

"Shall we?"

"We shall." She responded with a smile.

20

MARK

He was in the detective's house. Well, not that this was a new thing, after all, he'd been here before. But it seemed more special now that he had decided that she would be perfect for his project.

He wanted to go and look at her room, but he wasn't sure how to do that without drawing attention to himself. He looked around the room, all the other men seemed to be involved in the Call of Duty bracket they had going on, but he couldn't be sure, and he couldn't afford to have any suspicion on him at this point in his plan.

He would just have to come back another time and do some snooping then.

The doorbell rang as the pizza they had ordered was delivered.

"I got it." Smiling as he headed for the door.

He found a pimple-faced teenager on the stoop with the pizzas. "Thanks." He said politely as he took the pizzas from him and closed the door. He hadn't done the ordering, but he was surprised to feel how heavy the four pizzas were.

"What did you get on these things?" He asked as he walked back in, lifting them up and down a couple of times.

Vance laughed weakly. "I think I got extra meat on all of them."

All the men in the room started laughing. It was quite funny that Vance had been the one to order such heavy pizzas when he barely ate.

Mark headed for the kitchen, setting the pizzas down on the counter and grabbing the paper plates from the cupboard where he knew they would be. He had already had time to snoop around down here. But of course, that was much less suspicious than snooping in Detective Largusa's bedroom.

He loaded up two of the hefty slices onto his plate, and placed a single slice on a plate for Vance. He turned to find the other guys had paused the game, and they, except for Vance, had followed him to load up their own plates with piping hot, greasy pizza.

He returned to the living room and handed Vance his plate before sitting on the floor and digging into his. The others returned and soon they were all eating pizza and throwing jabs at each other about who was going to win the bracket.

This was all so mundane to him, he only played video games because the other guys did. It had never been his thing.

He was briefly reminded of his wife, and his old life, where he had also pretended to be someone he was not. At least here the lies were fewer and less significant. Well except for the wig. He couldn't wait to kill the detective so he could ditch the itchy mass of fake hair on his head.

Soon, he told himself as the other men finished eating their pizza and returned to the game.

Very soon.

He glanced at Vance out of the corner of his eye. He was probably going to get in the way at some point. And that was unfortunate.

He would need to be taken care of.

And fate was on his side...

21

NAYA

Kevin had taken her out for Thai food at a place she had never heard of, but that wasn't a surprise since she hadn't been living here long. Naya was surprised at how well she had settled in here. It felt right somehow, like she was supposed to be here.

They had chatted while they ate their dinners, and afterwards Kevin had driven them out towards the mountains. Now they were sitting in the bed of his truck on some pillows and blankets he had brought taking in the view. Naya was curled into Kevin's side, her head on his shoulder and he was absentmindedly running his hand through her hair. They were both looking up at the stars which were exponentially more numerous away from the light pollution of the city.

"What are you thinking?" Kevin breathed in her ear, breaking the comfortable silence.

"Just how right it feels to be here." She realized after that she hadn't specified what she meant, but maybe that was a good thing.

"Here in Denver, or here with me?" He asked, reading her mind, again.

She thought for a moment. "I guess I would say both."

They settled into a silence again, until Naya remembered what she had been meaning to ask earlier. "My parents weren't there when we left, how did you ask them about tonight?"

He let out a low chuckle. "I have your mom's number. Vance wanted to hang out at home today, and they were excited about the city, so I think your parents were going out for an evening by themselves and giving your brother some space for the night."

"He doesn't want them to see him after chemotherapy." She deduced instantaneously.

"Yeah, Vance doesn't have much control in his life left. But he does want your parents to think he is managing. I think you'll need to send them away soon though."

Naya looked up at Kevin's face. "What do you mean?"

Kevin stopped touching her hair and moved his hand to the side of her neck. Naya leaned into his touch. "He doesn't want them here when things get worse. You know that as well as I do."

"But—" she snapped her mouth shut. Naya wanted to argue but realized she had nothing to say. If Vance felt he was getting worse, there was nothing she could do. It was his life not hers; he would know better than she.

"You should talk to him before you do anything though, make sure I'm not assuming incorrectly."

Naya dipped her head. "No, you're probably right. You notice these things so easily, it's uncanny. I guess the reason I was about to say something was because I truly want to believe Vance is getting better. But I suppose at some point I just have to—" Her voice broke. "To do what Vance wants me to do...for him." She would need to accept it, there was nothing to gain by avoiding it any longer.

Kevin was empathetic. "It won't be easy. But I can tell Vance is glad it's you here and no one else."

A silence fell over them once again, as they stared into each other's eyes, this one heavier than the last. After what seemed like ages, Kevin leaned in and captured her lips with his. She felt her body responding and began to kiss him back. The hand that wasn't on her neck came to rest on the small of her back and pulled her closer. Naya brought her hand up to rest on Kevin's shoulder while her other hand twisted in his hair.

They kissed for what felt like forever, until one of them, Naya wasn't sure which, pulled back and both took a moment to breathe. Naya laid her head on Kevin's chest, listening to his heartbeat.

"How would you feel about coming back to my place tonight?" He asked in a hoarse whisper.

Naya thought for a moment but didn't respond. Could she leave Vance on his own for the night? Would he be okay? He'd had chemo earlier that day—

"Trevor and Sebastian both volunteered to sleep on the couch if need be."

"Are you sure?" It seemed so weird that Vance's friends were always so willing to help, maybe it was just because she wasn't used to having friends the way Vance did.

"I'm sure. I think Sebastian brought about a hundred beers over. My guess is they won't be driving anyway." His hand moved up from her lower back and began rubbing her shoulders. "I can give you another back rub."

"Are you trying to bribe me?" She asked playfully.

"Maybe."

"You know bribing a cop is illegal right?" She looked at him and lifted one eyebrow.

"You won't tell on me, will you?" He plastered a pleading puppy-dog look on his face.

"Just this once." She joked, hoping the smirk on her face looked flirty and not weird.

"Shall we?" He asked for the second time that night, pointing towards the east where they had come from.

She bit her lip and nodded as Kevin stood and jumped out of the truck bed. Then he turned around and held out his hands to lift her down. She was still frequently amazed by how strong he was.

The minute her feet hit the ground she lifted her chin to look him in the eyes and he leaned down to kiss her again.

Before they could get carried away, she pressed a hand to his chest and leaned away. "I think we better get going if you know what I mean."

"You're right let's go." He laughed as he walked around the car to open the passenger door for her before walking back and climbing in the driver's side.

Naya couldn't believe how nervous she was, it was like going back in time. She had never felt this way about any of the guys she had dated in La Junta, it was a weird feeling. Before she knew it, they had pulled up in front of a small house which looked to be a similar style to the one she and Vance shared, they must've been built during the same time period. She could tell from the outside that Kevin's house was a tiny bit larger than theirs though, probably a two-bedroom instead of a one.

She opened the truck door and stepped out, to find her legs were shaky from her nerves. Or maybe anticipation, she couldn't be sure.

She followed Kevin up the walk and stood awkwardly by while he unlocked the door. But as soon as they were inside, they picked up right where they had left off and began making out in the entry way.

It was Kevin who pulled back this time. "I was going to give you the grand tour but...want to just skip straight to the part where I show you the bedroom?" He smiled shyly and Naya couldn't help but marvel at how cute he looked with his hair tousled, as he invited her to his bedroom.

"Sounds fair." She whispered, surprised by how husky her voice sounded.

Kevin's smile grew more confident and mischievous, and he grabbed her hand and led her up the stairs.

It was her alarm that awoke them the next morning. Naya groaned and rolled over, putting a pillow over her head.

Kevin just chuckled. "Late night?" He asked, knowing the answer. He rolled out of bed and crossed the room to where her phone had been tossed the night before, shutting off her alarm.

"I blame you." she grumbled from beneath the pillow, knowing very well that she needed to get up and go home to change before she could go to work.

"I have a spare toothbrush here if you want to brush your teeth."

She lifted the pillow. "So, you have guests often then?" She was joking, but also a little curious.

"No, but my mother taught me to always be prepared. I honestly think I bought the toothbrush I'm offering you almost three years ago. And at the time I even bought a five-pack, just so I wouldn't have to restock."

"Wow. I'm impressed." She stretched her arms over her head, trying to convince her tense muscles that they had to get up and be active, even though they were clearly pissed they didn't get enough sleep. She groaned exaggeratedly, annoyed at having to be a responsible adult.

"Should I call Atlas and tell him you're sick?" Kevin cocked an eyebrow, a playful smile rising on his face.

Naya chucked the pillow she had hid under at him.

"Don't you dare."

"Just checking." Kevin stepped over to the closet and began pulling on a pair of jeans. "Well, come on, the Kevin Express pulls out of the station in fifteen minutes."

"Will refreshments be served?" She climbed out of bed and began putting on her clothes from the night before.

"Yep, I have coffee on the auto-timer, so I believe it'll be ready when we walk down the stairs."

"My God," Naya stage whispered, "And you are sure you're single?"

Kevin laughed. "Well about that, actually, I had wanted to ask you last night but you fell asleep too quickly." He poked her gently in the side as she pulled on her sweater. "But how would you feel about being an item?"

She followed him down the stairs, her socks in her hands. "Is that your way of asking me to be your girlfriend?" She jabbed him playfully.

"Kinda, I mean, yes. I just always felt the term 'girlfriend' wasn't a very mature word for a grown woman in a relationship."

Naya was surprised. "Wow," she mumbled. "I thought I was the only one who thought that."

They walked into the kitchen, where he poured them each a cup of coffee in travel mugs and laid out creamer and sugar. He held hers out to her then held up the carton of half and half. She shook her head, snagging the sugar from the counter and adding some before she took a sip.

"So, what do you prefer to call someone you are in a relationship with then?" He asked as he doctored up his cup.

"You're going to laugh because of my profession, but I always liked the idea of 'partner'. Once things got far enough along."

"Same here." He smiled as he put away the coffee supplies and began to head to the door. "It's shocking that you feel the same way. I feel like most people like the terms 'boyfriend' and 'girlfriend'."

She shrugged as she placed her coffee on the table by the door to slip on her socks and shoes. "I just like the idea of men and women being equals in a relationship. Again, maybe it's because I'm a cop, but this isn't 1890, if I'm with a man it's because I want to be, not because I need him to survive."

He opened the door and held it open for her as she grabbed her coffee and exited, then he handed her his coffee so he could use both hands to lock the door.

"And as a man, I don't want a woman who relies on me for everything. I want her to be able to stand on her own two feet. It's crazy how quick emotions and stress can get out of control when someone is relying on you for everything."

Naya had never thought about it from the guy's perspective, but he was right. If you were expected to single-handedly support your woman and any children, it could put a lot of stress on your shoulders that may be hard to handle.

She handed Kevin back his coffee as they headed for the truck. Once they were inside, she set her coffee in the cup holder and sent a quick text to Vance, making sure he was feeling alright, and that everything had gone well the night before.

"Did you want to stop for food before I drop you off?" Kevin asked politely. "Usually, I would have offered to cook but that would take time, and I know you're in the middle of a case right now."

She shook her head. "Thanks, but I'm already going to be late as it is, and I'll have to explain why to Atlas."

She pinched the bridge of her nose. Like Kevin always did, she knew Atlas would be able to read her like an open book and he would know exactly why she was late.

"So is you not answering a 'no' then?" Kevin asked as he kept his eyes on the road.

Naya looked over at him, observing the way his jaw was clenched. It seemed like he was a bit nervous too. "Can I think about it? It just feels a bit fast for me is all." She explained.

Kevin kept his face stoic but she saw his shoulders drop a bit. He was disappointed. "Of course."

They pulled up in front of her house and Naya noted that there were indeed two additional vehicles parked out front with the ones that belonged to her and Vance. Trevor and Sebastian must've both spent the night.

She leaned across the center console and gave Kevin a quick peck on the lips.

"Can I see you tonight?"

She nodded. "Yeah, I can text you when I get off?"

"Okay, I'll probably be here anyway. I'm going to go home and shower and stuff, but I told your parents and Vance that I would spend the day with them."

Naya rolled her eyes. "How is it that my parents instantly adopted you into our family?"

"Because Vance isn't the only one who can tell I'm a good guy." He smiled at her seductively as she stepped out of the car.

She rolled her eyes again. "Sure, bye, text me." She sassed, shutting the door she sprinted inside to change.

She was done and back in her car within five minutes. She had peaked her head in on Vance on her way out and he had been sound asleep. She had been tempted to check the living room for Trevor and Sebastian but hadn't wanted to risk waking them.

It was just after nine when she got to her desk, but sure enough Atlas was already there and her late arrival didn't escape him.

"Tsk-tsk You're late to your overtime Saturday shift. How dare you have a life outside of work." He didn't even look at her as he said it, clearly too engrossed in whatever else he was doing though he said it lightheartedly.

Naya tossed her pad of sticky notes at the back of his head but she was blushing and didn't say anything about it for fear he would look up.

She slid into her chair and powered up her computer to check her emails. She had access to them on her phone, but it was almost dead from not being charged at any point during the night. She hoped what measly battery power remained would be enough for the seven or so hours she was about to spend here.

"Any new developments?"

"Nada. I was hoping maybe something would miraculously come through late last night, but I'm sure now we won't see anything 'til Monday."

"Does that mean we're taking tomorrow off?" The minute the words left her mouth she could tell they sounded much too excited and that she shouldn't have said anything.

Atlas finally lifted his head and looked at her. "Why, you have a hot date?"

She blushed bright red and Atlas chuckled.

"So that's why you were late. This is a development!" He spun his chair to face her. "So, you better tell me about him just in case you wind up missing." The beaming smile on his face teasing.

"Like anyone could kidnap me." She retorted as she noted there was nothing of use in her inbox and minimized the screen. He was far too excited in her opinion.

Atlas was still waiting patiently for the details, but Naya ignored him and instead pulled up an internet search engine to resume her research from before.

Realizing he wasn't going to get any juicy details out of her, he changed the subject as he pulled up his own search engine.

"What should I be looking into?"

"Well, he is clearly injecting them with something that doesn't show up in an autopsy. So, it must be something that is already in the human body. I want to know what benefit he would get from injecting these women and what the substance is, to figure out what his motive might be."

Atlas typed something in his computer as he mulled her statement over. "Do you think the injection is part of the abduction?"

She shook her head. "No, because Shanice didn't have any injection marks on her. I think it's something he does after and I want to know why."

"You have a point. But I also know that sometimes people do crazy things because they are well, crazy, and there simply is no explanation that makes sense to anyone but them."

"And that's what you think is happening here?" Naya was reading an article about what a large dose of potassium would do to the human body, but she turned to look at Atlas who was looking straight at her.

He nodded. "You're analytical, so you naturally want to find a reason behind everything. But I'm telling you, this isn't like any case I've ever seen before. I mean we still need to analyze his behavior to find him, but I think when we do, we'll find that he is simply crazy."

She wasn't going to argue with Atlas because he was entitled to his opinions and she hated the thought, but he could be right. She turned back and clicked through a few more windows about potassium as her mind raced.

"So, you think he's just crazy?"

"I do." He answered, his voice level, no hint of playfulness now.

"Do you think he is able to hide his crazy? Or do you think people around him notice it?" Naya turned to face him once again, crossing her legs and spinning a pen around in her right hand.

"What do you mean by that?"

"I guess what I'm saying is, do you think this guy can hold down a normal job, or do you think he's too crazy for that?"

"I guess I hadn't thought about it. "

Atlas leaned back and rubbed his stubble. "What if he's too crazy for a professional job, but not too crazy to hold down a job? You know, something menial like a janitor or gardener. And while he's there, he feels out of control of his life. So maybe he tries to get control back by abducting women."

They were both quiet for a moment as they considered the new theories on the table.

"I wish I could say we were getting somewhere, but that only eliminates less than half of the professions in this city." Naya grumbled dejectedly as she set down her pen.

"There's got to be something big we're missing. Something this guy missed that will lead us to him." He leaned back, crossing his arms behind his head.

Suddenly, a thought hit her that she realized they should've investigated a long time ago. "How easy is it to get needles here?"

"Well, not easy, but not hard either I'd imagine." He appeared to be deep in thought for a moment. "If you are in the medical profession, I think it would be quite easy. Now if you're not, I don't think it's hard necessarily, but definitely can't be that easy either."

Naya turned back to her computer and typed a few words in the search bar. When the results came up, she muttered in frustration and turned her screen so Atlas could see.

"Well, I'll be damned; you can order needles on Amazon. Who knew?"

Naya rolled her eyes as she scrolled through the online needle options. "Amazon, making it easier for serial killers since 1994."

"Really, it's been that long?" Atlas had picked up a stress ball from his desk and started tossing and catching it.

"Yep." She leaned back in her chair, exhausted even though she had just started. "You think we should canvas?"

"Once we get the information from RunTracker, for sure." Atlas was still tossing the ball.

"So where does that leave us for right now then?"

Atlas shrugged and put the ball down. "I guess you can help me research these chemicals."

Typical Atlas, getting out of his work. "No problem. Let's research separately and compare notes?" Atlas nodded his agreement so Naya quickly turned to her computer and got to work. She skimmed the article on potassium overdose. It could cause an irregular heartbeat, which could lead to death. She couldn't tell if that was instantaneous, or if it would take time. Surprisingly, there wasn't that much information about taking potassium by injection. Go figure. But something did catch her eye, it said prolonged exercise could cause elevated levels of potassium in the body without taking any supplements, and that meant because these women were already working out, their potassium levels could have already been high. She put a star next to potassium on her paper.

She went back to her list of naturally occurring minerals in the human body and clicked through to the next one which was magnesium. Surprise, surprise, magnesium overdoses could also be life threatening. And, like potassium, it could cause an irregular heartbeat. It didn't seem like it could kill someone who didn't have kidney problems, she would have to dig further into that for sure. She was sure the amount of magnesium found in a supplement was nowhere near the levels this guy was potentially dosing them with.

She clicked the back arrow again and went to the next mineral. Calcium. She chanced a sneak-peak rolling her eyes to the side to see if Atlas was still working. It appeared that he was, as he was reading something on his computer, but she supposed he could also just be scrolling Facebook. She went back to her own screen and began scanning the article, like the two previous minerals, calcium overdose was also possible. And if you took in too much it would cause blood toxicity, which could weaken the heart and be lethal. She was sensing a theme. It still didn't quite seem like their smoking gun, but she it was definitely a possibility all the same.

"Are you thinking what I'm thinking?" Atlas' voice interrupted her thoughts.

"That all of the minerals that the body needs are also apparently fatal in large enough doses?"

"Yeah, I'm thinking I should watch what I eat now." He joked while scrolling down his screen slowly.

"As if you would ever get too many minerals from your diet. I think you'll be fine." She teased as she clicked on the next mineral. Copper could apparently also cause death, specifically heart failure. However, it claimed it had to be over a long period of time, which didn't sound like their culprit. Unless of course he was injecting these women with an amount that had never been studied—

"Wait. Do you think he's performing science experiments on these women?" The thought was disturbing.

Atlas shrugged. "I'm still going with just plain crazy, but you do have a point, there isn't much existing science on these sorts of things it seems."

Naya's phone buzzed in her lap and she looked down to see a text from Kevin. The battery bar in the upper right corner blinked once to remind her it was dangerously low at three percent. Kevin would just have to wait until she got off work.

"Well, I don't think this mineral research is getting us anywhere." Atlas leaned back in his chair. "The cop in me wants to go canvas but I don't even know where we would start a canvas. At least not without the information from RunTracker."

"And that won't be until Monday." Naya pinched the bridge of her nose.

"So, we've got one day to solve this crime?"

"Basically."

22

MARK

He really hadn't wanted it to come to this. But here he was. Someone not a part of his plan had to die.

Mark was in the kitchen at the detective's house preparing lunch for Vance. He had suggested they order Thai food, and now he pulled the bottle from his pocket and plopped an entire dropper full of liquid into the bowl of Pad Thai before sliding it back in his pocket and stirring the food.

He walked back into the living room where Vance was right where he had been when he left him, playing video games. He handed Vance his food when he paused the game.

"Damn." The other man in the room exclaimed. "Of course, it's lunch time right when I'm about to win.

"Story of life." Mark shrugged and dug into his curry with gusto. "There's plenty more in the kitchen if you want some."

"Thanks man."

After a few minutes later Mark looked up from his food to see Vance staring at him. "Everything okay?" He asked politely.

Vance shrugged. "I just got a weird feeling is all."

"Like you're not feeling well?"

Mark took a quick glance at Vance's bowl to see he had hardly eaten.

Grr. This was going to be more difficult than he had thought. He would have to find a different way to do things.

Vance's eyes followed his own, "No, I feel okay. Just something feels really wrong, like in the mood." He was looking pointedly at Mark again, and he felt himself lean back a fraction of an inch.

"Maybe you should call your sister?" He suggested, trying to think of what a normal person who wasn't trying to poison someone would say in this situation. He began to second guess himself. Had he been sneaky enough? Or had he spent too long in the kitchen?

The doorbell rang before Vance could speak again and Mark got up to answer it.

It was Vance's parents.

He opened the door wide to let the two of them in, watching as they removed their shoes, placing them on the mat by the door and then headed into the living room. He stood by the door a moment longer to make sure they would already be in a conversation with Vance when he returned.

When he walked back in, he was glad to see that the four people in the room all seemed to be chatting animatedly. Phew, that was a close one.

"Anyone else want Thai food? There's plenty in the kitchen." Mark offered.

"Nah, we just ate." Vance's dad chimed in as he turned back to whatever conversation they were having. Well, it seemed like he wouldn't be missed for the moment.

Mark walked into the kitchen and messed with the takeout boxes a bit making it sound like he was cleaning up. He thought about actually taking the time to clean up, but he didn't want to be that nice to the detective. He flipped the lid open on the trash can, noting it was a new bag, and a plan formulated in his mind.

He quickly undid the trash bag, shook it out, then placed the bag back in as if he had just emptied the trash. Then he paused to see if there was any movement from the other room. He heard the four muffled voices, still absorbed in conversation. They wouldn't miss him one bit.

He walked towards the door, but instead of going out of it, he turned left and headed up the stairs to detective Largusa's room. The walk up was silent until he reached the top step which let out a creak as he put his weight on it. He paused for a second to see if he had been noticed, but no one called up after him.

He gingerly moved his second leg over the spot that had creaked, checking to see if there were any more spots he needed to be aware of, but it seemed like the rest of the floor was silent. He remained cautious as he crossed the room towards the wardrobe and began peeking in rummaging through her belongings.

There was nothing of interest, just clothes. Besides, he didn't even really know what he was looking for. It just seemed exciting to be in the detective's room.

She really didn't have much, so his snooping didn't take long. But once he finished, he had a decision to make. What should he take? He wanted the detective to know he had been there, but he didn't want it to be too obvious. He glanced at her running shoes and thought for a minute that could work, but then he realized that could affect his plans. That's when he spotted a rainbow scrunchie tied around the edge of her hairbrush.

Perfect.

He crossed the room and slid the scrunchie off the hairbrush and into his pocket.

When he returned to the stairs he was careful to skip the creek on the top step and made his way back down and to the living room.

Vance and the other guy were back to playing video games while his parents looked on, chatting to him as he did.

Well, this was boring. Mark spotted the bowl of half-eaten Pad Thai next to Vance. Maybe he hadn't gotten enough. Maybe he had. He would have to wait until later to know for sure.

He bid everyone a quick goodbye and headed for the door. He had better things to do than watch a dying guy play video games.

23

NAYA

She walked through the door at exactly four, tossing her keys in the dish and removing her shoes. For such a uneventful day, she was beat. She smiled as she remembered the night before with Kevin, well, that explained it.

She crossed the entry way thinking about going upstairs to change, but decided she would check the living room first. She walked in to find Kevin and Vance playing video games.

"Hey you two."

They both jumped as if they hadn't heard her at the door, but the minute Kevin saw it was her his face broke out in a smile. "Hi." He said back quickly before turning back to the game.

"How was your day?" She asked as she sat down on the couch next to Vance.

"Good, Mom and Dad came over for a bit. They're leaving tomorrow so we're having dinner with them."

"Ah." Naya leaned forward to glance in the kitchen and then checked her watch. "Where's Derek or Elliot? They're supposed to stay until six."

Kevin waved his hand in her direction. "Something came up and he had to go about an hour ago. I texted you to see if it was okay but when you didn't answer I told him he could go since I was here."

Naya felt her pocket for her phone but then remembered it was dead. "Oh yeah, sorry about that, my phone died. I didn't charge it last night."

She watched as the corner of Kevin's mouth rose slightly in a smirk. It was clear he wasn't going to say anything more in font of Vance, but he was obviously remembering the night before.

She stood to head upstairs to change, but then remembered she had wanted to say something. "So, it turns out, I'm off tomorrow. And I was thinking us three, and Elliot or Derek or whoever's day it is, we could all go on a walk together? After mom and dad leave?"

Kevin glanced at Vance out of the corner of his eye, waiting to see what he would say.

"Sure, sounds fun. It's Elliot tomorrow by the way." Vance's eyes didn't stray from the screen. "Did you have somewhere in mind?"

Naya looked at Kevin. "I was hoping either you or Kevin would know somewhere."

Kevin nodded, groaning as his character died in a replay on the screen. "Damn, I was so sure I was going to win that one." He set down his controlled then seemed to remember that Naya had asked a question. "Oh right, I know a place, no worries."

"Good. Alright, I'm going to go change before mom and dad come back." She headed up the stairs. It wasn't until she took her shirt off that she noticed the change in the air. She looked over her shoulder to find Kevin standing on the second stair from the top, staring at her.

"You know you could frighten a woman doing that."

Kevin shrugged and walked up behind her to give her a hug. "So, tell me, how was work?"

"Not much to report, just waiting for some information to come in, which will hopefully be on my desk when I walk in Monday."

He released her from his hug so she could finish changing. When she was done, he gave her a peck on the lips.

"What would you say to spending the night with me again?"

She leaned against his chest and looked him in the eyes

pondering his request for a moment. "I don't know how I feel about leaving Vance again. Why don't you just stay here?"

"Oh, I don't know, maybe because you don't have a door?" He motioned to the stairway. It was private enough that you couldn't see anything from the bottom of the stairs unless she changed right at the top, but he did have a point.

"I just feel like I can't keep leaving Vance and relying on Trevor and Sebastian to help when they aren't being paid or anything. How about you ask Vance and if he says he doesn't want you to stay here, then we can discuss the alternative."

Kevin nodded. "Fair enough. I'll go do that before your parents get here." He winked and disappeared down the stairs.

Naya sighed and plugged her phone in on her nightstand, watching as it slowly came back to life. It was so weird how much her life had changed in a matter of weeks. She hadn't been expecting a huge case like this to fall on her lap so soon, and she certainly hadn't planned to start dating one of her brother's friends.

She glanced around her room, it was fairly neat except for a few piles of clothes. She quickly picked them up and placed them in the hamper. There, now she was ready for company. She chuckled slightly at herself and headed back downstairs.

Kevin and Vance were talking in the living room and Naya didn't want to interrupt, so she went into the kitchen where she was greeted with boxes of open Thai food. She quickly packaged everything up and placed it in the fridge. She was a bit annoyed no one had cleaned up, but she didn't want to complain because at least Vance was eating something. Every time she looked at him, she felt like he was getting skinnier.

She grabbed a towel to wipe down the counter when she heard the doorbell ring. She would have to finish later.

THEY RETURNED HOME MUCH LATER that night than Naya had anticipated, it was almost midnight by the time they walked in the front door. It was her parents' fault, they had wanted to spend as much time as possible with Vance, and she couldn't really blame them, they were going to go back to La Junta in the morning. But they had made plans to come back in a few weeks and spend more time with Vance then.

Naya unlocked the door and Kevin wheeled Vance up the walk in his wheelchair. Vance had an apprehensive look on his face and Naya couldn't tell if it was because he was thinking about if Kevin could spend the night or because of something else.

After she opened the door for them, Kevin wheeled Vance to the bathroom where he dropped him off and then folded the wheelchair against the wall. They both stood in the front hall quietly as they heard Vance brush his teeth.

"So –?" She asked quietly, a yawn sneaking through.

"He's fine with it."

"That makes it easy then." She smiled at Kevin just as the bathroom door opened, and Vance shuffled out.

"Need a shoulder to lean on?" Naya offered, holding out her hand.

He shook his head. "I think I can manage to the bedroom, but thanks." The two watched as Vance walked ever so slowly into his bedroom. Naya motioned her head to the stairs, hoping that Kevin would get the message.

Kevin nodded and went up the stairs two at a time, careful to hop over the top step. Naya shook her head. "Show off." Kevin beamed and then moved away from the doorway, presumably to make his way over to the bed.

Naya knocked on her brother's open door.

"It's clearly open." He grumbled from the bed. He hadn't bothered to change his clothes.

"I know, but I was being respectful." She motioned to what he was wearing. "You don't want to switch into something more comfortable?"

He shook his head glumly. She moved towards him.

"What's going on, you're never like this."

"Nothing." He mumbled. "Some days it just hits harder than others I guess."

Naya quietly sat on the bed and put her hand on his shoulder. They sat in silence for a few minutes, both contemplating his future.

It was Vance who finally broke the silence. "I told them yesterday when I went in for chemo that I wouldn't be coming back."

Naya turned and looked at what remained of her older brother. "But Vance, the doctor, he said your best chance—"

He held up his hand. "The chance was so slim in the first place Naya. And it's not working. At all. And at this point, it's drained my savings, and now we are draining yours, and I won't stand for it. This is it Naya. Whatever happens now is what happens."

Naya put her head in her hands, tears rising in her vision. "But Vance—" She tried to argue.

"No, Naya. I've made my decision. You need to be able to live your life after I'm gone. I can't steal your life when my destiny is set in stone."

She reached her arms around Vance and rested her head on his shoulder. "How did I end up with the best older brother ever, and I don't even get to keep you."

Vance smiled sadly. "That is definitely not what you would've said when I was twelve and intent on you being the butt of my practical jokes."

It was Naya's turn to smile sadly, tears were sneaking down her cheeks. "Yeah, and remember when Mom said someday we would be best friends?"

He nodded, "Why did we wait so long?" He finished her sentence for her.

"I love you, Vance," Naya whispered.

"I love you too, Naya. And I always will." Vance continued to look down at his lap.

"Why do I feel like I'm saying my goodbye to you?" Naya realized suddenly. "You aren't planning anything crazy, right?"

Vance shook his head. "Besides stopping the chemo, no. I promise

I'm not planning to off myself or anything like that. You're stuck with me until the end."

"Then why?"

He shrugged, clearly fighting back his own tears. "I just, I don't know, something weird happened today. And I got the sudden notion that I should say my goodbyes." He took a deep breath and closed his eyes.

"And mom and dad?"

"I talked to them this afternoon. I know they say they will be back in a few weeks. But Naya, I never thought I would be saying this at thirty-two years old, but I can feel it. My time is coming. And soon."

Naya tried to brush away the tears that were flowing freely now, but it was no use. "I want to argue with you and tell you that you're wrong. But I can't." The feelings she had been trying to hold back these past few weeks were finally starting to make sense.

"Because you can feel it too." Vance whispered quietly.

She nodded. "I think I knew when I first moved in."

They sat quietly for a few more moments just enjoying being there. It was Vance who broke the silence again. "Tomorrow, on our walk, I want to say goodbye to Kevin. When the time seems right, can you and Elliot leave us alone? Please."

"Anything for you." She promised in a whisper, she didn't trust herself to speak any louder for fear she would begin sobbing uncontrollably.

"And I don't have much of anything left, but can you call a lawyer? I need to draft up my will." His voice transformed from emotional to businesslike. "The house is yours." Naya knew he was serious about it, there was nothing for her to say.

"I'll have one come on Monday."

"And I want to be cremated. Don't waste money on an urn or anything, spread my ashes somewhere in nature. Please. Don't spend any more money on me."

She felt her tears slow, realizing that after all he had been through, Vance was more worried about messing up her life than his. When he didn't speak for a few more minutes, she squeezed him and then slowly stood and headed for the door. She planned to clean herself up in the bathroom before going upstairs to see Kevin.

"And Naya?" Vance called as she was almost to the door.

"Yes?" She asked, turning back around.

"I'm sorry."

This confused Naya, and she tilted her head to the side. "Sorry for what?"

"That you changed your whole life for the last few weeks of my life." His voice cracked, and he dropped his head to his hands.

Naya quickly crossed to the bed and hugged him again as tight as she could.

"Never see it that way, Vance. I've only been here a few weeks and already they've been some of the best weeks of my life." She remembered the huge case breathing down her neck, well, best except for that she reasoned. "In La Junta, I had reached the end of my rope. There was nothing else for me to do but stare at the same few cases for years on end. Coming here was the shock I needed to show me there was more to life." She realized she was crying again. "And for that I thank you." She whispered the last part.

After another minute of hugging each other, Naya pulled back and stood. "Goodnight, Vance."

"Goodnight Naya." He replied as she slowly closed the door behind her. She turned to go to the bathroom and ran straight into Kevin, who was leaning against the wall, a solemn look on his face.

"How much did you hear?" Naya whispered.

"All of it, I think." He whispered back. "I didn't mean to. I came down to brush my teeth and when I heard you guys talking, I froze." He embraced Naya in a hug, and she felt herself somehow still crying. Where was all this water coming from anyway? He smoothed a hand through her hair.

"Come on, let's get you upstairs."

She nodded as he took her hand and gently led her up the stairs and around the creaky step. Both were silent as they stripped to their underwear and slipped into bed. Kevin lifted his arm, and Naya snuggled into his side.

"I'm sorry I ruined the mood for the evening." She grimaced, remembering his playful mood earlier.

"It's not your fault." He must've realized how bad that sounded because he quickly amended his statement. "And it's not Vance's either. I just wish there was something I could do to keep the inevitable from happening.

"Me too." She sighed as they fell into a companionable and comforting silence. Naya was so tired that sleep came quickly and soon she found herself in that weird place between waking and sleeping.

A place where everything was pleasant and safe. She was back in La Junta, running through the long flowing grass, her older brother running right alongside her...

~

MORNING CAME ALL TOO SOON. Technically, she could've slept in, but the light from her window woke her up around seven. She was still cuddled up to Kevin, who was fast asleep, snoring lightly. As quietly as she could, she slid from the bed and pulled on her hiking clothes.

She ran her brush through her hair, noticing that it felt weird in her hand. When she pulled the brush away from her head, she noticed her scrunchie, which had always been on the end, was no longer there. She paused. Maybe Kevin had borrowed it for...something? Well, it was just a scrunchie, she would just have to grab a regular hair tie from the bathroom to put her hair up.

Trying her best to hold her ponytail in her hand as she stepped down the stairs, she made her way to the bathroom, where she grabbed a hair tie and brushed her teeth. Then she made her way to the kitchen to finish cleaning up the mess she had left when they had left for dinner the night before.

Luckily, it wasn't too bad, just some sauce residue and a little spilled fried rice on the counter. She quickly cleaned it up and then looked in the fridge to see if there was anything she could make for breakfast.

No such luck, she hadn't been to the store in over a week. The fridge was crowded with a random smattering of take-out boxes from probably every restaurant within a three-mile radius but nothing else. They would have to go out, like usual.

She heard movement in the bathroom and was in the process of trying to guess who it might be when Kevin appeared in the doorway.

"You're up early." He commented, raising his eyes at her clothing choice.

She pretended to check her watch even though she wasn't wearing one. "I could say the same, I've only been up for a few minutes." She paused and looked back at the fridge. "So, we have absolutely nothing to eat, so once Elliot gets here, let's plan to grab breakfast somewhere near wherever this walk is."

"Sounds like a plan. I was thinking about this trail up north a bit, it's called Sand Creek National Greenway. It's fairly flat and will be easy enough to manage with the wheelchair, I think." He stopped for a second to think. "There's not a whole lot right by it, but we could stop at Snooze on our way north."

"What's Snooze?" It certainly sounded like a breakfast place, but she hadn't heard of it before.

A Cheshire grin appeared on Kevin's face. "What is Snooze? Only the best breakfast place on this side of the Mississippi. Man, you are in for a treat."

It was almost four hours later, and the four of them were walking on the small path on the northeast side of Denver. Kevin was pushing Vance's wheelchair while Elliot and Naya walked behind them.

Naya was glad she had suggested a walk, because after the delectable pancake flight she had just downed at Snooze, she could use it. But the pumpkin creme pancakes had been so worth how uncomfortably full she was feeling now.

They all walked together for a few hundred yards before Vance gave Naya a nod. She then began to walk slower and slower to create some distance while engaging Elliot in conversation.

"So, Elliot, why did you become an at-home care nurse? Wait, is it okay that I call you a nurse? I just realized I don't know if that term is gender-neutral or not..."

Elliot laughed. "Yes, you can call me a nurse. They don't have different terms for us." He ran a hand through his hair, his mood changing. "Well, my sister had cystic fibrosis, and I spent most of my childhood caring for her. So, as an adult, this came easily to me, so I just continued with what I was good at, I guess." He shrugged, watching as Vance and Kevin edged even further ahead.

"Don't worry, Kevin has him." Putting her hand on his arm to quell his nerves.

"I know. And I know I've only worked with him for a week, but Vance is great. I usually only have older patients. It's so rare I get a patient that's so easy and fun to hang out with. We mostly just play video games."

Naya nodded. "I know. It doesn't seem fair."

Elliot shook his head. "And it never will."

Vance and Kevin stopped up ahead, and Naya put her hand on Elliot's shoulder again and came to a stop as well. "Let's give them a minute, shall we?" She said as she turned to give them some privacy. Elliot followed her lead.

"So, how long have you lived in Denver?" He asked, probably finding it odd to stand there in silence with her.

"I came to help Vance a few weeks ago. But he always acted so strong I had no idea...I mean...when I got here..." Guilt rose up in her throat as she considered how she had basically gotten here and hired help.

"Hey, don't worry about it. Sometimes, getting extra help is all you can do. And I don't think Vance would have wanted you to give up your career either."

She nodded. "You're right. This might be weird, and you don't have to tell me, but how old are you, Elliot?"

A small smile ghosted his lips. "I get that a lot, actually. I'm twenty-six. But I know I look younger, and I was forced to grow up fast. I think I've been an adult since I was about seventeen."

"Well, you're good at what you do, Vance simply raves about you and Derek until the cows come home."

"Thanks." His cheeks dusting with pink from being put on the spot. "But really, that's Vance. He makes my job easy."

Naya glanced over her shoulder to see Vance getting out of his wheelchair and giving Kevin a brief hug. Anyone looking on might think it weird, to see two guys hug, but if either cared, they didn't show it. After another minute, Vance sat back down, and Kevin did a one-eighty with the chair. They quickly made their way to where Naya and Elliot were standing.

"Alright, shall we start making our way back?" Kevin asked. Though neither of them was as visibly emotional as Naya had been the previous night, she could tell the talk had affected them both.

Vance nodded, and Naya began walking back up the path to the car.

Kevin seemed a bit on edge, whether from his talk with Vance, or because of Elliot, Naya couldn't be sure. He was tense, his hands white-knuckling the wheelchair.

"Anyone want lunch?" Naya asked with a smile on her face, knowing they had all just eaten loads of food at breakfast.

Vance grabbed his stomach, "If you try to put another bite in me, I will simply explode."

"Says the person who ate like three bites of a pancake." Elliot chimed in the banter light; he was clearly more comfortable with Vance than he was with Naya.

Naya noticed how Kevin said nothing at all, and she fell back a step so she could put a hand on his arm. He relaxed slightly under her touch, but she could still tell he was tense. She would have to ask him what was going on when they were alone.

Elliot, Vance, and Naya chatted comfortably as they walked along the nature path towards the car. Kevin did interject occasionally, but he didn't volunteer anything of substance to the conversation, which wasn't like him at all.

The conversation continued much of the same way during the drive to the house. As soon as they got Vance through the door, him and Elliot were off to the living room to play whatever video game they had been talking about in the car. Naya was starting to think that Vance used video games to keep his mind off of things, and if that was the case, she didn't have a problem with him playing so frequently.

She made eye contact with Kevin as soon as they were alone.

"Do you want to talk about something?" She asked him quietly.

He shook his head and moved his arm out from under her hand. "I'm going to go. I'll talk to you later." And then he was out the door and down the walk before Naya could even give him a kiss goodbye. As the door shut, she found herself standing there still holding out her hand and wondering what had just happened.

Just what had he and Vance talked about?

24

NAYA

The night was all too short, and as Naya rolled out of bed the next morning she checked her phone to see if Kevin had messaged her. Nothing.

Her heart fell a little bit, but she couldn't focus on being bummed now. She had a case to solve.

She slid on her work clothes and clipped her gun and holster to her belt. Forgoing coffee, she looked in on Vance quickly, who was still sleeping, then was out the door not more than fifteen minutes after she had woken up.

She didn't know why she felt such urgency, she just had a feeling this case was about to break. Some piece of information they were waiting for today had to be the piece they needed to put the puzzle together.

Naya pulled into the work lot just after seven-thirty, incredibly early, only to spot Atlas' truck in its usual spot. Damn! She wondered how he always managed to beat her?

Slightly defeated, she stepped out of her car and made her way in the building.

By the time she got to her desk, Atlas was already reading some sort of report that had landed on his desk. She saw another copy on her desk.

"I don't know how you do it." She huffed as she sat down and began reading, it was the RunTracker data for the three victims.

"Magic." Atlas snickered, still busy reading.

Naya knew she read faster than Atlas, and if she tried, she could surely beat him to the end of the report, but she also knew that a woman's life could be relying on this and she needed to read carefully. So instead, she pushed her competitive nature aside for the moment and invested herself in the reports.

Each stack was the print outs of the women's last ten runs, they included a rough map of where the woman ran, as well as their speed, and distance.

Naya looked over the maps for Julia Charles, the routes varied quite a bit; it seemed like she really had been committed to switching it up. When she got to the last page, her last run, during which she had been abducted, she stopped and tilted her head. The line just stopped. It was if she was beamed from her route by magic. She separated this page from the stack and then went on to read the ones for Shanice Woods.

She hadn't varied her route as much as Julia, but she had run much faster, after all, she had been a champion racer. But the story was the same, Shanice was running like normal, and then the route just suddenly ended. There was no visible struggle, or evidence of any kind, that the women even had a chance to attempt to escape their attacker. She separated this page as well, placing it with Julia's.

She didn't know what to expect from Alia Larson's RunTracker data, but it read a lot like Shanice's, a semi-varied route, less than Julia's but still as varied as it could be with limited options. But when she got to the last page, she saw that Alia had indeed finished her run just as they had seen. So, just as they had deduced, she had been abducted at some point after she re-entered the building.

Naya set Alia's stack of data aside and set the last runs of Julia and Shanice side by side.

"How do two women, who are fast and seasoned runners, just get beamed into space?"

Atlas must've been thinking the same thing, as he was looking at the last run of Julia Charles. "It's as if he knew they were going to be there."

Naya flipped through the packets again. "But both women varied their route regularly. There is simply no way to predict that either of them would have been in that place at that time.

Atlas suddenly sat up straight in his chair. "Wait. What if this guy somehow had access to the app?"

"What do you mean?" Naya could feel her brain was still waking up a bit. She shouldn't have forgone the coffee.

"I'm saying, what if this guy is a programmer for this app or something? How else would he have this information? Even if he was the girls' friend on the app, these women varied their route way too much to predict. But what if, he could access the app and watch them as they ran?"

Naya felt her mouth fall open. "My god." She whispered. "Call tech right now, I want to know how easy this app is to hack."

Atlas already had his phone in his hand. "On it. And can you contact RunTracker? Let them know there's been a possible breach, and our tech guys will be in contact shortly to discuss their security procedures and obtain a list of local employees."

Naya nodded and rushed to look up their phone number on the documents and dialed.

After she hung up, she turned towards Atlas. "Do you think the tech guys will have an answer for you today?" She was thinking about the clock ticking. Another woman was going to go missing tonight.

"I think so. They were already downloading the app to try to hack it while I was on the phone with them."

Atlas' phone rang in his hand, he hurried to answer and became consumed by his conversation with the person on the other end. Naya turned back to the reports, aghast at the possibility of what they might be dealing with here.

If this guy could really hack the RunTracker app, then no woman was safe, no matter how fast she ran or how careful she was.

Atlas hung up his phone. "That was the coroner. He can't be sure, but he thinks there's a chance there was an excess of potassium in her system."

"As in potassium chloride? Like what is used in the lethal injection?"

Atlas shook his head. "He couldn't be sure, as it's difficult to locate potassium chloride in the body post-mortem. But my guess is that is exactly what this guy is doing."

"So, he kidnaps them and kills them with a lethal injection within hours? And that's it?"

"I told you, crazy." Atlas made the gesture for crazy to his own head as he said it to emphasize his point.

Naya leaned back in her seat, biting the edge of the pen she was using to take notes. "Every time I feel like we are about to break this case open, I only get more confused. If only those tapes would show up."

"They're coming, I checked on them earlier this morning, they should be here before the afternoon."

Naya slid her phone from her pocket, checking the screen to see if she had a text from Kevin, man she really was reverting back to a high school girl. Her screen was blank, no messages, she put her phone back in her pocket.

Of course, nothing escaped Atlas' notice. "Everything okay at home?"

"Peachy." Naya lied, as if her brother hadn't told her goodbye two nights before and the guy she had been dating wasn't not talking to her.

Suddenly, Naya's email pinged, and she opened it up to see an email from the techs. Atlas noticed over her shoulder and quickly opened it in his own inbox.

It was a large file, and Naya knew reviewing the footage might take some time.

"Conference room?"

"On it." Atlas stood and disconnected his laptop, turning towards the conference room. "Grab me a coffee while this finishes downloading, will you?"

She shook her head, annoyed that he had been reading her thoughts, and knew she would be going to get coffee. Atlas was truly meant to be a detective.

She entered the conference room with a cup of steaming hot coffee in each hand. She handed Atlas his and then sat in a chair facing the projection screen. She grabbed the notebook she had left there and pulled her pen out of her pocket, ready to note any suspicious characters.

"Okay." Atlas pulled up the footage. "This starts at two hours before Alia left on her run. The techs have slowed it down for us and lightened it, as the cameras are old, and it's difficult to see some of these people, according to them anyway."

He pushed play, and Naya could see the empty lobby. They were looking for people, mostly men, who entered or left solo. In the first hour, there were three men who left the building in suits. Naya made a mental note but assumed they were going to work and wouldn't be back until evening.

A couple of families with small children left. One woman also exited the building dressed professionally as if she was going to work. Then Alia came into the frame, exiting out the door to go on her run.

"So, no one came in."

Atlas shrugged. "It was early."

They watched the lobby for the next hour of the footage. It was busier now as all the people who worked a nine-to-five job started leaving for work. One man did leave in what looked like gym or running clothes, with an armband on his arm; Naya made a note of him.

Before she knew it, Alia was back on the screen, crossing towards the stairs. Naya moved to the edge of her seat, watching for someone to follow her in.

"How is that possible?" Atlas grumbled, standing up from his seat.

"How could no one enter, and our girl go for the stairs but not make it up the stairs?"

It suddenly hit Naya, the conclusion they had dismissed. "He lives in the building." She gasped.

Atlas' eyes went wide. "Damn it! She was probably still in the building while we were there!" He balled his hands into fists, looking like he wanted to punch someone.

"Quick, let's get that list of residents, we'll go over there tonight. And get squad cars, I don't want anyone able to enter or leave the building tonight with anything unusual without being thoroughly inspected. We're gonna get this guy."

They rushed back to their desks and began frantically making phone calls and arranging to get the list of residents as soon as they could. As soon as they were done with the arrangements, they were in the squad car on the way to the building.

"Here's the game plan, we knock on every door. If a woman answers, we move on. I don't think there's any way this guy can live with anyone." Atlas surmised.

"Are you sure?" Naya didn't want to question his plan, as it was a big apartment building and would take them a while to process even with his plan. "What if this is a couple or something?"

"Fine, fine. But single men first, let's make note of the places with adult couples and no children and we can look into them after the men. If we don't catch him tonight, another woman's life will be on the line. We need to work fast."

Atlas was right, they were going for speed and efficiency, they were under the gun. Statistically, this was a lone male perpetrator acting alone anyway. They could go back and look at the couples later.

"Let's split up. I'll start at the top floor; you start at the bottom." Naya suggested.

"Deal. I've got patrol cars on their way too. We can have them start checking when they get there. Take notes about every household. Hopefully, we will have a list from the complex by the end of the evening so we can make sure no one is lying to us. Also, write down any apartments that don't answer."

"We will get this guy. We're close, I can feel it." Naya felt anxious and she wasn't sure if it was because of the case, or what was going on at home right now. She glanced at her watch, noticing it was already three. She needed to find someone to come help Vance tonight because she would probably be out late. As much as she didn't want to bug Kevin, she hoped he wasn't too mad at her to help take care of Vance. She quickly pulled out her phone and typed out a quick text.

Naya: Hey I know you're upset about something. But there's been a break in the case, I won't be home, but can you, Trevor or Sebastian check in on Vance around bedtime?

She didn't have time to wait for the reply as they were pulling up at the apartment building. Naya slid her phone into her pocket and followed Atlas inside. As she pressed the button for the elevator, Atlas ran up the first set of stairs. As she stepped into the elevator and pressed the button for the highest floor, she took a deep breath.

The elevator dinged on the thirty-first floor.

They could do this. It was go time.

25

MARK

"Hello!" he called as he entered the house using his key. It was so convenient. He considered sliding off his shoes to be polite, but decided against it.

"Yo!" Vance called from the couch in the living room as Mark entered the room. Elliot was also there; they were playing video games per usual. "How's it going man?"

"Good, you guys playing Call of Duty still?"

"Yeah, you want in next round?" Vance's eyes didn't even leave the screen.

"Nah I'm good. I was actually just thinking of ordering food, you guys want anything?"

Elliot checked his watch. "No, I'm off in an hour so I probably won't even be here when it gets here."

"Is Kevin coming?" Vance asked as he continued to hit buttons on the controller. Mark wished he could find this entertaining, but he just couldn't.

"Um, I don't think so." He was actually pretty confident Kevin wasn't coming, but he didn't want to reveal that information just yet. "So, I was thinking of ordering some soup from that one sandwich place, Panera or whatever. What kind do you want Vance?"

"I'll take a grilled cheese with the tomato soup please; I think it's a combo of some sort."

Mark stood and headed for the kitchen, pulling out his phone to order the food. God, he was so ready to be done playing this role. When he had stepped into it a few months ago, he had never imagined what an impact it would come to have on his plan. It had just seemed like a good idea to have work friends so he could have an alibi. Especially work friends who played a lot of video games and wouldn't necessarily notice if he was in the room or not.

But now, now he was done. He was finally going to get the perfect specimen, and he was going to do it tonight. He hadn't wanted things to escalate this way, but he found that he just couldn't wait any longer. He had wanted things to be painless for Vance because he did sort of think of him as a friend.

Well, as much as he could, considering his total lack of emotional attachment to anyone.

After the food arrived, with a glance over his shoulder first, Mark pulled the vial out of his pocket. This wasn't his usual stuff. Vance didn't eat enough for that. He'd had to go off script. He hoped that no one would notice, but he figured there was a chance. Hopefully, he would be long gone by the time they figured it out.

When Kevin had texted him, he had already been planning to vacate his apartment building. It just didn't seem right to have the detective there. Too risky because of the Alia situation. He had packed up his lab the night before, and everything was now in two trunks in the back of his truck. He had already been practically on his way to the detective's house when Kevin asked him to come over.

It had all been too easy. Now if he could just manage to pull this off.

26

NAYA

She was on the twenty-fourth floor. And she was burnt out.

They had been knocking on doors for hours. Some there were no answer, and others a woman would answer. It was the same routine each time someone opened the door, she would explain who she was, show her badge, and ask if anyone else lived there. Most people were cordial, but a few had been standoffish. One woman even verging on rude, she had refused to give any information, Naya had marked her down as uncooperative. According to Atlas' theory she shouldn't matter in the long run.

Each floor had at least six separate apartments, some even more if that floor had a lot of studio apartments. Naya had already knocked on so many doors she felt desperate like they weren't working fast enough, but there was nothing else she could do.

She raised her hand again and knocked on the next door. A young child answered.

"Hi," Naya said as she leaned down to the girl's level. "Is your mom or dad home?" She couldn't be more than five years old.

"Dad." A man said from behind the door as he stepped into Naya's view.

Naya stood and flipped out her badge, "Hello, I'm Detective Naya

Largusa from the Denver Police Department. I'm here to find out the names of the adults living in this apartment."

He raised an eyebrow. "Why?" Of course, he was one of the apprehensive ones.

She kept a smile on her face. "We are looking for someone who lives in this building who has information about a crime."

"Well, it's just me and my wife here. She's at work but will be home any minute." He listed their first and last names for Naya, which she quickly jotted down.

"Thank you, that's all. Have a good night." Naya waved at the little girl as the man closed the door. She double-checked her paper to make sure she had knocked on every door on the floor, then jogged down the stairs to floor twenty-three.

After the next apartment, her phone buzzed in her pocket. She picked it up without looking at the screen. "Largusa."

"Hey, I'm on floor ten, and I'm beat. Where are you?"

"Twenty-three. I'm tired too. Should we take a dinner break and pick this back up in an hour? We can eat in the car and change with the patrol guys if they want a break from monitoring the door to knock on doors."

"Good idea. Meet you in the lobby in five." Naya slid her phone back in her pocket and looked down at her paper. How had Atlas finished nine floors while she had only done seven and one apartment? Oh well, she would ask him when she saw him.

THEY HAD PICKED up roast beef sandwiches from down the street and were sitting in the car watching as people went in and out of the building. It was dinner time now, so there were lots of delivery men and couples going out to the restaurants nearby. But so far, no one had tried to enter or leave with a bag that seemed larger than normal.

"Any emails from the apartment company yet?" Naya asked when she was halfway through her sandwich.

Atlas shook his head. "Course not. I bet they'll respond tomorrow morning."

"Are we staking out tonight?" In La Junta, they had such a skeleton crew that she would definitely personally be doing a stake out if there was a stakeout to do, which was rare. Here, she wasn't sure what the protocol was.

"Nah, someone will come relieve us at midnight. They'll need us fresh for tomorrow. I doubt we will get to all of these doors tonight before a decent hour, and I had so many on the lower floors that didn't answer. At least we will be able to eliminate some when the tenant list comes in."

Naya was glad she wouldn't be out there all night. Then at least she wouldn't feel as guilty. She checked her phone to see if Kevin had replied, but he hadn't. She really hoped he had called someone, she wished she had Trevor or Sebastian's numbers, but she had never needed them before.

"The techs called while I was knocking on doors." Naya looked over at Atlas, pausing between bites to give him her full attention. "Turns out RunTracker was ridiculously easy to hack. They said all it took was the user turning on their Bluetooth connection while using the app, and I guess if you knew basic hacking you could get in while it was running. They weren't sure if the connection would still be accessible after the run stopped, but they think there's a chance if you were good enough at programming that you could set something up so you could re-enter the app at any time."

Naya turned back to her sandwich and took another bite. "I guess that makes sense, but how is he finding these girls initially?"

"I was thinking about that." Atlas took a bite of his sandwich as well, and the car was quiet while he chewed. "And when you showed me the app the other day, I saw that you could connect it to your Facebook. So, I think there's a possibility that all three of these girls posted their runs on Facebook. Then he was able to use their profile to get enough information to get close enough to them during a run to hack into their Bluetooth connection."

"Jesus. That is why I don't have social media." Naya shook her head. Most people had no idea the amount of information that could be discovered about them from a simple glance at their profile.

"My sentiments exactly. But I was thinking we should give the families a call and see if what I said was true; if they posted their runs on Facebook. Because think about it, most of the runs start and end at their homes. Even though you can't zoom in, if this guy knew the area well enough, he could just hang out in that area and watch for the Bluetooth connection. And most people just label their headphones with their name."

Naya felt her eyes widening. That was definitely the name of her earphones. "But wait, none of the girls had wireless earphones in when we found them."

"Bingo. I bet whatever hacking he is doing on these Bluetooth connections would show up if we found the devices."

She finished the last bite of her sandwich and crumpled the wrapper. "This brings up the fact that the man we are chasing is probably highly intelligent. When we get the apartment building tenants, let's have your tech guys or someone comb them for prominent people in technology. Even if this guy isn't famous, sometimes these people can be in scientific papers or magazines for their discoveries or designs."

"True. Alright, you ready to go back in?" Atlas glanced at her empty hands, and she noticed he had also finished his sandwich.

"Yep. Let's do this."

27

MARK

It was done. He had poisoned Vance.

It had been much easier than he anticipated with the soup. Vance had eaten almost all of it. About an hour later, when he had started not to feel well, Mark had helped him to his bed.

That had been hours ago.

Mark wanted to look in on him and make sure he really was dead, but he also didn't want to miss Naya returning. The minute she was almost to the door he would have to get his rag soaked in ether and get into a position where he could get it over her mouth before she could fight.

She was a cop. And she was armed. This would be his most difficult abduction yet.

It was almost midnight and he knew Kevin had called him because she would be back late, but he was starting to get a bit anxious and wished he knew just how late.

Whatever. It would be fine. After all, luck had been on his side so far. Kevin had not been here tonight for the first time. Then again, Kevin had no reason to not trust him.

Well, not yet.

After he got Naya in the truck he would need to restrain her. Tape her mouth. Get her on the floor so she couldn't signal. Then he would need to ditch his phone. He had another set of plates in the cab for his truck, he would put them on before they crossed state lines.

He already had another Airbnb lined up in Kansas.

Now, all he was missing was his specimen.

28

NAYA

It was midnight and they had reconvened in the car.

"Anything?" She asked, exhausted.

He shook his head. "According to both of the RunTracker runs, he had abducted the women by now. But I don't think we missed him."

"Remember he took Alia on Tuesday morning." Naya closed her eyes and leaned against the headrest for a second.

"Yeah, but I feel like that was an opportunistic victim, not one which he selected. But maybe I'm wrong."

"Good point." Naya felt her eyes becoming heavy and quickly snapped them open again before she could fall asleep.

Atlas still noticed. "As soon as the night watch pulls up, we will head for the station."

They sat in silence for a few minutes, both beat from having knocked on doors all evening. Eventually, Atlas started the car.

Their welcome call came over the radio. "There they are." Atlas quickly pulled forward so they could take the spot he and Naya had been occupying, once the radio call came confirming that they were officially on watch Atlas pulled away, headed for the station.

"I know it's late, but what do you say to a seven-a.m. start?" He asked as the city lights blurred outside the window. Naya hadn't been this tired in a long while.

"Sure. I'll just grab a shower and a couple of hours of sleep and come right back." As long as she got four to five hours, and about a gallon of coffee, she would be good to go. She felt bad that she wouldn't have time to spend with Vance, but he would understand. Once they caught this guy, he would have all of her attention for a couple of weeks.

When they got to the station, they switched from the squad car to their personal cars, wishing each other a safe drive, and headed home. Naya was so tired she was a bit scared to drive, but she kept some candy in her center console for this exact purpose, and quickly popped a few pieces in her mouth to chew to keep her mind awake.

When she pulled up in front of her house, she noticed a truck parked right out front. For a second, she was excited, thinking it looked a bit like Kevin's, but after a closer look, she realized it was Trevor's instead.

So, something really was bothering him then. His avoiding her seemed so out of character for what she knew about him. She was going to have to confront Vance and find out what their talk was about.

She unlocked the door and stepped into the front hall. The house was quiet; she assumed Vance was in bed, and Trevor must already be passed out on the couch. She leaned down to slip out of her work boots.

Before she understood what was happening and reacted, there was a body pinning her to the ground and chemical-smelling rag over her mouth. Her mind immediately sprang into action to figure out what was going on, her body started running on autopilot and she tried to move her arms to reach for her gun, but whoever was on top of her was strong and had a size advantage, they had her completely pinned. So, she stopped breathing.

She struggled feebly for a few seconds to no avail, they wouldn't budge.

When the air ran out in her lungs she was forced to breathe again, knowing full well what was about to happen. She tried to make out the identity of whoever was on top of her, but he was purposely keeping his head out of headbutt range. He knew all the self-defense tricks.

That was the last thing she thought before sliding into unconsciousness.

29

KEVIN

He could hear his phone buzzing on the bedside table.

It was probably work. He had called out for the entire week, but they had spent all of the previous day calling him for approval and instructions for random things.

It could also be Naya, but it was only about seven in the morning and he figured she would just be waking up if she was awake at all.

Kevin felt bad for stonewalling her, he really did, he just wasn't quite ready to talk yet. But he was feeling better today than he had the day before, maybe he could go over and at least visit with Vance today before Naya got home. He would face her later this week. His chest physically hurt at the fact that he was probably hurting her right now, but he just needed some time to process.

It was so hard knowing he was going to lose his best friend. And he felt like if he didn't deal with the emotions now, he was going to really lose it when Vance actually died.

Maybe he was being dumb. Maybe he should just call Naya, at least make sure Trevor had checked in on Vance.

Yeah, that was a good idea. He would do that in an hour or two when it was a decent time.

He couldn't deny that his feelings were rapidly growing for Naya.

She was beautiful and smart, and she had such a caring heart. He kind of wished he could see her in action at work, he imagined she was quite sexy.

He really hadn't planned to fall in love with her, it had just sort of happened. He had volunteered to help with Vance because he was his best friend and when Vance had mentioned his sister had moved to town, he never dreamed that she would be the girl he'd been waiting for all these years.

The first time he had seen her, he couldn't even explain it. Watching her try to be kind and cook food for all of them in that small kitchen. Biting her lip when she realized there wouldn't be enough. Something within him had changed in that moment. He knew she was different, and he had needed to know more.

So, yeah, he was definitely an idiot for ignoring her right now, but she had said the case had just broken. So, maybe she was happy to have a little break from having to worry about him? His excuse sounded weak even to his own ears.

He closed his eyes, fully intending to take advantage of his rare day off from work, when his phone started buzzing again. Okay, even for work, they were calling a bit early. Maybe it was an emergency.

He blindly reached for his phone and brought it to his face. It was a number he didn't recognize, but a local area code. It was probably a sales call. He silenced it.

Not even a minute later, the screen lit up again. The same number. Dammit all.

"What do you want?!" He answered angrily. He was pissed and wasn't about to be cordial.

"Hey Kevin, this is Atlas, Naya's partner, she was supposed to be here at seven. I'm guessing she slept through her alarm, and I was just seeing if she was with you?"

What. The.

"How did you get this number?" As far as Kevin knew, he had only met Atlas once, and it was in passing, without so much as an introduction, at the hospital. The guy couldn't know more than his first name.

"Dude, I'm a detective. It's not that hard. But seriously, is she with you?"

He was annoyed. Maybe he would feel better if she was here, now that he thought about it. He really was being stupid. "No, she's not here. You should probably call her number."

"I'm not an idiot, I already did. Straight to voicemail."

Kevin thought for a moment about how Naya's phone battery was always low. "Her phone probably just died, and that's what she uses as her alarm."

The phone line was silent for a minute. Clearly, Atlas wasn't buying it.

"This isn't like her, I'm going to have an officer go to her house."

As much as he wanted to hole up in his room, Kevin knew that if cops showed up at her door, Naya would be embarrassed. Decision made he spoke up.

"No, no, I'll go over there now. I have a key."

"Okay, have her call me as soon as you wake her, please."

"Will do." Kevin grumbled as he got out of bed and pulled on clothes. Maybe this was good. Clearly, avoiding Naya wasn't going to solve his problems; he just wished he'd had more time to think.

He spent the entire drive grumbling about how bright the sun was this early in morning. Man, even for him, he could admit he was being grouchy.

When he pulled up in front of her house, grimy from not having left bed the previous day, he wished for a moment that he would have at least had the forethought to shower before he came over here. Oh well, Naya would probably run right out the door after he awoke her anyway.

He parked right behind her car and walked up to the door. He pulled his keys from his pocket, slipping them into the keyhole, only to find the door wasn't locked.

That was odd.

The moment he walked in the door, he knew something was wrong.

"Naya?" He called out as he stepped over the rug, which was bunched in the doorway. "Vance?"

There was no answer from either of them. He glanced at Vance's door, but it was closed, and since it was still early, he decided he would check on Naya first. He walked up the stairs and peered around the corner into the loft to find her bed empty. Not just empty, but it was made. He headed back down the stairs and poked his head in the bathroom. Empty. He roamed through the kitchen and living room. There was no sign of anyone. It was definitely time to wake Vance.

He knocked on his door. "Hey, it's Kevin, you up?"

He waited for an answer, but when none came, he turned the knob and opened the door.

What he saw would be burned in his memory forever.

"Vance?" Kevin stood there in shock.

It took another second for his mind to flip into gear and for him to cross the room, he reached for Vance. The minute he touched Vance's arm; he knew.

He was cold.

He backed out of the room. He could feel himself panicking. He tried to search his mind for what to do and found himself blindly pushing redial on the number that Atlas had called earlier that morning. He stumbled out onto the front porch, gasping for air.

"Atlas." He answered after a single ring.

Kevin found himself tongue-tied for a second before he was able to choke anything out. "Uh..."

He cleared his throat and tried again. "It's Vance. I, uh, don't think he's alive." Kevin felt himself going into shock.

"I'm sending a bus right now. How's Naya?"

Seeing his friend dead had almost made him forget the reason he had come over in the first place. "She's...she's not here."

"Jesus. I should have driven her home I knew she was too tired to drive, I need to check the accident reports—"

What Atlas was saying sunk in, and he rushed to cut him off. "Her car is here. I'm looking at it."

Now, it was Atlas' turn to be at a loss for words. The phone was silent for a moment.

"Fuck." He whispered, then he took a deep breath. "I'm on my way. And I'm bringing the cavalry."

Kevin doesn't remember hanging up the phone. Maybe he never did. Maybe it had just gone dead while he was holding it against his ear, he couldn't be sure. He didn't even remember sitting down, but he was sitting frozen in the exact same position on the cement step with the front door still hanging open behind him when the ambulance and police officers arrived.

An EMT began asking him questions, and all Kevin could do was motion to the open door behind him. The EMT went in only to come out a few minutes later and speak to one of his colleagues who had stayed outside with Kevin.

A different EMT offered him water and a cookie, saying what he was experiencing was shock. Kevin kind of wanted to yell at him because he clearly knew that, but he couldn't find the energy to do so. He was still holding the bottle of water and cookie when Atlas pulled up an intangible amount of time later.

He got out of his car and headed straight for Kevin.

"What happened?" He quickly turned and shouted orders over his shoulder, ordering the officers who had pulled up behind him to secure the scene after they removed the body.

Kevin shook his head. "I knew something was wrong when I walked in. The front mat was all bunched up, and the door was unlocked. Naya wouldn't just leave it like that."

Atlas nodded. "What else? What did you do next?"

"I went up the stairs. Her bed was still made. I knew then that she probably hadn't made it to her bed. But I checked the rest of the house to be sure. I knew it was dumb, though. I had called her name when I walked in. If she had been awake and cooking breakfast, she would have answered. Then I checked on Vance and..." He couldn't bring himself to describe what he had seen then.

Atlas stood up and went to talk to the other officers that were there in a whisper. Kevin couldn't even bring himself to listen in. But the more he sat there, the more it began to set in that Naya was missing.

Where was she?

Kevin remembered that he had called Trevor the night before to check on Vance. He wondered if he had spent the night and just left early or had left the night before.

He pulled out his phone and dialed Trevor's number. The phone rang and rang. Finally, a recorded message came on to say the number did not have a voice mailbox set up yet. That was odd…

Atlas came back over. "Were you with Vance last night?"

Kevin shook his head and stood. He was finally getting his wits back. "No. Vance and I had a bit of a heavy talk on Sunday. So, I was taking a little break. Naya texted me last night and asked me to have someone check in on him. I called my friend Trevor."

"Trevor, who?"

"Carlson. We work together. He and Vance are buddies, too." After the words came out of his mouth, he gulped. He couldn't say those words anymore.

Atlas put a hand on his shoulder. "What's his number?"

Kevin held out his phone. "I just tried to call him. He didn't answer."

"Okay, I'll have some officers see if they can intercept him at work. Can you tell me where you work?"

Kevin nodded and gave him the cross streets of the construction project Trevor had been on this week.

"What do you think happened to Naya?" Now that the shock was wearing off, panic was setting in. What was Naya going to do when she found out Vance died while she was working? This was going to crush her. Where was she? Had him not coming over last night caused her to do something rash?

"I have no idea. But my best guess is someone was waiting for her."

"But who would want to take Naya? She doesn't have any enemies." As he said it, he realized he actually didn't know that for sure. She could have had enemies in La Junta he didn't know about.

Atlas shook his head. "She's a detective and was a Sheriff. She's probably pissed off any number of people over the years. I'm having a colleague send up her files from La Junta now." He checked his phone for the time. "This is just really bad timing because our case was about to break. And now she's missing."

"Do you think they're connected?" Kevin asked apprehensively.

Atlas thought for a second, he clearly hadn't considered the fact that they might be yet. "I don't know. But if they are, this isn't good."

"Why?" Kevin asked, even though he knew he probably wasn't going to like the answer.

Atlas shook his head. "Because this man is crazy."

Another officer called Atlas over to ask him some questions. Kevin felt the guilt beginning to settle in. If he had been here last night, Naya wouldn't have been taken. Maybe Vance would still be alive.

Then it hit him. If a crazy man really did have Naya, would he kill her? Would he ever get to see Naya again?

Oh God.

And he hadn't been nice to her the past couple of days. Kevin felt sick to his stomach.

This couldn't be happening.

He had just found the first woman to hold his interest in years.

And he might have already lost her.

30

NAYA

aya felt herself slowly coming to. It took her a minute to realize that something was wrong, her eyes were open, but it was still pitch black. And she couldn't move her mouth. She tried to move her arms and legs and found she was bound, tightly.

The night before came rushing back to her. She had been drugged. And kidnapped. Her detective mind kicked into overdrive, trying to think of every person she'd ever pissed off and who would possibly want to kidnap her, but everyone she had put behind bars was still there as far as she knew.

Her mind snapped back to her current case.

What if? It had been Monday after all.

She felt a cold dose of fear run down her spine. If the guy who kidnapped her was their guy she didn't have much time before he killed her. He only kept most of the women alive for an hour or two. She needed to think of a way out, and now.

She tried to relax so she could think clearly. She felt motion. Okay, so she was in a car. She was wearing a long-sleeved shirt and pants. Probably her work clothes, so he hadn't stripped her or anything. She rolled slightly so she could feel the material she was on. It felt like the floor of a car. She tried to listen, to see if she could notice anything distinct that would tell her where they were, but all she heard was the sound of the vehicle she was in. She barely had room to move; she had to be in the back of a car with no legroom.

Okay, now time to think back to the night before. When she had gotten home, Trevor's truck had been out front. She had gone inside, leaned down to take off her shoes, and someone had been waiting for her.

But the door had been locked when she had put her key in the lock.

Whoever had her either had a key or had been let in by Trevor and then locked the door behind them.

She felt dread settling as she came to realize that she probably knew her attacker. And that wasn't good at all. What could Trevor want with her?

Naya started thinking back to all the interactions she'd had with him. But honestly, besides meeting him, she couldn't remember having that many interactions with the guy, nothing noteworthy for sure.

She thought briefly about Vance and she hoped that Kevin would stop by and check on him today at least. She wondered what time it was; if it was light or dark outside. He had grabbed her at about one, which meant that no one would be missing her until about seven, when she was supposed to be back at work.

Dammit. She had been so tired the night before, Atlas might just think she had overslept.

She tried to see if she could move at all. If there was any weakness in the ropes where she could slip out a hand.

"Don't even try." Came the gruff voice of her attacker. So, he was keeping an eye on her.

She wanted to engage him so badly but couldn't with the tape over her mouth. So instead, she decided to see what would happen if she kept struggling.

"I said stop. We're almost there."

Almost where? She wanted to ask, but nothing physical had

happened so she continued to see if she could mess with the ropes. Nothing seemed to budge.

Trevor slammed on the brakes, and she felt herself go forward into the seat in front of her. "I said stop it!"

She could hear he was getting annoyed. But, he was definitely acting alone. If he had been able to do anything other than slam on the breaks he would have done so. And honestly, his slamming on the brakes didn't bother her that much, so the joke was on him. Okay. She was going to keep struggling.

"STOP IT!" He screamed from the front seat, and she felt the car swerve. He was clearly being distracted by her actions; she could tell he liked control, and her refusing to comply was driving him nuts.

Suddenly, the tires screeched to a halt, and she felt them swerve again. The ride got bumpier as he was apparently heading off the paved road.

"Goddamn it. I wanted to go further, but fine, you win. We will do this right here!" He roared as she felt him tear open the car door and he dragged her out by her feet. She dropped and hit the ground with a crash and a sharp jolt of pain traveled up her shoulder.

The ground was rough, and she could feel what felt like blades of dried grass cutting into her arms. Her mind immediately went to the fields Benjamin Rodgers worked.

Wait a minute.

Was Trevor also her perp? Had the guy who had been kidnapping and killing these runners been under her nose the entire time?

Oh God. She suddenly felt like an idiot.

But she had no time to work through it because this also meant that death was probably right around the corner unless she could act quickly. She immediately started going over every personal defense class she had ever taken. The answer had to be somewhere.

The way he was roughly dragging her across the ground had moved her blindfold just enough that she could tell it was daylight. Or it would be soon, she hadn't been out for all that long.

Trevor stopped suddenly and tossed her legs roughly to the side. She braced herself, waiting for him to do something, but nothing happened. She heard the grass rustle, he apparently was returning to the truck.

If this guy really was her murderer, he was going to kill her with an injection. She needed to get moving. And fast. She didn't know where he had gone, but he hadn't dragged her for that long, so she didn't have much time.

She began struggling with her wrist restraints again; they were really tight, but she knew some tricks. That was probably the reason he had gotten so upset before. She began to rub her hands together, allowing the sweat to make her hands slick. She rubbed more vigorously until she finally felt her left hand coming free.

She quickly tossed the rope aside, pulling off her blindfold and looking around. She was lying in a grass field, as she had already deduced. She lifted her head a little, Trevor was already walking back with a trunk in his arms. Although this slowed him down considerably, she needed to get her legs untied too, and fast. She leaned down as inconspicuously as possible and began working on the knot. It went quickly, but not fast enough for her taste. She could hear his heaving breathing, he was almost back. She would have to fight to get the head start she wanted, and then she would take off.

She rolled over onto her stomach and into a crouch position so she could spring the minute he noticed she had untied herself. She glanced down at her hip, confirming her fears. He had her weapon.

He wasn't dumb. He noticed something was up with the way she was lying when he was still a few paces away. Well, she was going to have to skip the attack and go straight for the run.

Just as he slammed the trunk to the ground in a fit of rage she popped up from her position and began to sprint.

She ran faster than she had in her entire life. She didn't care where she was going, everything around her was yellow field. But the mountains were further than where they had found the other women, so this wasn't the same spot.

When he had knocked her unconscious, he had taken her work boots. Which was good because she wasn't sure how fast she could run in them, but it was also bad because she could feel grass and bits of the ground cutting into her bare feet.

She chanced a glance over her shoulder to see, he was indeed pursuing her. She knew she couldn't run like this forever, maybe another minute or two at most. She looked to the horizon, looking for anything that wasn't flat grassland. There was nothing. No cover. Just grass for miles.

Where was the road they had been on? If she could head towards that maybe she would have a chance of someone spotting her. It was still early, but it was her only chance.

Knowing the mountains were to the west, which was the direction she was heading, she made a sharp left, hoping that was the correct direction for the road.

She peeked over her shoulder, he was still behind her. He wasn't as fast though. If she could run like this forever, she could probably outrun him, but her legs and lungs were already burning, protesting her exertion. She hadn't gotten much sleep in the past twenty-four hours, the adrenaline wasn't going to be enough to sustain her.

She had never been religious, but now she started begging anyone who would listen to her to get her out of this situation.

She felt herself slowing, her muscles were screaming. She tried to push herself faster, but it didn't work.

Before she knew it, she felt herself being knocked to the ground from behind.

She felt her head hit the ground as the wind was knocked out of her. She gasped for breath.

For the first time since her abduction, she was face to face with Trevor.

"Goddamn it. Get up." He dragged her to her feet. She could tell she had surprised him when she ran. He hadn't brought anything with him to drug her.

She was still out of breath, so she complied with his instructions for now. He twisted one of her arms behind her back, and she heard her elbow pop. She didn't call out.

Naya knew that in order to save herself, she needed to keep him away from whatever was in those trunks. Luckily, her mad dash to freedom had taken them a ways from the place where he had parked. She had a few minutes before she would have to enact the next part of her plan.

She didn't know if it would work, but she had to try.

31

KEVIN

He was sitting in the waiting room at the police station, resting his head against the metal table. Atlas had set a paper cup of coffee by his head some time ago, but he didn't feel like moving.

"You okay?" Atlas came and sat next to him.

"No." Kevin mumbled, slowly lifting his head from the table.

"It's not your fault." He replied, and he heard him take a gulp of coffee.

"Easy for you to say. Why aren't you out looking for her?" Kevin regretted the accusation the minute it came out of his mouth, it sounded harsher than he had intended.

Atlas held up a hand. "I've got officers all over the state looking for her. But I am just one man, and besides me, you probably know her best. So, if I can figure out who took her, it will save us time. I can't just knock on every door in the state. Otherwise, I already would have."

Kevin was quiet. He was embarrassed by his outburst now.

"I need you to tell me what you know about Trevor."

Now he was confused. "What about Trevor?"

"He's missing as well. The Foreman at the site said he never showed up for work today. We triangulated his cell and found that the last place it had service was at Naya's house. He hasn't been seen or heard from since, and his cell has been shut off."

Kevin felt his mouth drop open. "Seems like you know way more than me."

Atlas rolled his eyes. "Not like that, tell me what kind of man he is, how long you have known him et cetera."

"Well, I met him about six months ago when he showed up at the construction site I was running at the time and asked for a job. We always need people, so I gave him one." Kevin rubbed his chin remembering the day. Back when Vance had just gone on leave and they were constantly shorthanded.

"Did you do a background check or anything?"

Kevin hadn't noticed, but Atlas had, at some point, pulled out a notepad and a pen and was taking notes.

"Uh. No. In the construction world, we don't really do much paperwork. If the men want direct deposit, we do need a check from their bank. Otherwise, a scan of their ID showing they live in the US and they are good to go."

"So, you don't run social security numbers through the system?" Atlas had one of his eyebrows raised.

"No." Kevin shook his head. "That's part of what makes construction so appealing to recent immigrants, they can work the job with just a green card or driver's license."

"Well, what kind of car does Trevor drive?"

"A Chevy Silverado truck, black, I'm not a huge car guy, but if I had to guess it is about the same age as my truck, so 2018 or 2019." Kevin didn't like where this conversation was going. "Wait, do you think he took Naya?"

Atlas pulled out his phone and sent a quick text, probably the car information if Kevin had to guess. "Well, I think there's a chance, yes. Do you have any idea where Trevor lived?"

Kevin rubbed his forehead. "He gave me the address when he first started working for me of course, I would have to call the office to get the exact address now, but I believe it was somewhere on Blake Street."

Kevin watched as Atlas froze. "What did you say?"

"It was an apartment on Blake Street, he was subletting from someone. I never went there. We always just hung out at Vance's place because it seemed to be easier."

He put down his pen and pinched the bridge of his nose.

Kevin was really confused now, but he didn't want to make himself look like an idiot, so he just stayed quiet.

Atlas pulled out his phone and dialed while Kevin looked on.

"Get all the units you can head out east. Yeah, I think it's our guy. Black Chevy Silverado. I've got guys looking for the plates now. Yes, keep the units at Blake Street in case he comes back there."

He hung up the phone. "You're welcome to stay here if you want, or you can leave. But do me a favor, can you contact Vance's parents? We can do it if you don't want to, but I think it will sound better coming from you than me."

Kevin nodded as Atlas left the room in a hurry. He pulled his phone out from his pocket, pausing when he unlocked it, and the background picture was a photo from a hiking trip he and Vance had taken a few years before.

On Sunday, when Vance had pulled him aside to say goodbye, it had sounded so much like he was giving up. And Kevin had said so. They hadn't exactly argued, but now Kevin understood why he had wanted to say goodbye so soon. He had known something bad was coming.

Why hadn't he gone to check on Vance last night instead of sending Trevor?

He knew there was no use in thinking about the past now, but he just hoped Naya was okay wherever she was. And that Atlas would find her, and quick.

He found Vance and Naya's mothers' number in his phone and pressed dial, closing his eyes and leaning back in the chair while he waited for her to answer.

"Hey, Kevin! How's Vance?" She answered in such a cheerful voice Kevin found himself tongue-tied for the second time that day.

"Uh." He choked as he tried to formulate the words.

"Kevin?" Vance's mother could immediately tell this was not a social call.

"You better come back. He... uh... this morning." He managed to get out eventually, trying to hold himself together by avoiding the actual words.

"No!" Vance's mom started sobbing into the phone. "Naya, let me talk to Naya."

Kevin's chest seized as he realized that he had not one piece of bad news but two to deliver.

"Uh, oh God, Mrs. Largusa I-I-I..." He paused and took a breath; he could do this. "Naya is missing."

"WHAT?!" She screamed into the phone, and then she heard her call for Naya's father, who must have been in another room. He heard her babble incoherently away from the phone for a second before Mr. Largusa answered.

"Wait, tell me from the beginning. Just what is going on over there?" Kevin could see where Naya got her police officer tendencies from, her dad was all business. He let no emotion into his voice.

Kevin took a deep breath. He could do this. "Naya's partner called me this morning because Naya didn't show up to the office. I went to their house to look for her, and instead, I found Vance, and he was uh..." He trailed off and the phone line was silent for a moment.

When he spoke again, his voice was much more somber.

"So, are you out looking for Naya, do you think she was depressed enough to hurt herself?"

Kevin thought back to the night when Naya and Vance had said their goodbyes. This was not what this was about, and he knew it. She had been at peace that night. Sad, but at peace. "No sir. I'm at the police station right now, you see, Naya's car was at the house, and the rug was messed up. They think she may have been taken."

"Jesus." Kevin could tell Mr. Largusa was having trouble dealing with the double blow that he may just be losing both his children at once. "I'm going to have someone drive us up there at once. We will meet you at the police station."

"Yes. See you soon." Kevin hung up the phone, the sound of Mrs. Largusa's sobs still echoing in his ears. He laid his head back down on the table.

Atlas came back in at that moment, his face grim. "We have a problem."

"What?" Kevin sat back up.

"There is no Trevor Carlson who owns a truck like you described in the entire state. Not only that, but when we ran the numbers from the driver's license your office had on file for him, they came back as fake. Trevor probably printed that license himself."

Kevin's jaw dropped. "You mean his name isn't Trevor?"

Atlas shook his head and took a seat once again, his notepad and pen ready to go. "I need you to tell me everything you know about this man, right now. Where he came from whatever you can think of."

Kevin thought for a moment, and the more he thought the more he realized he didn't know all that much about Trevor. The guy really hadn't talked much when they hung out. And at work, they had talked about trivial things.

"Wait, he mentioned once that he was divorced." That was how they had connected. Kevin had mentioned the end of his recent relationship and Trevor had said his divorce had been finalized recently as well. Now where had he said that it had happened? "I think he moved here from Chicago; he had insinuated his divorce was recent when I met him."

"Okay good. Anything else? Did he mention what he did before? Anything about his family?"

Kevin shook his head. "As weird as it is, I'm suddenly realizing just how, well, little, I know about the guy. We connected over our recently failed relationships when we met, but I think I mostly talked about mine and he would say things like 'the same thing happened when my divorce was final' and so on."

"Hm." Atlas stood from the table. "I'm going to go to my computer and do a few searches. If you think of anything else, can you come tell me right away?"

"Sure." Kevin put his head in his hands, trying to think of all the conversations he had with Trevor over the past six months. They had all just been so one-sided. And then, recently, he had begun asking about Naya.

The guilt came crashing down on him at that. Maybe he had made Naya his target.

Why had he ignored her the last few days? This was such a mess.

Wait! He remembered something. He rose from his chair and walked towards Atlas' desk. "Atlas, I remembered something, his wife, he said her name was Katie."

Atlas didn't look up from his computer. "Of course, the most generic name ever. But thanks, Kevin."

"No problem." Kevin turned and went to grab his coffee from the table where it had long gone cold. He took a long sip from the paper cup. He had never felt so ineffective in his life.

32

NAYA

She walked quietly alongside Trevor for a few yards. He kept her arm twisted behind her back in a painful position which she was sure had dislocated her shoulder, or elbow, or both.

She saw a dot come into her field view and she quickly realized that it was Trevor's truck. Time was up. It was fight now or die.

Before he could tell what was coming, she lifted her leg and kicked him as hard as she could in the groin. She was pretty sure she had missed her mark, but it was enough for him to release the powerful grip on her arm. While he staggered in place, she quickly used a trick she had learned in college to relocate her elbow. It fell back into place with a painful pop. She rolled her shoulder, it seemed to be in place. Good enough.

Trevor stood up straight, clearly baffled by why she hadn't run again.

Using his confusion as a distraction, she quickly rammed the heel of her hand into his nose, hearing a sickening crack as the bone broke. She still had her edge.

As he grabbed his nose, she used her knee to hit him in the groin again, and this time, she hit her target, and he doubled over in pain.

Naya could tell immediately that he wasn't used to dealing with women who could fight back.

She stepped closer to try a move to get him on his stomach so she could try and get the car keys from his pocket, but he was too quick. He knocked her off her legs the minute she was in range of his long arms.

She caught herself this time though, as she hadn't exhausted all her energy running and her will to live keeping her going The minute she propelled herself into a standing position she kicked his stomach as hard as she could, a little bummed he had taken her shoes when he drugged her the night before as it didn't quite have the impact she wanted.

He aimed another punch towards Naya's head, but she was able to dodge and grab his arm, twisting it behind his back in the same way he had done to her. She kicked his feet out from under him, landing with one knee on his back and the other on his neck.

Naya was under no illusions; although she was a good fighter, she knew she was smaller, and she could feel herself tiring; Trevor was definitely going to gain the upper hand and quickly if she didn't make a move. She frisked his pockets, trying to find the car keys.

"Ha, enjoy your last few moments being a cop." Naya crushed her knee tighter into his neck. She had about three seconds to come up with a new plan. Trevor's pockets were empty, the keys were probably in the truck.

She glanced out of the corner of her eye. The truck was a bit too far to make it on how tired her muscles already were, but she could go for it. Or she could try to make it to the street.

She made her decision. She quickly pressed her knee into the back of Trevor's neck, feeling satisfied as he gasped for air. His arms started flailing but she didn't let up. He was trying to roll over, and Naya found her grip loosening; it was okay, though. Her plan wasn't to kill him. She Just needed to hopefully knock him unconscious or tire him enough to get a running start.

She couldn't tell if he realized it or not, but at some point, he stopped struggling for just a moment and Naya used the opening to jump up and began running in the direction of the road.

Her feet immediately protested, not happy about being put to work again. This time she was almost certain she was headed in the direction of the road, and as she looked over her shoulder, she didn't see Trevor pursuing, which made her feel like she had made the right choice.

For someone she had been chasing for weeks, Trevor was never someone she would have suspected, which made her think her and Atlas' profile of the guy had been somewhat incorrect. But there was one thing she knew about this guy, and it was that running would never best him. She would have to outsmart him.

Please Atlas, she thought to herself, please send cops out east. She hoped that he was already on it and had made the connection that this was their perp. But she wasn't holding her breath, it was quite the leap to make.

She noticed something peeking out from the grass up ahead. It was asphalt! Yes! She had made it. She quickly moved to the centerline and began running west. Please, someone be driving this way, she pleaded with the universe.

After what seemed like forever, she began to slow, her energy stores exhausted at the same time she heard the sound of an engine from behind her. She peeked over her shoulder to see a black truck coming straight for her.

Fuck!

She quickly jumped off the road. When she had made her run for the road, she hadn't thought he would get to his truck that fast. And she had hoped she would see a car before he did. Dammit!

She pleaded with her feet and legs to keep going as she ran in the grass still west, but also heading slightly north to try and get away from the road a little, to make her harder to follow. She cursed this area of the state of Colorado for having nowhere to hide.

Suddenly, she heard something in the distance. Was that police sirens? Was she dreaming? Just the thought that she had heard police sirens spurned her legs to move faster. Then she heard an engine rev...

She looked behind her as he maneuvered the truck off the road. She needed to stay near enough to the road that if those were sirens, that they would see her. But getting him off the pavement had slowed him down considerably, and she needed any help she could get.

But not enough. He was still gaining on her. And her body was giving out.

She pushed herself harder than she ever had before, her legs moving almost mechanically. Off of what energy, she wasn't sure.

It wasn't enough. She heard the car squeal to a stop, and soon enough, he was behind her on foot again. And not far.

This time when he knocked her off her feet, she felt the cool metal of her own gun pressed to her temple.

"Get up. And no funny business this time. Or I will shoot you."

She stood. "What do you want from me anyway?" Naya decided if she couldn't fight, it was time to use the last tactic she knew of: conversation. "You know maybe we can help each other out if you tell me just what you plan to do with me."

Trevor laughed maniacally. "Ha! You help me? I don't think so."

It was time to prove the theory that had been formulated in her head. Hopefully, it would be enough.

"Come on, I know those other girls weren't what you wanted. Julia, Shanice, Alia. But I'm different."

"That you are." She could almost hear the cruel smile that must have spread across his face from where he stood behind her.

"So why don't you see if I can help you?"

"The only way you can help me is by dying."

Naya gulped. This had been what she was afraid of. Whatever he needed these women for, death was involved. "Are you going to perform science experiments on me?" She asked bravely.

"Just your blood."

Naya felt her throat go dry, she really was just an unnecessary accessory to him. And that's why they never found any of the drained blood. Not because he was afraid of getting caught. In fact, now that she thought of it, he wasn't even wearing gloves now as he held her arm. She wasn't sure if he usually wore gloves or did away with his prints another way, but whatever this meant, it wasn't good.

"Can I ask why?" She mentally crossed her fingers hoping he was the type of killer who liked to brag about the superiority of his reasons for murdering.

"Nope. And that's enough questions." He jabbed the gun further into her temple and Naya felt her luck waning. "I'm going to enjoy killing you." He said, just as they got to his truck.

Suddenly, the glass of the cab door shattered, a bullet had whizzed by their heads. Naya instinctively ducked.

"Freeze!" Came the order, just as he was about to shove her in the back seat. He slowly spun, keeping Naya as a human shield although the cab door was already protecting him.

There were two officers standing in the middle of the road. Naya could see their squad car parked not too far away. They must've turned off the sirens as they had gotten closer.

Naya didn't recognize either of the officers, and she guessed this might be their first situation like this. They couldn't shoot Trevor without shooting her, but she couldn't move with the gun to her temple. And if he removed the gun from her temple for even one second, she would react to get her weapon back.

"Put down the gun Mr. Carlson." One of the officers called out. "Let Ms. Largusa go, and then we can work this out."

"My name isn't Carlson. And I'm not stupid. I know she's a detective and I'm not interested in going to jail for life." He tightened his hold on her arm and Naya felt her recently dislocated elbow protesting.

"We can make a deal. But you need to let Ms. Largusa go, now."

Trevor clearly didn't like this situation at all.

"Back up or I shoot." He threatened as he cocked the pistol. Naya made eye contact with the cop who hadn't spoken and raised her eyebrows hoping he noticed the signal. He raised his eyebrows back. Okay, he understood.

She blinked three times to indicate that he had three blinks before she acted. She wasn't sure this was going to work, but she knew she was out of time and that Trevor had no mental attachment to her whatsoever. He was merely trying to save himself right now.

She blinked once. She blinked twice. She blinked a third time.

Then with all her might, she pulled herself downwards, her arm howling at her in pain. Almost simultaneously, she heard the gun fire. From where, she wasn't sure. Then her world went black.

33

KEVIN

One minute he was just sitting there thinking about how much his life had changed the past twenty-four hours. The next thing he knew, Atlas was screaming on the phone as the office broke into a flurry of activity.

He sat back and watched, trying not to get in anyone's way, but at the same time, he wanted to know what Atlas was saying and what was happening.

"Black truck? That's him. Turn your sirens off. NOW!" Atlas screamed. "Do NOT let him know you're coming. Naya may become expendable."

He hung up the phone and grabbed his keys, noticing Kevin looking at him with a stricken look on his face.

"They've spotted her. I've got to go as backup. Don't leave. Once the scene is safe, I'll have an officer bring you." He stormed out of the office before Kevin even had a chance to agree or disagree.

He could feel the panic seizing his chest as he thought about what Naya was possibly facing at that moment. But deep inside he knew she could handle it. She was stronger than him emotionally, she had shown that this past weekend. She would keep her head clear under pressure.

Suddenly, Atlas was back in front of him.

"Come on. Let's go."

Kevin stood and followed Atlas towards the door without hesitation. "Wait, what happened? I thought you were going to go help?"

Atlas shook his head. "There was a standoff. But it didn't go well. We're going to meet them at the hospital."

He felt as if someone had punched him in the gut for the second time that day. "And Naya?"

"She's been shot."

Kevin felt all the breath leave his lungs and he felt like he was about to collapse, but somehow, he was able to make himself sit in the passenger seat of the car just as he felt he was about to faint.

"Is she...is she okay?" He whispered as Atlas started driving, lights and sirens blaring.

"She's alive. I don't know her condition, but they have her in an ambulance on the way to the hospital."

Kevin wasn't reassured. And he didn't think he would be until he saw her for himself. The two of them didn't speak for the rest of the ride.

When they arrived at the hospital, a bigger one than the one that they had brought Vance to a couple of weeks ago, Kevin stood as slowly as possible. Taking deep breaths to keep himself calm.

Atlas power walked from his side of the car, almost to the doors already, and motioned for Kevin to follow. His expression was more somber than Kevin had seen before.

They walked to reception, where the emergency room seemed far too quiet for someone who had just been brought in with a gunshot wound. Kevin didn't know what he was expecting, but the movies certainly hadn't prepared him for how normal this all seemed. As if they were just calmly coming to the hospital to visit someone who had gotten a routine surgery, not a life-or-death situation.

Atlas spoke to the receptionist in hushed tones as Kevin stood by. He sent a quick text to Naya's parents, letting them know he was at the hospital now and the address. He also gave them an update on

Naya, hoping it wasn't too preemptive. Then he slid his phone back in his pocket.

Atlas finished talking to the receptionist and turned to Kevin.

"They brought her in just minutes before we arrived. She's in surgery now. As soon as the surgeon is done, he will come and speak with us."

Kevin almost felt angry as he and Atlas both sat down in the chairs in the waiting room, as if this were just another day.

He pulled out his phone and began to mindlessly scroll through social media. Everything seemed so trivial now. He knew he hadn't known Naya for long, but he didn't think he could handle losing his love interest and his best friend on the same day.

He had no concept of time as he sat there and ran through every hypothetical scenario that could happen from this point forward. It must've passed the time at least, because next thing he knew, a nurse had come over and was leading them back to a private office.

"The surgeon will be right in. Have a seat." She instructed as she closed the door behind her. Kevin could feel his palms sweating. He was sure his nerves would be shot after this. Atlas seemed unnaturally calm still, and Kevin craved nothing more than to be that calm.

After what was probably about another three years, or so it felt to Kevin, an older man in scrubs entered the room and sat behind the desk.

"Hello, gentlemen; I hear you are here on behalf of Ms. Largusa?"

Atlas held up his hand to Kevin before he could speak. "Yes sir, I am her partner, and this is her boyfriend."

Kevin knew that he and Naya hadn't started discussing the status of their relationship just yet. But he also knew that Atlas said it on purpose so he could get more information.

"Okay, well, she's stable," As the words left the surgeon's mouth, Kevin felt a huge weight lifted off his shoulders, and he could breathe for the first time all day. "The bullet skimmed her temple. Mostly just superficial damage it seems. She sustained some other injuries as well. But honestly, they were fairly mild. A dislocated shoulder and lacerations to her feet. She's on some pain medication for the shoulder, but honestly, she should be awake any minute, and you can go see her."

Kevin felt a smile spreading across his face. Naya was going to be fine.

"Thank you, doctor." Atlas rose and shook his hand. "Can we go in now?"

"Sure, the nurse will show you the room."

Kevin followed Atlas back to the hall where the same nurse appeared to lead them down the hall. They stopped in front of a room and the nurse opened the door for them.

Her face was all bandaged, and her arm was in a cast, but the moment he laid eyes on her, Kevin knew everything was going to be okay.

EPILOGUE
NAYA—TWO WEEKS LATER

She stood just a few feet back from the edge. The urn clasped tightly to her chest with her good arm. The other was still in a sling to let the tendons heal from where they had been stretched all too painfully.

They had just finished Vance's funeral, it had been a beautiful ceremony. Although she had been given her chance to say goodbye, she still cried at the funeral. Actually, she had probably cried more these past two weeks than she had during her entire adult life.

Kevin had been nothing but supportive and understanding. Although Vance had left her the house, Naya had taken up residence at Kevin's place. She was probably going to sell the house. She couldn't imagine living in it ever again. In fact, as much as she had loved growing up in the state of Colorado, the recent events had left a sour taste in her mouth and she fully intended to move as soon as she could request a transfer.

She was on an indefinite leave from work. Not that they wouldn't take her back, but she needed time to heal and work through what had happened.

What had happened in that field still hadn't quite sunk in. It seemed like another woman in another lifetime, rather than something which had happened to her. And she knew the only way the nightmares would stop is if she could learn to confront what happened. She just wasn't ready yet. But she knew she would go back eventually. The unsolved cases in her desk drawer wouldn't let her leave the force for good until they were solved. At least, that's what she told herself.

She clutched the urn tighter to her chest as she thought about all the details that had emerged about the case over the past two weeks.

Based on a hunch, Atlas had ordered an autopsy for Vance, even though they were ready to attribute his death to the cancer and leave it at that. Although Vance did have highly progressed stage-4 Non-Hodgkin's Lymphoma at the time of his death, the coroner discovered he had been poisoned with cyanide the night of his death. Likely Trevor trying to make sure he wouldn't interfere.

Trevor had died at the end of the standoff. Thanks to her quick, but not quite quick enough, ducking skills, he was killed with two shots to the head by the officers on the scene. He had been dead before he even hit the ground.

They never did discover just what scientific experiments Trevor had been planning to run on her, or what he had already done to the other women. He hadn't left any notes that they could find, and the equipment in his truck had been less than helpful. It seemed like Atlas may have been right, and he was just simply 'crazy.'

They did find out that his real name was Mark Jackson and he had fled the Chicago area after some crazy occurrence with his wife. The police there were re-opening that case.

He had fooled them all. They weren't sure if Naya had been his intended victim the entire time, or if he had just spent time at her house and found her fascinating. Whichever it was, Naya wasn't planning to give anyone a key to her house ever again. Well, except maybe Kevin.

Things were going well between them. And while she had been healing these past few weeks, he had been her rock as she mourned the loss of her only sibling. Who's ashes were in her arms now.

She glanced over her shoulder to see her parents and Kevin

watching her patiently. She had asked to be the one to do this and they had obliged. But now she wasn't so sure.

"Hey Vance." She whispered quietly as she turned back forward and looked out over the range of the Rocky Mountains. This was such a beautiful place.

"I know you're not really in this urn, but I feel better holding what is left of you close to me." She swallowed as the tears streaked paths down her cheeks.

"I know we said goodbye while you were still alive, so I'll keep this brief. I just want to let you know that you are the best big brother. I know you were worried about draining my finances. But money is just money. I would give up everything to have you back." She choked as the words died in her throat. She stood there silently with tears trailing down her face.

"I'm going to let you go now. But first, I just want to let you know that I'm going to be just fine. You made sure of that. You left me with a new home, and new friends. And we will always love you. Enjoy the next life, whatever that may be. And I'll see you there someday."

She stood there silently for an immeasurable amount of time before she turned and gave Kevin a slight nod. He walked up next to her and held out his hands.

Naya handed him the urn so he could take the top off and hold it for her as she used her hand to begin releasing his ashes into the wind.

She felt her parents come to stand behind her, her father putting a hand gently on her injured shoulder as they, too, said goodbye to their only son.

After she was finished, they all went and sat on the bench which was a few feet back from the cliff. They sat in silence, just watching as the mountains changed colors as the sun set behind them. Once they were fully cloaked in darkness, they said their goodbyes and headed to their separate cars. Naya's parents were headed to their hotel, and she was headed to Kevin's place with him.

Once they were safely in the car away from her parents Kevin turned to her and placed a hand on her leg. "How are you feeling?"

"As best as can be expected."

"That's not what I meant." Naya looked over at his profile, illuminated by the headlights through the windshield. Kevin knew firsthand the nightmares that had been plaguing her since she had gotten home from the hospital. Every time she closed her eyes all she could see was the abduction. She was basically living in a state of chronic sleep deprivation.

She tried not to let her nightmares keep Kevin awake. Often times she would quietly leave bed and go read in the living room after they happened, but if he woke and noticed she wasn't in bed, which sometimes happened, he would always come join her on the couch, even though she protested for him to go back to sleep.

"Are you avoiding the question?" He asked, making Naya realize she hadn't answered yet.

"I don't know." She responded honestly. "I think I need to talk about what happened, but I don't feel ready yet."

"Well, I'm here when you are. You know that, right?" He gently squeezed her thigh.

"I know." She looked out the window for a minute as the dark scenery passed by, not taking in any of it. Besides making their relationship official over the past couple of weeks, they had also discussed what had happened during that last chat with Vance. And Naya knew Kevin was battling a large amount of guilt, which she wanted him to seek help for as well.

She placed her good hand on top of his. She knew they would work it out though. They were both strong individuals. And she was sure they were even stronger together. Whatever lay on the road ahead...

They would face it together.

∽

BENJAMIN RODGERS STOOD on his front porch, looking out over all the land he had acquired over the past few years. Most of it he had purchased, but some of it had come from old Dave, and that other farmer who used to be out here.

Benjamin was glad they had finally caught the culprit who had been killing those women and leaving them on his land. It had brought way too much attention to him and events that should have been long buried.

He felt a little bad for the women who had died. But, well, stuff happens.

Benjamin crossed the porch and walked across his driveway, toward the spot where he had told the detectives that he had buried old Dave. And he hadn't lied about that. No, old Dave had died very peacefully of old age.

Benjamin couldn't say the same about the rest.

He let his eyes move from the obvious mound of dirt to those alongside it, which were becoming less and less obvious as the years went by. There were seven now.

He had told himself that seven was enough, a nice round number. But after hearing the tales of the recent murders, something within him had stirred. He had thought he was done. He thought he had only murdered to gain more land which was rightfully his to begin with.

But now he had all the land, and the urge had returned.

He was suppressing it for now. Best to let things die down in the county. Especially because he needed to report Old Dave's death soon. But then...well...

Then he would have to return to the work that he had been designed to do.

WHAT'S NEXT?

If you enjoyed *You Can't Run*, please take a moment to leave a rating or review and check out Hope's other mystery novels, *Before Now*, *The Fate of Ava Miller,* and *Deceptive Perfection*!

Now available on Amazon in both paperback and kindle!

Follow Hope on Amazon or her socials for information on upcoming books!

ABOUT THE AUTHOR

You Can't Run is Hope's fourth novel. When she isn't writing, she is busy traveling the world, trying new foods, or hanging out with friends. A graduate of Metropolitan State University, Hope grew up in Colorado but currently calls the Netherlands her home. To find information about her other novels and be notified of her newest releases, follow Hope on Twitter @thehopeopera, Instagram @hopeedavisauthor, and Amazon Hope E. Davis.

www.ingramcontent.com/pod-product-compliance
Lightning Source LLC
Chambersburg PA
CBHW072300130726
47910CB00012B/2211